When Summer Ends

ALSO BY JESSICA PENNINGTON

Love Songs & Other Lies

When Summer  *Ends*

JESSICA PENNINGTON

A Tom Doherty Associates Book *New York*

WHEN SUMMER ENDS

A Tor Teen Book
Published by Tom Doherty Associates
175 Fifth Avenue
New York, NY 10010

www.tor-forge.com

Tor® is a registered trademark of Macmillan Publishing Group, LLC.

Library of Congress Cataloging-in-Publication Data

Names: Pennington, Jessica.
Title: When summer ends / Jessica Pennington.
Description: First edition. | New York : Tor Teen, 2019. | "A Tom Doherty
  Associates Book." | Summary: Aiden, former star pitcher and golden boy
  of Riverton, and Olivia, whose life is falling apart, connect during the last
  summer of high school as both seek a new direction.
Identifiers: LCCN 2018051010| ISBN 9781250187338 (hardcover) |
  ISBN 9781250187345 (ebook)
Subjects: | CYAC: Self-perception—Fiction. | Fate and fatalism—Fiction. | Dating
  (Social customs)—Fiction. | Vision disorders—Fiction. | Family life—Fiction.
Classification: LCC PZ7.1.P44737 Whe 2019 | DDC [Fic]—dc23
LC record available at https://lccn.loc.gov/2018051010

Our books may be purchased in bulk for promotional, educational, or
business use. Please contact your local bookseller or the Macmillan Corporate
and Premium Sales Department at 1-800-221-7945, extension 5442, or
by email at MacmillanSpecialMarkets@macmillan.com.

First Edition: April 2019

Printed in the United States of America

0 9 8 7 6 5 4 3 2 1

When Summer Ends

Chapter  One

Olivia

I've been stabbed in the chest. Literally. My eyes dart down to my bridesmaid dress, but somehow, it's inexplicably blood-free. It's also about four sizes too big, engulfing me in swaths of loose fabric.

"Sorry about that, honey." Deb, the seamstress, puts a pin between her teeth and talks around it. "We just need it a *little* tighter up here." She pulls at the minty green and pale blue fabric that wraps across my chest, pinching until it feels like it may slice me in half.

My boyfriend Zander's mom, Trudy, gives me a sympathetic glance from her perch on a kitchen stool. "The first fitting is the worst. Next time will just be little tweaks." She looks at the seamstress, who is now crouched down at my feet. "Right, Deb?"

Deb nods as she slides another pin into the dress.

It feels like I've been trapped in this dress for a short eternity, even though the clock claims it's only been twenty minutes since I stripped down and traded my clothes for the eclectic floral confection that now drapes over me. *Eclectic.* That's what the bride, Becca, called it when Trudy pulled it from the bag and presented it to me, one hand under it, like I was setting my eyes on a great award and not something that looks like an old watercolor painting in dress form. When Trudy slides a magazine across the counter and begins thumbing through it, I worry that maybe this is going to take a lot longer than the "quick second" she promised.

I take a deep breath and remind myself that this is what I wanted. To be in the wedding. Being in Becca's wedding is the epitome of acceptance into Zander's family. *Wedding pictures are forever.* It wasn't a huge surprise though. Sure, Zander and I are only juniors—almost seniors—but I'm not a regular girlfriend. The kind you meet on the first day of math class and start dating on a whim when you get partnered up for a project. The one you break up with before the first school dance rolls around. No, I'm the opposite. I'm the friend-turned-girlfriend, the one his mom has been begging him to date since way before it was even appropriate. I'm the pseudo daughter-in-law. The girlfriend who no longer gets asked to dances or out on dates, because we just *know.*

The door slams and I tear my eyes away from Deb—who I was hoping wouldn't poke me while I was actually watching her—to see Becca coming through the kitchen with a small black tote bag slung over her shoulder. Zander's sister looks like a younger version of his mom, with sandy blond hair that is always in soft curls at her shoulders and blue eyes that are soft and kind. Even when she's curled up on the couch watching a movie with her fiancé Chad, Becca looks like she has somewhere to go.

"Oh Liv, you look so beautiful," she gushes when she sees me. Like her mother, Becca has the ability to say that sort of thing without sounding as if she felt obligated to.

"It's a really gorgeous dress," I say, and for the first time I feel like it's true.

She shakes her head as she sits down on a stool next to her mother. "It's a really gorgeous *you*." She sets the black bag on the counter and dumps out the contents, sending little squares of fabric sliding across the granite breakfast bar.

Trudy claps her hands. "Wow," she says, fingering a few swatches. "Madeline sent all of these?" Madeline is Becca's wedding planner, but I've never met her, because she lives in Indianapolis where Becca and Chad live, and where the wedding will take place in one of the loft spaces downtown on Labor Day weekend.

Becca nods. "We're supposed to pick our top five. I'm thinking something darker for the table"—she grabs a shiny taupe fabric and sets it aside—"and lighter for the napkins. And something with some sparkle for the cocktail tables." She holds a sequin beige square in the air and shakes it in my direction. "What do you think about this? I sort of love this one."

"Are there going to be any colors?" I ask.

Trudy laughs. "These *are* colors. Neutrals are elegant." She pats Becca's hand on the counter. "It's going to be so beautiful." Trudy pushes a curl behind Becca's shoulder, and leaves her hand there, and my heart aches for how sweet it is. I so want that to be me someday, sitting with Trudy and Becca, obsessing over fabric swatches and appetizer choices and the guest list.

"Liv." Zander's voice comes up the stairs just as he does, and pulls me out of my thoughts. "We gotta go."

I look down at Deb, who shoves a pin along my hem before sitting back on her knees. "You're good," she says. "I'll see you in a few months for the final."

I look up at Zander, who is striding over to his mother and sister. He picks up a piece of fabric. "Why are they all brown?"

Becca lets out a dramatic gasp. "It's not *brown,*" she says, scrunching her nose up in mock disgust. "It's cappuccino."

"Whatever you say." Zander puts his hands up in surrender. "*Your* wedding, *your* poop-brown napkins."

Becca comes at Zander with an open hand that lands across his bicep, and he breaks out into laughter. "I'm just kidding! Jeez!"

"Leave your sister alone." Trudy's voice is sugar, like it always is with her youngest. "I didn't hear you come in."

"I snuck in the back. Liv and I have to go to a . . . thing. Okay if I steal her?"

I don't move, because I know how this routine goes when I'm in the midst of wedding prep. Trudy and Becca can spend hours talking over every detail of this wedding, and Zander and I have been putting on this show for months. He insists we leave. I act like I just can't, I have to help. He insists, I give in (because *Ugh, what can you do? Guys.*). And then, finally, I'm free. Tonight's performance is no different. After a few groans from Becca about needing a tie-breaker vote, the door slams behind us and we practically leap onto the back porch. And no one can be mad at me.

Zander grabs my hand and leads me down the steps toward his car. "I am a human pincushion." I sigh dramatically, like there was a chance I wasn't going to make it through my fitting unscathed. "I could kiss you for rescuing me."

"You could." Zander is smiling when he pulls me toward him, his blue eyes locked on mine, his cropped blond hair shining in the sun. His arms wrap behind me as he walks me back, until my butt bumps into the car door. Zander's lips are warm and soft, and so sweet when they meet mine. I sometimes still think about how surreal it is that I kiss him now. That after years of thinking about it—and okay, I'll admit it, obsessing about it—I finally get to do it. I grope around for the handle behind me and slide away from Zander before our driveway PDA gets out of hand. I'm not making out with him in front of his house, not with all of the Peeping-Tom neighbors at their windows. I drop myself into the front seat and he does the same. As we back out of the driveway, I don't even know where we're going, but I don't care. I'd go anywhere with Zander.

﹖

As we're pulling out of his subdivision, Zander turns the music down. "Don't be mad, but I can't hang out tonight," he says.

"But you just said—" *What was that whole song and dance at his house for?*

"I didn't want you to be stuck with my family on a Friday night."

"Thanks. I guess . . ." Instead I'm going to be stuck by myself on a Friday night, because there's no chance my best friend, Emma, hasn't already been scooped up by her new boyfriend, Mani. "*Why can't we hang out?*"

"Peterson has a thing at his house."

Tim Peterson is a senior on the baseball team—one of Zander's teammates.

"And this is a no-girlfriends-allowed type of thing? It's not just a party?" I say.

He doesn't respond right away, and I wonder what exactly is happening over there that I can't come along for. "It's a party, sort of. But, like . . . okay, it's a tournament."

I've been to a lot of Zander's tournaments, and none of them happen at anyone's house.

"Peterson got the new Madden and the draft is tonight." He looks at me like I must not understand. "You know, picking our teams."

"I know what a draft is." We're pulling onto my road. "And that's going to take all night?"

"We'll probably just hang out after," he says as we pull into my driveway. "I could maybe stop over after?"

When did it became such a chore for him to work me into his schedule? I think about telling Zander that it's the second time he's ditched me this week. But instead he kisses me, and tells me he loves me as I close the door behind me. And I don't say anything, because he's already said the one thing I've always wanted him to say.

⁂

"What's the buzz, little bee?" Aunt Sarah flicks me on the shoulder as she passes me in the kitchen. I'm perched atop a stool at the island,

and while my math book is open on one side of me, my computer is filled with words. I tip the screen down just slightly, to obscure it. "Still writing, I see." She laughs at her rhyming. I'd roll my eyes at anyone else, but something about how much she doesn't give a crap just makes me love her so much more. "Oh em gee."

"Okay, just stop." I laugh as she opens the refrigerator and pulls out the carton of lemonade.

"Sorry. When you wear that, you know I just can't help it. Brings back memories." She mock sighs and looks up dramatically, like her memories are locked up in a little cloud hovering overhead in our kitchen.

I look down at the yellow shirt and black leggings I'm wearing, and it does bear a slight resemblance to the bumblebee costume I was obsessed with in elementary school. It had black tights and a striped black-and-yellow body that looked like I'd gutted a giant stuffed animal, and inserted myself into it like a striped version of Big Bird. My mom had brought it home with her after she returned from wherever it was she had wandered off to. I didn't know back then, but if I had to guess now, it was probably somewhere with our neighbor, Mr. Hoyle, whose wife moved out sometime shortly after. She was always scowling at our house.

Every day when I came home from kindergarten, I would pull my bumblebee outfit on, and spend the rest of the night buzzing about my Oma's living room. Aunt Sarah would always come over for dinner when I was there—which was most of elementary school and the first half of middle school, before I moved in with her in seventh grade. She'd always greet me and my stripy legs with, "What's the buzz, little bee?" I bet she wished I'd still been that cute when I moved in with her in seventh grade. It probably should have been weird for me to move in with her when I was twelve, but Aunt Sarah and I clicked right from the start. Probably because I never had a "normal" life. Aunt Sarah always made me feel like she wanted me at her house, and that's all I ever wanted.

"She called yesterday." Aunt Sarah doesn't have to say who, because anyone *other* than my mother would just call my cell phone. Normal people actually *want* to talk to you, because they care. My mother just wants the *illusion* of caring. Next time I see her—which will likely be around my birthday next spring, because she's senti- mental like that—she'll point out how many times she tried to call me. Like I've got a scorecard and she's earned some points. In reality, I stopped keeping score when I was nine and she told me she was moving back for good and then didn't. And I stopped caring around twelve, when I moved in with Aunt Sarah and knew that the illusion of my mother figuring her crap out was officially over. I don't even know what state she's currently in. She seems to just pop from place to place, without a care in the world.

When I think of family, I think of Aunt Sarah and my Oma— even though she's mostly in Florida these days—and Zander, and his family. And Emma, my best friend since kindergarten, who is walking through the back door right now, letting it slam behind her.

"I did it!" she belts out.

"I'll leave now." Aunt Sarah glances at Emma and her eyes go wide. It's not that Aunt Sarah isn't fun, she just likes her fun a little quieter. And with fewer sweeping arm movements.

"You don't have to," I say. Unlike me, Emma doesn't care what people think about what she says, or how she dresses, or anything, really. Aunt Sarah's probably worried she's about to hear Emma's "first time" story. *That ship has sailed.*

"Oh yes, I do," Aunt Sarah says, glancing down at my computer as she passes by. "But let's talk later, okay?"

I love that Aunt Sarah doesn't ask about my writing. I guess maybe it's out of habit, since when I started, it was a journal my therapist gave me. At first I wrote about my mom, because I thought that's what they wanted, but they never asked to look at it. So eventually I just started jotting down little thoughts I'd have. Usually it was a note about my life—something I wanted to change, a wish I had for how things actually were, something I felt bad about. But eventually they turned into little stories. My own little world where *I* controlled the outcome. And I suppose maybe that was the point all along.

Unfortunately, tonight I'm not writing anything. I'm staring at my blank screen, trying to think of a topic for a "dynamic personal essay" that doesn't require me to splash my family problems across the page, but could still win me an internship at a major teen magazine next summer. Which would be a very exciting step up from the job I have lined up this summer at our local tourist magazine, *Lake Lights*.

"What are you working on?" Emma does *not* have a problem asking me about my writing. Or anything.

"It's an essay contest for this—" I pick up the magazine from the counter next to me, the lead actress from my favorite book-to-screen adaptation smiling on the cover. "The winner gets an internship this winter."

"Oh my god, in New York or something?"

I wish. "No, remotely. But it would look amazing on my college applications."

"True story." She sets a pile of red and white fabric on the counter in front of me. "I have news too." She smiles. "I got the job at The Cherry Pit. You're looking at one of Riverton's newest worst-dressed waitresses." She pops her hands at her shoulders and dips in a little curtsy.

"Congrats," I say, and I mean it, because it's not easy finding a job in a small town when all of the college kids swoop back in for the summer.

"So what are you going to write about?"

I stare at the screen, filled with completely unrelated paragraphs that are all dead ends. Usually I write short stories—love stories. But this? I don't feel like I've actually experienced anything worth writing fifteen hundred words about. "I have no idea."

Aiden

Just put it in his mitt, and you can get off of this field. When I stand on the mound, that's what I think about now. When I'm standing on the mound, or sitting in the dugout with moon dust caked on my pants. Or when I'm riding my bike, wishing I were still behind the wheel of my car. I played summer league when I was a kid, and I don't remember wanting to get off of the mound as badly as I do now. I'd think about the way the sweat and dirt would make my face red and scratchy. How the short stocky kid who played right field always lost his white uniform socks and would come in his dad's black dress socks. When I was twelve, I'd think about impressing the girls who had come to watch us play. Or I'd think about the motions I was about to go through. About how I needed to present the ball for just long enough. Shifting my weight at the right moment, squaring up to the batter after releasing the ball. I don't remember my dad's yelling back then, but I'm sure it was always there, like a soft static that was drowned out by all of the other thoughts. The girls and the pizza after the game were louder than he was.

But now, standing on the mound, the ball sticky in my hand, all I hear is my father, saying out loud all of the things I'm thinking. He's standing behind the fence next to the dugout, his brow almost as wet as mine. At least mine is hidden by my Hornets hat. His is shining red, matted with damp brown hair.

"One more, Emerson!" he screams, his voice getting a little hoarse from the last eight innings. "Make it count!"

The ball leaves my hand and I can feel the verdict before the plate ump delivers it. "Ball two!"

My father's hands slam against the wire cage in front of him. "No! Head in the game! You've got this, Emerson!"

There's something really weird about my dad calling me by my last name. I think it's a habit that carried over from little league, when he was my coach and wanted to treat me like the rest of the team. I can't blame my dad for yelling today. He's just saying out loud what I'm thinking:

What are you doing, Aiden?

Focus!

Get this over with already!

I'm the fastest pitcher in our district, by just one percent. And if

I could simply focus—do what my dad is begging of me—this game could be over.

Focus, focus, focus. I squint my eyes against the glare of the sun, and cock my head to the side. *Better.*

I wipe my fingers down the side of my blue pants and pat my palm against my thigh. Left. Right. I crank my neck back and forth, as if that's going to fix the knot in my arm, the pain in my head, or the real problem—the blurriness as I stare straight ahead at the worn brown glove of my catcher, Zander. He's clad in black and blue gear, flashing me a two, then four, then two, with his fingers between his knees. Two is my curve ball, and I shake my head at him, telling him it's a no-go. I don't trust myself today. He flashes it again and jerks his mitt to where he wants the ball, close and inside.

"Two up, two down!" Mani, our shortstop shouts to our teammates, letting them know we're going to get these next two outs. We're up by one with runners on first and second, in our last game of the regular season. The last win we need to take us into regionals. Back-to-back-to-back titles could be ours.

I bring the ball to my chest and feel the power charge through me as I release it toward the plate. I can feel that one percent. Feel it racing through my arm, feel it slip past my fingertips. This. Is—

I hear the unmistakable groan as leather meets skin. A grunt, a lurch, as the batter crumples to the ground, the ball falling off of his bicep down to the plate.

The ump stands. "Take your base," he yells in a booming voice. There's a special tone that umps save for pitchers who hit batters. There's always a warning to that particular command: *Don't do it again.*

"Emerson!" my dad yells, the metallic clang of the fence in harmony with him. His voice has an edge of knowing sympathy. "It's just muscle memory! Focus!"

Zander throws his face guard back and puts his hands in a T over his head as he trots out to the mound. I jab my toe into the hard dirt.

"Shake it off, bud."

Despite his best efforts, Zander and I really aren't buds. We're more of a codependent two-person ecosystem. Without me, he can't do his job. He can't be amazing until I am. You can be an amazing catcher, but without the right pitcher, you're just catching the ball. With a bad pitcher, you're chasing the ball.

He grabs my head in his hands and pulls it toward him. Zander loves these big shows. The whispers of, "Look at him, bringing Emerson back down, getting him focused." People love the idea that we're some sort of dynamic duo, on the field and off. "Shake it off. He had it coming. He leaned into it, man." I know he didn't, I know I was off, too tight, too wild. I shouldn't have tried for inside. I *told* Zander. I don't say it, because this is a show, not a conversation. "You've got this next guy. You hold them here." I twist my head and pull away—I *don't* like his little shows. I nod, because I know he won't let up until I do.

My best chances for a strikeout are now on first, second, and third, and the top of the lineup is striding out to home plate. He stops behind the plate, rolls up his sleeve, and pats his bicep. He's inviting me to hit him, egging me on, mocking me. The all-state pitcher who just nailed a batter. All they need is one run and it's over. I grit my teeth, and remember what my dad said.

Muscle memory, muscle memory, muscle memory.

I lock my eyes on Zander's mitt and lean back. I try to relax, let my arms and legs do their thing. The same thing they've done for the last ten years. Thousands of batters, tens of thousands of pitches, probably.

I let the sticky leather roll around in my hand, squeeze it tight, and let it roll off the tips of my fingers. When I was a kid, I had to remind myself what to do after the ball left my hand. I'd count it out step by step: present . . . cock . . . knee up . . . release . . . pivot . . . so much of it is natural momentum. But at the end, when you bring your body back to the center, position your glove in front of you, and stand ready—that takes thought. But even that is muscle memory now. I'm not even thinking as I let my weight shift to my left leg; as my right comes down and swings to the side. There are no thoughts as my glove comes up to my chest and my leg pivots out. Not a single thought as the white blur of leather leaves the bat and makes contact with my face. No thoughts as I hit the ground, my mother's shriek hanging in the air.

Chapter  Two

OLIVIA

Baseball games are so not my thing. The uncomfortable metal bleachers, the bees that always seem to be hovering around the concession stand, following me and my ritual sixth-inning hot dog. We're all squished into this one tiny set of bleachers, and I have to make a conscious effort to keep from grazing the hairy dad-arm next to me. *Gross.* Why couldn't Zander have picked basketball—or any sport, really, that doesn't take place out in the blazing sun? Of course the only thing worse than sitting in the hot sun, watching his back while he catches a ball, is sitting in the cold, watching as he's pummeled again and again on the football field. *Oh, the joys of fall.*

"He needs to chill." Emma jabs her head in the direction of our dugout, where Mr. Emerson has taken his usual spot along the fence outside. If she had ever gone to games before this year, when she started dating the shortstop, Mani Flores, Mr. Emerson would be background noise to her by now. I don't even hear him anymore; I'm sure the coaches don't either. It really does drive Zander nuts when he gets like this though.

Next to me, Emma shakes her head, her brown eyes squinting at the middle-aged man who bears a striking resemblance to the Hornets' star pitcher, Aiden Emerson. The chain-link clangs every time his open palms slam into it, screaming "Come on, Emerson," or "Focus!" Which has been a lot this game—Aiden is struggling. He's been struggling for weeks, ever since he showed up to a game with an unexplained black eye. The black eye is gone now, but it seems our all-state pitcher has disappeared along with it.

I hit Emma's knee with mine. "Emma."

"Olivia." She draws out my full name, long and slow.

"Stop staring."

Emma doesn't turn away. "How is *anyone* supposed to concentrate with all the *yelling*?" Her voice is loud enough that I expect Mr. Emerson to look at her—to come tearing into the stands toward us, to shake us like he does that poor fence—but his eyes stay glued to his son, out on the mound. We're background noise to him too. The woman in front of us looks back at Emma with annoyance in her eyes. "Not you," Emma whispers, with a sweet smile and shake of her head. Emma's boyfriend, Mani, turns from his spot between second and third and looks at the outfielders. He yells, "We got this, two up, two down," just as Em screams, "Nice butt, Flores!" He smiles and she laughs, amused with herself.

And I wish I could magically sink down under these bleachers. I shake my head and Emma smacks my leg with a smile. "*Your* boy-friend's isn't bad either." She winks one blue eye at me. "Wouldn't kill you to get into the spirit of things."

"I don't think the objectification of players is the 'spirit' of base-ball." I take a sip from my water bottle—it's unseasonably warm for Memorial Day weekend in Michigan.

"You wouldn't."

I groan, and it sounds like there's a baby bear stuck in my throat. I'm not telling my boyfriend he has a nice butt—which he does—in front of a bleacher full of students, teachers, and parents. *His* parents. My head instinctively tips toward their location two rows behind us. I sat with the Belles before Emma started coming to games. *Those were quieter, less embarrassing days.*

Just as Zander takes his spot behind home plate again, Emma does what I won't. "Nice butt, Belle!"

Zander shakes his head as his mitt stretches in front of him, ready-ing himself, and I can't help but wonder why he puts up with me and my shameless plus-one.

"Ball two!" the umpire yells, eliciting more screaming from Mr. Emerson and glares from Emma.

"Two up, two down!" Mani yells, once again reminding every-one on the field that only two batters might stand between them and regionals. There are runners on first and second and a tied score. *Please let this be over soon.* Zander's mom, Trudy, catches my eye and gives me a little wave as she passes a paper bag of neon yellow popcorn to her husband, Dean, sitting behind her. I give a little wave to her and Becca. I would be surprised by most college juniors driving three hours to watch their little brother's baseball game, but not Becca.

There is nothing average about the Belle family. Which is what I love most about them.

Smack! Another ball hits Zander's mitt, pulling me out of my thoughts.

My phone buzzes, and a white box pops up. It's a text from my Aunt Sarah, who was supposed to be here an hour ago, taking the place of Hairy-Arm Guy, who is still disturbingly close on my right.

Aunt Sarah:

Concession stand

I turn to make my way out of the bleachers.

"More hot dogs?" Emma doesn't wait for my answer before starting to make her way to the aisle. "These baseball games are serious business, I've gained ten pounds this season."

I follow her, trying to keep my eyes on the game as we walk to the bright blue two-story stand that holds the concession area down below and the announcer's nest overhead. Just as we reach the counter, I hear a loud grunt, and gasps fill the stands.

"Did he just *hit* a batter?" I say to Emma, who is craning her neck to see over the man behind us. I haven't seen a pitcher hit a batter in years. I've *never* seen Aiden hit a batter.

The ump stands. "Take your base," he yells in a booming voice.

Zander throws his face guard back and puts his hands in a T over his head as he trots away from home base. The two stand on the mound, Zander clearly giving Aiden the pep talk he needs.

Next to me, Emma sighs. "I *adore* concession-stand nachos."

My eyes are still on Zander making his slow-walk back to his spot.

Giving Aiden every extra second he can. I catch his eye as he reaches the plate and smile. He meets my eyes but he still looks angry. Even so, it's a little barb that he can't just suck it up and smile back.

Aunt Sarah appears at the metal counter just as I'm given my pop and gumballs. She fidgets with her phone, then quickly shoves it into her pocket. I hand her a can of Diet Coke and am turning back for the bleachers when a tug at my wrist stops me. She pulls me a few steps in the opposite direction and looks at me nervously. "I have to tell you something, and I've been meaning to, but then there's never a good time." She rambles nervously. "And I'm going to be gone this weekend, so . . ."

"Tell me what?" I pop a piece of baseball-shaped gum into my mouth, my eyes still fixed on the back of my boyfriend's head, over Aunt Sarah's shoulder.

"I got an amazing job offer. In Arizona." The words make me flinch. My eyes dart from the batter to my aunt, standing in front of me looking like she's about to throw up all over my shoes. *The feeling is so mutual.*

I've never heard Aunt Sarah mention Arizona before. Or wanting a new job. "Why would you want a job in Arizona?"

"Well, it pays better, and it's with a bigger company. And there are more opportunities for me if I get out of Riverton." Okay, I guess I have heard *that* before. Aunt Sarah is a programmer, and rural Michigan is not a technology mecca.

"Do I have to move to Arizona?" I can't. Not my senior year. Not with Emma and Zander here.

"We'll . . . figure something out," she says, but she doesn't look as optimistic as she sounds.

Behind her, the whir of the bat catches my eye. *Arizona?*

The ball flies, and from our spot behind the fence it almost looks as if it's going straight for Aiden. But he's not moving, and when I see it happen—the way the white leather deflects off of his perfect cheekbone—I can't help but gasp. He crumples to the ground and it feels a lot like I'm right there next to him—both of us victims of something we didn't see coming.

AIDEN

When I enter the locker room on the last day of school a week later, the sour smell hits me like a line drive to the face. I wish I didn't know what that felt like, but my face still says otherwise. I'm lucky all I got was some serious bruises and broken skin, and that my eye didn't explode, or something. *Has it always smelled this bad?* It's lunch hour on the last day of school, so the locker room is empty, but I know Coach Martinez will be here. He teaches freshman algebra, and is always in his office during lunch time. It's usually open tutoring time, for guys with at-risk GPAs. Not at risk of not graduating, just dangerously close to being kicked off the team. But those guys are usually cleared out by now, making their way toward classes. They're not sticking around one second longer than they have to.

"Hey, Stevens," I say to our third baseman—the biggest asshole on the team—who is leaving Coach M's office as I come down the dark tiled hallway. He nods as he passes me, and keeps walking. Everyone acts like this is all my fault, and it's hard to even argue.

Losing the game meant the end of practices, so aside from the occasional side-eye from Zander in our physics class, I've gotten off pretty easy.

I knock on the window before I step through the door. Coach M is sitting at his desk, a Riverton Hornets hat pulled over his shaggy black hair.

"Emerson, you're just in time." A giant grin fills his face; if the loss is getting to him, he hasn't let on. "We've got a few minutes. You need a quick session?" He laughs, because I'm far from needing tutoring, and he knows it. Our team was academic all-state last year, thanks to GPAs like mine pulling up slackers like Stevens.

"I'm good."

His eyes drop to the pile of blue in my hand, and scrunch up in confusion. "Problem with your uniform, kid?"

I swallow, trying to make the words come out. I've played baseball since I was four. Summers of tee-ball, then little league, then three years of varsity. I have a shelf around my ceiling, lining my room with metallic trophies—red and green and blue—all topped with bat-wielding gold or silver men, ready to swing. Now I'm standing here, after the last game of my junior season, and I can't say the words that I know I have to. Even though it took me fifteen minutes to force myself into that smelly hallway. Even though I feel like I might puke all over the tiled floor.

"Emerson?" Coach M tips his head and perks his brows. He looks nervous, like maybe I'm about to tell him I decided to run track and I'm going to miss a few games. That shit really pisses the coaches off. There's nothing they like less than a guy who's lacking 110 percent allegiance. *God forbid anyone be multitalented.*

"I'm . . . out," I mumble, not sure that the words were actually audible.

Coach M looks around him, like he's missed something. "Out of what?"

"Out of baseball." I set the uniform on his desk and look at the clock. There's exactly ninety seconds until the bell sounds. Ninety seconds until I have to flee, no matter what. I'm not an idiot, there's a reason I skated in just under the bell. Because I can't take being berated about this. I'm maxed out on guilt.

"Like hell you are, son." Coach M is out of his chair, two hands planted on the desk, leaning toward me like he's trying to keep himself from lunging. His face is already turning red, the way it looks when he screams "Gimme one more" as we run wind sprints—third base line to the mound and back, first base line and back, right field fence and back, our arms pumping until they're tingling and almost numb. Only he doesn't scare me then, because all I have to do is run. Just run, run, run and the screaming will stop. Run, run, run and eventually you get to go home. But I can't run now. There's still sixty seconds until that bell sounds, and even when it does, I don't know that he's going to let me leave. "You're our starting pitcher. Have you lost your fu—" He looks around like he forgot he was in the school. His voice gets just a hair softer but it's just a different kind of yelling. When it comes to yelling, it's actually about tone, not volume. That's what people don't get about my dad yelling. I know what my dad sounds like mad; really mad, like I've done something wrong. It's different from the frustrated yelling I hear from behind the fence every game. "Have you lost your mind, Emerson? You're not quitting right before your senior year."

"I just did." The bell sounds, and I feel like a racehorse just set free, the metal gate pulled away. Except that I'm not running toward anything, I'm being chased—by everything I could have had. I turn to the hallway and walk away as Coach M slams something in his office behind me. I exit the locker room hallway and head into the bright expansive gym. There are signs plastering the gym walls, left over from the last pep rally. The blue walls are spotted with white rectangular blotches. Banners, likely filled with player names and numbers, and notes reading GOOD LUCK, YOU CAN DO IT and WE'RE #1. By September they'll be gone—everyone will have forgotten the last game and the big loss. The same way they'll have forgotten about me, and everything I could have been. I hope.

༂

When the final bell of junior year rings, the hallway is filled with excitement. Locker doors are slamming and feet are pounding as everyone darts outdoors. Everyone has somewhere to go. Usually I'd be headed to the gym to lift weights. Even on the last day of school. We wouldn't get much done, but we'd still sit on the equipment, lifting half our usual and shooting the shit. Martinez would come in to lecture us about being responsible over the summer and not getting soft and worthless, lying at the beach and eating concession hamburgers. The guy always has something to say about concession food. *So who has the* real *problem?*

Zander passes me with a nod, and I know he doesn't know. For now. Because no chance he'd let me just pass by if he did, and no way Coach M doesn't fill everyone in. I guess the guys will get a different kind of warning this summer. *Eat all the hamburgers and nachos you want, just don't lose your shit like Emerson.*

When I close my locker, I look down the quiet, almost-empty hallway. It's my last time standing here as Emerson. In three months I'll come back as a senior, and I won't be Him. Emerson, the Golden Boy of Riverton Baseball. I've already noticed the change the last week, as I've navigated the hallways with my mangled face. I've had to wear my failure like a mask.

I push the doors open and walk into the courtyard where the bike racks are. My yellow Schwinn is the only one left. It's still dusty and scratched from two years of sitting in the backyard shed since I got my permit and abandoned it. I brush off the black handlebars and give it a squeeze in my palm. *It's just you and me this summer.* As I roll out onto the sidewalk I can see a few of the guys out by the double doors leading out of the gym, at the opposite end of the building. They're looking out into the parking lot.

When Stevens's eyes meet mine, I know they know. I hear my name in a loud shout—not angry, just loud—and steer myself in the opposite direction. They can't fix this. And I don't want to hear about how I'm letting the team down, or ruining senior year, or driving away scouts. I know I'm doing it. I let all those thoughts infest my brain for the last week, until it got so messed up I had to let them out. I'm used to baseball being on my brain—games, scouts, college plans, all of it. But not when I can't have it. Not when I know it's out of reach.

Because there's no such thing as a legally blind pitcher. Even if it's just one eye. I close my left eye as I pedal, and watch everything get soft and shaded like a watercolor painting. I can still see the road—the dark strip stretching out in front of me. The grass and trees are all shades of green, blended together, lights and darks, like little puddles of paint against the blue background of the sky. I close my other eye as well, just for a second, feel the breeze against my face, warm sun in my hair. My shoulders suddenly feel so much hotter.

I jerk as a rush of air goes by me. My eyes whip open as the car flies by down the country road, my tire sliding just off the shoulder into the gravel, crashing me down to the ground.

"Fuck." I push myself up, pulling my bike with me. My forearm burns, covered in dirt and tiny pieces of gravel, the blood starting to seep out in thin lines and splotches. *Fantastic.* Because I didn't look like enough of a freak show with my mutilated face. My mom's going to lose her shit when she sees this. She's already convinced I'm going off the rails. That I'm being hasty quitting the team. Things will get better, she says. Which is probably true, but what she doesn't understand is that baseball isn't going to wait for me. That the idea of a baseball flying in my direction is fucking terrifying now. That even before I took a line drive to the face, I flinched every time Zander lobbed the ball back at me in practice. I knew as soon as I left the ophthalmologist's office a month ago that I probably shouldn't play, but I've let my parents' optimism keep pushing me forward. *Until the hit.* I knew that hit was the end of more than just our chance at regionals.

My phone is buzzing in my pocket and there are only three possibilities:

1. The guys, ready to trash me about baseball
2. Ellis, my cousin and best friend, making sure I survived
3. Dad, checking in about River Depot

When I finally pull up to the house and take my phone out, it turns out I was three for three.

> Zander: WTF Emerson!!!
>
> Stevens: Come on man, get your ass back here
>
> MISSED CALL: Dad
>
> Ellis: You alive?
>
> Still have all your beautiful teeth?
>
> Your face needs all the help it can get at this point.

I laugh out loud, because Ellis is obsessed with the current status of my face. A few days ago he tried to put concealer on my eye, and he's already looked up the area's best cosmetic surgeon, in case—his words, not mine—my face doesn't "pull together" soon. It's not really that bad. The swelling is gone and in another week the bruises will hopefully be gone completely. There's a healing cut on the outside of my cheekbone, but the little white strips across it look kind of badass. Like I was in a fight or something. By the time I throw another bandage on my arm, the look will be complete.

❧

When I pull into the driveway, Dad's giant red truck is in front of our massive garage. Most people would just call it a pole barn, but to me it's always been the garage. Except it's the kind of garage where you winter fifty canoes, a hundred kayaks, and piles and piles of life jackets. Even now, with the season getting started, a third of the space is still covered in red, blue, and green boats.

My car is sitting in the unopened bay at the far end of the garage, and even though I can't see it, I can sense it like a cosmic pull. I can almost feel the worn leather interior, like a phantom limb.

"Aiden." My name rings across the yard as I dump my bike in the grass.

"Hey." I make my way toward the porch where my dad is coming down the steps in his unofficial summer uniform—khaki shorts, Birkenstocks, and a Riverton t-shirt. My dad owns every t-shirt River Depot sells. This one says SALT-FREE SUMMER FUN with an outline of Lake Michigan, and RIVERTON across the bottom. It's so weird to live in a place where people buy everything from shot glasses to kid's slingshots with the town's name slapped on it. It's not like we're New York or Chicago or Paris. I doubt some dude overseas visits the Eiffel Tower and then thinks, "Now all that remains is to see Riverton, Michigan, and I can die happy." It's a nice enough place though, if you like the water, which my family does. We've spent most of our summer free time outside for as long as I can remember. Canoeing and kayaking; hiking in the dunes along Lake Michigan.

"Help me load up?" Dad nods toward the garage. "It's good practice for you."

"Sure." I toss my backpack onto the porch and make my way to the garage. Dad looks at my wrist, then holds it up in his hand. "What's this?"

"Bike ride home." I lightly brush at the dirt still stuck to my arm. "Wiped out." The blood is starting to dry and it's going to hurt like a bitch when I finally get a chance to wash it off.

"You're killing me with this stuff." Dad laughs softly, but I can tell he's irritated. "Throw your mom a bone and try to be more careful, okay? I'm tired of hearing about how you're mangling the body she spent nine long months growing."

"Limb by limb," I mutter, and Dad laughs. I look down at my arm, barely bleeding at all but clearly not looking great. Life has been more dangerous lately. "Sorry."

Dad grabs one end of a canoe and I grab the other. "How'd it go?" he says, as we make our way to his truck. "Martinez give you crap?"

I hoist my end of the metal boat up onto the rack that sits atop the bed of my dad's truck. "It was fine." I don't know what else to say. This isn't the kind of talk we usually have about baseball. Dream colleges and major league pipe dreams is our usual thing. Stuff that's less depressing.

He nods but doesn't say anything else about it. We load five more canoes onto the rack, and then start shoving oars in the empty cavity of the truck bed. Dad climbs into the driver's seat and hangs his elbow out the open window. "You sure you're up for this?"

I know what Dad means—you're sure you want to work at River Depot? Sure that after all these years avoiding it with baseball camps and pitching clinics and extra workouts, I'm not going to let him down this summer? I won't be in charge—I don't know enough now to do anything other than grunt work. Ellis starts training me this weekend, getting me up to speed on all the things I didn't learn the last four years, while he was working there without me.

I'm excited to work with my best friend. Excited I'll mostly be helping tourists who don't know me, and not locals who will ask questions. A three-month break from teammates, classmates, and coaches sounds like a best-case scenario. This summer I need to figure out who I am *without* baseball, and I don't need to be reminded of who I was *with* it.

Olivia

"I could stay here." I turn my eyes from the ceiling and look into Zander's blue eyes. It's the first day of summer break, and I'm lying on his bed in a post-lunch food coma.

"In my room? You're not supposed to be up here to begin with."

I think of what Aunt Sarah would say, and snort a little. Even when we were in middle school and just friends, I always had strict instructions not to be in Zander's room. I'm not sure what the goal was, because Aunt Sarah is far from conservative and I wasn't even thinking about sex back then—I certainly wasn't about to do it with his parents down the hallway. Maybe it just made her feel more like a mother figure? I had just moved in with her full-time, and she was still getting used to the whole pseudo-parent thing. Sometimes I think she still is.

"*Your* parents don't care," I say.

"I guess." Zander doesn't sound convinced. He sounds indifferent. He's been weird the last week, ever since I told him I was potentially moving. *Weird*, because he's taken a temporary hiatus from ranting about his baseball woes, and is now talking about almost nothing.

Potentially, because I still have no intention of actually leaving. Aunt Sarah seems to be open to options, so now I just need some options.

It's true about his parents though. They really don't care. As far as they're concerned, my joining the family someday is just a technicality. They've introduced me as their "other daughter" for as long as I can remember; since I was the sometimes-neighbor girl at Oma's house down the street. Then in ninth grade, when Zander had his first serious girlfriend, I didn't come around as much. It was hard, seeing them together. Even harder getting the side-eye from Ellie Henderson. *It won't last*, his dad said to me with a wink, when I found myself early to his house one night and Ellie and I crossed paths. She glared at me from across the kitchen as I sat at the island with a glass I'd gotten myself from the cabinet. I wanted to cry then, thinking about how I wasn't The One. But six months later Ellie was gone. And his mom said, "It's always been you" when we told them we were officially together.

"Are you listening to me?" I flick his hand with mine. "I'm serious. Maybe I could stay in Becca's room."

"She's coming home for the summer. *She'll* need her old room."

He's right, of course. "But she's getting married at the end of the summer. And she'll be moved into their new place before that . . . so maybe I could stay *here*." I look around his room, at the posters and trophies and dents in the wall I know by heart. "You'll be gone most of the summer, anyway. I could stay in your room while you're gone, and then move into Becca's before school starts."

I'm proud of myself for thinking on my feet. Though I wonder how the Belles—or Aunt Sarah—would feel about me being in the house alone for so long.

"I'll be gone all summer," he corrects me.

No one knows better than me how long my boyfriend deserts me each summer, when he pilgrimages to his family's lake house five hours north. *Leaving one beach town for another—ridiculous.* For ten weeks every summer I'm at the bottom of the state, and Zander is at the top. And for one glorious week in the middle, I get to stay at the lake house with him—with all of them. *The Belles.* Becca lying out on the float until she's an unnatural shade of red, Zander's mom, Trudy, making elaborate meals every night, and her husband Dean manning the grill.

The lake cabin is just the right mix of new and old and the lake is always rippling gently with the light shimmering across it like tinsel on a Christmas tree. I'm always there during the Fourth of July, when the little town puts up flags and buntings. Like a freaking Norman Rockwell painting. Just thinking about the lake house makes me giddy with anticipation. Zander and I used to share a room with twin bunk beds when we were up there, but when I had gone from best friend to girlfriend that summer after freshman year I was promoted to the spare bed in Becca's room for the week.

"I'm staying the whole summer this year." Zander shakes his head, and his blond hair falls across his forehead.

"Since when?"

He doesn't say anything right away, just stares up at the ceiling. When I push myself up and sit on the edge of the bed, he closes his eyes. "Does this have to be a thing?"

"That I'm possibly leaving, and you're not going to see me all summer?"

He shakes his head. "If you're leaving, what's the *point* of the summer?" he mumbles.

Ouch. It had never crossed my mind that my moving would mean that Zander and I were over.

"So you don't want to waste your summer with me if I'm going to be moving . . . but you also don't want me to move in, which would keep me here? That sounds like us breaking up either way."

Zander doesn't say anything, and I can feel the tears pricking at my eyes. I don't say anything, because talking about feelings is hard. It was hard when I was in therapy, talking about my lousy mother, and it never got any easier when I had to start talking to Zander.

"Maybe we should, Liv. I mean—" His voice is soft but rough, and the words stick into my ribs like they were wrapped around the blade of a knife.

"Fine." I don't know what else to say when it's clear he's over this. That he's fine with leaving me for the summer, and for forever.

Zander rolls off his back and sits on the edge of his bed, his back to me. I've spent so much time in his room, I almost forget it isn't mine. That *I'm* the one who has to retreat from this match. "I still want to be friends . . ."

"Unbelievable." I push myself up from the bed and don't glance back as I make my way out the door. Of course Zander would think he could have it both ways. I was the friend, and then finally when it was convenient I was the girlfriend, and now the tides have turned again.

The hallway that runs along the upstairs balcony feels endless as I pass the doors to his parents' room and his sister's. *I can't believe I was thinking about moving in here while he was ready to dump me.*

He's just done? It doesn't make any sense, and the irrationality of it all gives me a certain sense of calm. Tomorrow he'll text. I'll wake up to "Love you"—Zander's version of an *I'm sorry*—and all will be right. Because serious relationships don't end like this. They don't end without tears or yelling. Over the years my mother's boyfriends just left. One day they were there and the next they were gone. Zander isn't some guy I met at the grocery store and brought home on a whim. *Why did he have to kiss me?*

I had almost gotten used to him and Horrible Ellie Henderson, to the idea that we'd never get together. I had a crush on Joey Hammond that spring. He had just started texting me, and showing up at the ice cream shop after my shifts. But then Zander broke up with Ellie, and we sat on his bed, and he kissed me. *He* changed everything. Now I wish he had just left me in my little bubble, loving him in secret. We wouldn't have anything to lose. But no, he just had to go and kiss me.

As I make my way through the kitchen I give Trudy a quick smile. She's leaning her hip against the counter, hunched over a notepad as she scratches at it with a pen. Her hair is long and blond and everything about her is soft-looking. Not like my mother, who is all sharp angles, straight lines, and cropped dark hair. Trudy has always felt like what I thought a mother *should* be. Not just soft, but warm. I want to stop, to tell her what a jerk her son is, but it's embarrassing to admit how dysfunctional we can be. Plus it isn't fair to her. Or to me. Because she'd march me right back up there and somehow fix this. I'm not sure if I'm ready for it to be fixed.

I want the text.

I want to ignore it for a few hours, to make him wait and wonder.

I want to be on the other end for once. I never realized how much I needed it until this moment. I'm out the door before Trudy can even say a word. And as I walk out of Zander's house, along the brick walkway and down the driveway, where the family's speedboat sits, waiting to be hauled five hours north, I realize that my problems have only multiplied since I arrived. I still don't have anywhere to live next year.

This isn't how I imagined summer starting.

Chapter
Three

All I can think about is how Zander has ruined everything. How it might never be what it was, the two of us lying on his living room floor, sorting through our history homework while his mom hovered around us with bowls of popcorn (and then chips, and then pretzels). Eventually I'd stay for dinner, because Aunt Sarah works late, and Trudy thinks I'll starve, because I'm basically a bottomless pit. The Belles were my family, my safe place, the universe's reward for all the crap. And Zander ruined it.

"I hate boys." The cupcake wrapper crinkles as I peel it back, letting my fingers sink into the softness. I think about the sappy text message I almost sent to Zander this morning, the one still sitting on my phone about how I wished he had never kissed me two years ago. *Don't do it, Liv.* It felt good to write it, even if I'm not going to send it.

"I don't," Emma says, her mouth full of chocolate. There's a smudge of pink frosting at the corner of her lips. The ridiculous uniform for her new job at The Cherry Pit is laid across my bed waiting for her shift to start in an hour. Emma and I are on the floor, sitting cross-legged and face-to-face, while I eat my feelings. Yesterday was the crying—today, I'm just mad.

"Fine, I hate Zander, not the whole gender."

"No you don't."

I glance at my phone, lying on the gray carpet next to me. Forty-eight hours, and still nothing. "I seriously do." I unlock my phone, checking to make sure I didn't miss anything.

"You wanna eff up his house?"

"Em," I scold. Because she's right, I'm not quite ready to give up yet.

"No, come on." Emma springs into a stand. "Let's torch it!"

"Torch what?"

"His house! I'm ready if you are." She grabs another cupcake.

"You're ridiculous."

"See!" She points at me accusatorily. "I knew you weren't ready to admit this is over." She shakes her head, looking at me like I'm a straight-A student who just brought her first B home. "*You're* ridiculous." She takes another bite and rolls her eyes. "You should be happy you've been saved from your own boring-ass future."

"Our future wouldn't have been boring."

"It *would*. Because the two of you are boring together. B-O-R-I-N-G."

Emma and Zander have never been best friends, but there's never been any animosity there. None that I've noticed before, at least. But here she is, telling me what she really thinks, apparently for the first time.

"Honestly, Liv . . . I don't think this is the worst thing that could happen. You could use a little drama in your life."

"Drama is the last thing I want," I say.

Emma obviously doesn't get what Zander and I have. The steadiness of it. I can't remember the last time I imagined my future without Zander. Even before we were together, I always hoped for it. His was the future last name I scribbled in my eighth grade notebooks. The yearbook photo I drew a heart around (and then shoved in the back of my closet to hide, like a stone-cold weirdo). I'm not interested in dating a bunch of guys and piecing my heart back together a million times. I'm not interested in the excitement (translation: drama) that Emma is interested in.

"Trust me, I know," she mumbles.

"What is that supposed to mean?" *Since when is it a bad thing to not want your life to be a freak show?* I've had drama, and she knows that. My mom's first, middle, and last name is drama. Drama Drama Drama.

"Nothing. You have the perfect GPA, the perfect boyfriend, the perfect summer job." Emma rolls her eyes. "I guess everything is perfect . . ."

"And?"

"And it's fucking boring," she says, around the chocolate cupcake in her mouth. "And safe. And it's getting really old watching you live like a fortysomething soccer mom."

"Oh come on, *now* who's being dramatic?" I say.

"Did you, or did you not, spend the last two Saturdays planning a wedding with his mom and sister?"

"I did. Because his sister is my friend, and I actually *like* his mom. And then I went out with my boyfriend."

Emma scowls and a little rumble escapes her throat. "Did you? Did you go out and do something *fun*?"

We went to a movie. Movies are fun. Last time I checked, taking your girlfriend to a movie wasn't a criminal offense. *Where is this coming from?* Zander and Emma have always gotten along. "What's wrong with a movie?"

"Nothing, it's perfect. *He's* perfect. Just like you've been telling me since we were ten."

"And?"

"And before you know it, you're going to be going to the movies that Zander picks out for the rest of your life," she says.

"And that's the worst thing?"

"It's not very romantic."

"They make movies about falling in love with your best friend, Em. It *is* romantic."

"Yeah, but they're like . . . *Hallmark* movies." Em squishes her nose up, like just the word offends her. "*You* need to be in the kind of movie that gets leaked on the internet because it's so hot."

She makes a sizzling sound when she touches my knee and I want to laugh but I can't quite make myself. I hate that she's putting these thoughts into my head, making me question what I've always wanted. Because I have *always* wanted Zander. I *still* want him.

"Okay, but seriously." Em's eyes are soft. "You've been in love with

Zander since you were ten or something. You've never kissed another guy. You've never been wooed."

"Wooed? Seriously?"

"Don't you want to know what it's like?"

"What?" I can feel the warmness rising up in my chest, the feeling when I know I'm in trouble, when I've done something wrong, been caught. I feel the panic rising up, the anxiety and anger. The sadness. I breathe slow through my nose, so slow Emma won't even notice it. But *I* do. I feel the air filling my lungs, feel the blood cooling down, my nerves starting to settle. 1 . . . 2 . . . 3 . . . I can't remember the last time I had to calm my nerves like this, had to do my breathing exercises from therapy. But I feel so unwanted right now.

"Don't you want to know what it feels like to be chased?"

She's right. I was most definitely the chaser with Zander. Even though he's the one who made the move that turned us into a couple, I was the one sitting on the sidelines, waiting for it. Deep down, I know he knew how I felt about him. For years. So yes, it's a little sad that I just waited around all of those years, until he was ready. But it never mattered because I ended up with what I always wanted. "Maybe I don't *want* to be chased," I say.

"And maybe you do."

Yeah, maybe I do.

⁓

The building that houses *Lake Lights* is short, fat, and gray, like the lady who is sitting at the reception desk when I walk in a few days later.

"Hi," I say. "You must be Brenda. I'm Olivia, we spoke on the phone a few weeks ago."

"Oh." She looks at me like I've caught her off guard, and she isn't making me any less nervous. "Wait here and I'll get Mr. Harris for you." I expect her to get up, but she picks up the phone and mumbles a few words as I sit down in one of the chairs next to the desk.

"Great. Thanks." I hope she can't hear my toes tapping away in my shoe like they might bust right through the bottom and hammer a tiny toe-shaped hole right through the floor. *Property damage on the first day of work.* When I was here two months ago for my interview, the office felt alive. People were scurrying about and phones were ringing. Now it's dead quiet, and it's almost eerie how still everything is. I look to the receptionist, whose eyes dart away as soon as they meet mine.

Oh crap.

Maybe they're rethinking their willingness to take on a high school student as part of the summer staff this year. If I could cross my tapping toes right inside my shoes, I would. This job is perfect for me. A staff writer for the busy summer season at the area's weekly tourism guide. They pick up a handful of extra staff for the summer, and I spent the last six months preparing my portfolio, finding an in at the magazine, and getting letters of recommendation from teachers. It's not unheard of for them to take a high school student, but it takes a lot more work. And I know they won't send me out on my own for a while, but it will be a great start. By the end of the summer I'll have published articles. Just the thought of my name in print gives me shivers. Maybe having assignments will help get my brain moving, and I'll actually think of a topic for the teen mag essay contest. *One problem at a time, Olivia.* I feel like I've been telling myself that a lot lately. That I'll deal with Zander once I've figured out how to stay in Riverton.

Lake Lights is perfect because it's something I could come back to every summer, when Zander and I are home from college. The thought stops me in my tracks. *Will there be a Zander and I?* It doesn't feel like it, but it also doesn't feel like it could be over. It's been almost a week since I walked out of his room. Three days since his family left for the cottage. Not that I've driven past his house or anything, but their boat is gone, and his mom has the spare key lockbox that looks like a frog statue set out by their garden. *I have to fix this.*

"Olivia . . ." My name floats out of the hallway, and I can tell just by the way he says it—like he wishes I weren't here—that this isn't good. "I'm so sorry you came all the way down here."

"It's no problem." I smile. "I live in town, so I'm happy to come any time."

"Right. Well." He pats the side of his leg. "I'm sorry, everyone was supposed to have been mailed a notice." He glances back at the elderly woman at the desk and I do the same.

"A . . . notice?"

"Of our closing," he says.

No. Oh please, no. "But—"

"I'm so sorry—"

"When will you reopen?" I ask.

"Closed for good, I'm afraid. Just not enough advertiser interest last summer."

"And that's it? One bad summer and that's it?" *What's wrong with this guy? Lake Lights* has been around *forever.*

"Well, it's been a few summers now, but yes, one bad summer and I've decided I could be spending mine elsewhere."

Apparently everyone *wants to get out of Riverton this summer.*

"But, I—"

"I'm sorry you weren't notified. Here, you should take a few of these." He shoves a handful of magazines into my hands, and he's walking toward the door, and I'm following without thinking, my six copies of the April issue clutched against my chest.

"But—"

"I hope you have a wonderful summer," he says.

And by the time the last word is out of his mouth, the door is closed. And all of my hard work and planning is gone with the slide of the dead bolt.

☙

After multiple online searches, I'm starting to worry there aren't actually any jobs within a five-mile radius of me. At least not any that don't look sketchy as hell. I finally resort to the newspapers. The regional paper and two smaller local ones are spread out on the kitchen table. I feel so old-school. Aunt Sarah would be really proud of me for resorting to digging through the newspaper pile in the garage, but I'm glad she's not here. Because she's on my blacklist. Last week I didn't even *have* a blacklist, and this week it's multiplying by the day.

1. Zander—Former love of my life, breaker of my heart. Officially MIA for a week.
2. *Lake Lights*—That magazine is dead to me. I gathered all of our old copies and burned them in the fire pit when I got back from what was supposed to be my orientation. *How's that for drama, Emma?*
3. Aunt Sarah—The Great Abandoner. Trading in her favorite (only) niece's senior year for an amazing promotion at a new technology firm. *I am the worst for being mad about this.*
4. Mom—Because I guess she's kind of always on this list. Because if she hadn't run off constantly, and left me with Oma, I wouldn't have taken up refuge at Zander's. And I'd be able to communicate with someone I love, like a normal person, and I'd have my own normal family, so I wouldn't have to attach myself to someone else's. Because if she had her shit together, maybe mine would be too. *Yeah, Mom's definitely on this list.*

An hour after sifting through ads for machine operators (too young), nursing assistants (unqualified), and truck drivers (too young, unqualified, and no thanks), it's official: My blacklist is longer than my list of job possibilities, which is a whopping one. A tiny newspaper ad and two hours later, Emma is enthusiastically shoving me out of her car in the parking lot of River Depot with a chipper "good luck." I haven't been here in years. It's a giant building of dark brown logs that sprawls next to the river. From the street you'd think it was a gas station, with its two old-fashioned pumps out front and the building's small visible footprint from the street. But inside, it's like a genie's bottle, spreading into multiple attached rooms and levels, built into the hill that slopes down to the river.

There's an area for kayak and canoe trips, another for lazy river rides—complete with floating inflatable coolers. Inside they sell everything you could ever need. *If* you're on vacation. It's the kind of place that locals avoid and tourists flock to. The parking lot is across the street, and as I cross, I can see the giant black bear that sits under the big wood RIVER DEPOT sign. The bear is at least twice as tall as me, and three times as wide. He's standing on his hind legs, with one paw outstretched in front of him at belly height. A mom is helping her daughter sit on the outstretched paw as Dad takes her picture.

I walk past the bear and into the front doors that lead into the gift shop. To either side are counters, and in front of me, there are souvenirs and knick-knacks more dense than any chain store. Shelves go to the ceilings with toy slingshots, polished rocks, foam guns, butterfly nets, and water toys. The left side of the store is filled with hats and t-shirts and sandals and visors, all emblazoned with RIVER DEPOT or other local touristy slogans. The right side of the store has overpriced boxes of cereal and pancake mix, paper plates, and graham crackers and marshmallows—all the vacation necessities.

I stop at the little desk to my left where a girl a little younger than me is clad in a red RIVER DEPOT tank top and khaki shorts. Suddenly the long sundress I was worried wouldn't be dressy enough for an interview is feeling like extreme overkill. "I'm here for an interview," I say, smiling.

"You need Ellis, down by the launch."

"Launch?"

"The boat launch, where they put the canoes in." She points to a pair of doors on the right side of the building. "Through those doors and down the stairs on your left."

Outside, a second story deck wraps around the concession stand called The Grill. A small staircase leads to a lower level surrounded by built-in benches that circle around a gas fireplace in the center. Past the fireplace, another set of stairs empties out onto a large deck full of colorful Adirondack chairs and round picnic tables that overlook the river. One last set of stairs dumps me onto a bed of gravel by the water. To my left, two large garage doors open up from the lowest level of the building. In front of me, towering stacks of colorful kayaks rest on metal bars. It's still early for vacationers—who will start pouring in next week—but there are a few boats being pushed from the docks on the right. Two guys in red shirts are standing in front of the garage doors with their backs to me, talking and laughing.

I walk up and announce myself with a few scuffs of the gravel under my feet. "Ellis?" I ask, hoping I haven't wandered to the wrong area.

Both guys turn around and the shorter blond sticks his hand out to me. "I'm Ellis. You must be Olivia."

"Yep." I shake his hand and smile. He's wearing at least three rings on each hand, and his hair looks better than mine. It's light, pushed up into a fauxhawk at the front, and held in place by . . . something strong. It's like the ultimate boy-band hair and I sort of love that I could potentially look at it every day. *My* hair—which is usually in loose dark curls around my face—is pulled up into a sloppy ponytail. I didn't want to look like someone who couldn't cut it working out in the heat, doing whatever it is they do here. Ellis is just a few inches taller than me, and lean, and really cute.

Almost as cute as the guy standing next to him. Aiden Emerson.

He still has a faint bruise on his cheek, around the little white strips that seem to be holding his previously torn skin together. And his arm is covered in a fresh patch of scabbed-up scratches. Even though Aiden and I have gone to the same school for years, and I saw him at all of Zander's games over the years, I don't really know him. Up until the last few weeks, Aiden was the kind of sports-star golden child you never heard a bad word about. But recently, he's all anyone is talking about, and not in a good way. A week after that epically awful game, he shows up to school on his bike, quits the team, and then just peaces out for the summer? Zander is probably still homicidal. Aiden was his ticket to college scouts. Scouts come for pitchers, not catchers, is what he always said. And Zander was hopeful that the better Aiden fared, the better he would.

"Hey." I nod my head at him, because I know he knows who I am. It seems weird to just act like I don't see him. Even with the remnants of his one-on-one with the baseball, Aiden is still hard not to look at. He's about a half-foot taller than me, easily six foot three, and he's a lot bigger than Ellis—or even Zander—is, with his broad shoulders and muscular upper body. His brown hair is short around the sides and longer on top.

Aiden nods back at me, and looks annoyed that he has to do that much. His eyes are vacant, like he doesn't know who I am. And then he's gone, turned toward the kayaks, making marks on the clipboard in his hands. *Whatever.* Maybe if he hadn't completely gone off the rails and I still had to see him at baseball games, I would care that he just looked at me like he had no idea who I was. Like we didn't go to the same school for most of our lives. I turn to follow Ellis over to a small wooden podium that looks like maybe it's used to register people. It's a giant stump covered in glossy lacquer.

"Thanks for seeing me, Ellis—" I feel like I should call him by his last name since he's interviewing me, but he also looks like he's about my age.

"Emerson," he finishes for me.

"Oh, you guys are—" I nod at Aiden, now in the distance.

"Cousins." Ellis pulls a paper out from the podium and sets it in front of me. "Fill out this top section. Make sure you include the emergency contact. That's not optional." He highlights the words in blue, and runs his finger down to the next section labeled AVAILABILITY. "Mark all the days and times you'd be available."

"I'm available any time." I draw a long skinny circle around the entire week. "I have zero life right now."

Ellis smiles. "Excellent." He hovers over me while I fill in my address, birthday, and school info. He hands me another sheet of yellow paper. "This goes over dress code. You'll get two RD tank tops, two shirts, and a hoodie, but you'll need to provide your own khaki shorts." He checks something off on his own clipboard. "Sneakers, no sandals. You're likely to break toes if you drop a boat on them."

Ellis tells me about River Depot and everything that goes on there. How I'll do a little of everything to start, until they figure out where the best fit for me is. I'll ring up customers, stock shelves, scoop ice cream, and make hamburgers and hot dogs, but I'll also work the canoe and kayak trips, hauling boats and reading the rules to riders and sending them on their way with paddles and life jackets and inflatable coolers in tow. That's where they really need someone, he tells me. When he's done, he pulls out flat plastic-wrapped red shirts from the podium. "Here are these."

I look at the shirts I've just been handed. "Is that . . . there's no interview?"

"I can ask you more questions if you want." He looks like he's serious. "Otherwise you can start tomorrow. We need all hands on deck to start orientation. They'll be here before you know it."

And by "they" he means the tourists. The thousands of summer residents and visitors who will take our tiny town from a two-thousand-person ghost town to a bustling summer destination. We may have a week before they start to trickle in, but by the Fourth of July, Riverton will be unrecognizable.

"I can start tomorrow." I smile, because I had no idea it would be this easy. That for the first time in weeks, something could go right. And so easily.

"See you at nine."

And just like that, I am officially employed for the summer.

AIDEN

Hauling canoes all day is suspiciously similar to baseball camp: I'm tired, hungry, and probably going to hurt in weird places tomorrow. Ellis hands Olivia a pile of red clothes, shakes her hand, and makes his way back to the riverbank, where I'm standing with an armful of red cushions.

"You hired her? Seriously, Ellis?"

He looks shocked. "She was nice. And she seems like she'll actually show up. She called four times yesterday."

I can't help but groan. This is not how my low-key summer at River Depot is supposed to go.

"You should have said something if you had a problem."

"You didn't give me a chance. You had to offer her a job on the spot?"

Ellis rolls his eyes and gives me a fake pouty face. "Oh, I'm *so* sorry you have to work with a nice, cute girl all summer. My sincerest apologies for burdening you."

I roll my eyes, because of course Ellis would have no idea who Olivia is or why I wouldn't want her around—he doesn't go to Riverton, he goes to South Hills, one town over. And yes, she's cute, I guess. But she's also got a boyfriend I'm not interested in running into this summer.

"Just hire some cute guys for yourself and don't worry about me. Please."

"What exactly is wrong with her?" he asks.

"She's Zander's girlfriend."

All I get from Ellis—who has been to most of my baseball games since forever—is a blank stare.

"Zander. My catcher."

Ellis shakes his head and turns away to go back to the boat shed. "Sorry, man," he tosses over his shoulder. "Just doing my job."

Fantastic. Now not only do I have to work with someone from school, I get to worry about Zander coming around. I rarely saw him around school without her. And the best thing about River Depot is that local kids don't hang out here. *Not yet, at least.*

℘

It's almost seven, close to closing, and River Depot is nearly empty. Everything is quiet, and I can finally hear the river sounds now that it's calm. The river is really shallow, and along the banks the water just barely skims over the tiny pebbles that line it. Even the deeper part, where we put the boats in, is barely past my knees in this section. The weeds that grow there float with the current, rippling just under the surface.

My mom is right, this would have been a beautiful spot for a house. That was the plan, fifteen years ago when my dad bought this place from my grandpa. It was struggling, barely getting by as a tiny general store and gas station. So my parents bought it with the plan of running it for a few years and then building a house here. But then my dad quit his construction job, doubled down on additions to the building, and started offering trips down the river. Our gas pumps are mostly for decoration now—the drive is usually too cluttered with boaters or shoppers, to actually pull in for a fill-up.

By the second summer, it wasn't a general store anymore, it was a local tourist stop, right along with the beach and the wineries, and everything else. And now it's my summer hiding spot. *Sort of.*

It's never pitch black along the river. There are houses dotting the banks, and then there's the moon shining off of the water, but I grab one of the lantern attachments anyway, because it could be late by the time I get back and my night vision is crap these days. I clamp the curved metal onto the canoe and step into the water. It's like bath water in the ankle-deep shallows of the river, even after a seventy-degree day. One foot, then the other, and I'm sitting on the hard metal, wishing I had thrown one of the red flotation squares under me. They're in front, shoved up under the seat, and I'll never get to them without tipping myself. A kayak would have made more sense for a solo trip, but the canoes have more room. My black bag is sitting in front of me, a thin line of water trickling under it.

It's early June, two weeks until the summer equinox, so the sky is still bright and warm, just like the shallow river water. I don't know why I'm so attracted to the outdoors right now. Maybe because it reminds me of when I was younger, and spent more time with my family in the summer, before baseball got so intense. Being outside makes me think, but it also helps me forget. It tricks me, with its colors and textures and sounds, into forgetting everything that I'm missing. When I'm anywhere else, every second is filled with the glaring reality of what is different. The assignment board that hangs in the shed is blurry. I circle every boat twice to double-check the number before jotting it down on my clipboard. I don't trust myself, don't trust what I'm seeing. What I'm not seeing. Everything is softer than it used to be, and not in a good way.

You should get your glasses. That's what some kid's mom said to me when I was filling out their paperwork, my face crowding the clipboard more than I had realized. I don't *have* glasses, I told her. She glared at me but didn't say anything. I don't know why I bothered; I'll never see her again. There's no need to impress her with my visual acuity, or shame her with a pity party over being seventeen with the vision of her kid's grandpa. *Just shut it, lady.* That's what I wanted to say. But it's my last day with the stupid little bandage by my eye, and my bruises are yellowing, and I'm *so close* to having my parents off my ass about everything.

I slice my paddle through the water, a mist of cool droplets spraying my hand. The river current isn't strong—that's why it's perfect for families and first-time paddlers who aren't paying attention—but it's enough to move me along. And this late I don't have to worry about traversing through red inner tubes and floating coolers. I rest the paddle across my lap and let the water push me. I close my left eye, letting everything go out of focus. I see three strips—the brown of the dunes, the darkness of the water, and the green of the trees on the right bank. I keep floating along. *Is this what it will be like someday?* I close my eyes. I don't think I believe in the whole "senses coming alive" thing, but I still can't help but wonder if there's something to it.

The rocking of the boat is more noticeable now, the sound of the water louder. Maybe it's just that I've stopped paddling. That I'm thinking about it. Everything feels off. The boat dips, and my eyes whip open, my body sliding to my right with barely enough time to balance myself. Alongside me, my paddle slides into the water, hitting the metal with a clank as it tips overboard. I didn't pack an extra paddle and I can't just leave it behind—there's no getting back upstream without it—so I use my hand to slow the boat down and when I'm over a shallow spot I put a foot over the edge. It's so shallow the canoe bottoms out on the rocks.

Grabbing the bow, I turn the boat toward a sandy spot on the shore, a little *C*-shaped crescent cut into the trees. My paddle is floating to my right, coasting toward shore, and I scoop it up and toss it back into the canoe. The bank is sandy, and I pull the front of my boat up onto the shore, far enough that it can't get pulled back out by the river. No one is going to steal my canoe—if they're out here, they already have one.

My backpack is slung over my shoulder in a quick motion and I'm headed into the woods, ready to put pencil to paper, to capture everything around me. I want to finish the sketches in my pad— the ones I started on family car trips, and buses to away games, and in classes that didn't hold my interest. I want to finish them all, while I still can. *You're being so fucking melodramatic.* Ellis's voice is in my head, and I know it's true, that I'm having a breakdown or something, but I don't care. I don't think wandering around in the woods and paddling down the river and drawing shit is the worst thing I could do. I'm not out throwing bricks through the windows of everyone with 20/20 vision, or egging my eye doctor's house, or something. *I'm creating fucking art.* And yes, I'm doing it in the middle of nowhere. *So sue me, Ellis.*

In front of me, the sandy shore stretches out and upward, and I duck under a branch as I make my way up, eager to see where this unexpected, sandy road will lead me tonight.

∽

I've been exploring almost every night for the past week, and every time I take a different path I find something new. I always have a certain destination in mind, but over and over I end up someplace I wasn't expecting. Someplace better. Ellis can't understand why I don't just sit down somewhere and draw. Why I insist on canoeing

and trekking through the woods, and making it "such a project."
But getting to my spot is half of the work. Because as I paddle and
hike and dodge the snapping branches and lumpy tree roots, my
mind wanders. If I sat down right after work, I can tell you exactly
what I'd draw. A canoe. Maybe, if I was feeling really creative, a
montage of canoes, all different colors. And I'm pretty sure a canoe-
themed portfolio isn't going to sway Mr. Winters into letting me into
Advanced Senior Art.

Because Advanced Senior Art isn't some humdrum slacker-fest
full of pencil sketches and watercolor. No, it's *Art as Life.* An in-your-
face, hands-on art experience, focused on real-world applications.
It's less instruction, and more experimentation. I took Intro to Art
freshman year with Mrs. Salsberg, and then Art II and III with Winters, but his more advanced classes were always at the end of the
day. I always opted for last hour study hall, so I could bail to the
gym for pitching practice and conditioning. Mr. Winters didn't seem
impressed by that excuse when I tracked him down on the last day
of school and begged him to let me into senior art. He was impressed
by my begging though, because he offered me the chance to show
him a portfolio at the end of the summer. "Wow me," he said. And
I'm going to. Because I need something to care about this summer.
Something to distract me from no baseball camp, no friends. I've
never felt like *Emerson* in art class. And that's all I want—all I need—
right now. To just be Aiden.

So I have eight weeks to make this happen. Less than sixty days
to show Mr. Winters what I'm all about. To show *myself* what I'm
all about. *Who are you, Aiden Emerson?* That's what he asked me as
I left his room. I still don't know the answer, but with every dune I

climb, I feel a little closer. *Who are you, Aiden Emerson?* I hike up the steep dune, an arch of branches just overhead, shading me. As I reach the top and the trees make way to open sky, I shield my eyes. The sun is making its slow descent toward the lake, already darkening to amber, as it prepares to be eaten up by the water. I look out over the sand below me, the sandy paths weaving through the dune grass. I didn't realize I had climbed so high—I'm above everything.

I set my backpack down, pull out my paper, and nestle my package of pastels down into the sand next to me. *This* is why I don't draw in my room or on a picnic table somewhere. *Who are you, Aiden Emerson?* I'm sure as hell not a boring collage of canoes you hang over the couch of your summer home. No, tonight I'm the world on fire. I'm end-of-days, burning water, apocalyptic beauty.

Chapter Four

Olivia

I sit down on the couch and set the bowl of popcorn between Aunt Sarah and me. If I had some sort of secret superpower, it would probably be my popcorn-making ability. I spend entirely too much time shaking and mixing, and making sure the butter and salt comingle perfectly so there aren't good bites and bad bites.

Aunt Sarah moans a little as she pops the first few pieces into her mouth. After I gave her the lowdown on my new job situation, we both decided to forgo a frozen dinner for popcorn.

"I haven't seen Zander lately." Aunt Sarah doesn't say it in a suspicious tone, more like she's genuinely curious. *That makes two of us, I suppose.*

"They left for up north."

She nods, like she should have known that. I think summer has caught up to both of us. Somehow it's the second week of June already, and in three short months I'll be a senior. *And Aunt Sarah will be gone.* The thought jabs into me. I keep forgetting about the looming change in my living situation. Aunt Sarah and I don't talk about the move. We've spent the last week deep-cleaning the house to put it on the market—so it's definitely happening—but we don't talk about it. I vacuum and she scrubs, and in the evenings we sit on the couch watching movies and just being us while we still get to.

I have less than twelve weeks to figure out how I'm staying in Riverton. Zander's house is obviously off the table, and Emma is lobbying her parents, but the Langes have four kids of their own to worry about, and Emma already shares a room with her younger sister Cordelia. I don't know where I would even fit in their house. Maybe on a couch or in the basement? I'd be open to either at this point.

"Are you excited to go up next month?" Aunt Sarah asks.

It takes me a minute to remember we were talking about Zander and his summer plans. I nod. I haven't told Aunt Sarah about Zander. About the breakup. I haven't told anyone but Emma yet. *Has he?* I don't want to have to say it out loud, but also I don't want her to start telling me all of the reasons I'm better off. What if, just like Emma, she isn't as Team Zander as I thought she was? Better to just wait and see how the summer pans out.

"She called again."

"And how is her latest boyfriend?"

"Olivia," Aunt Sarah scolds.

"What is she this month, a barista? A dog-walker?" I scoop popcorn into my mouth and chew. "Has she resurrected her short-lived private investigation career?"

"Olivia." For all of my mother's horribleness, at some point my aunt's sisterly allegiance always kicks in. Especially the last year or two. I don't get nearly as much mom-hating time as I used to with Aunt Sarah. "You're being a brat."

"I was raised in a barn . . ." I can't help myself. Truly. Any other time, Aunt Sarah says I'm an old lady in a teenage body. But talking about my mother brings out my inner brat. ". . . By my mother."

Aunt Sarah doesn't have to say another word, because she's glaring at me like she's thinking of grabbing the chair I'm sitting in and tossing me into the driveway. Though I'm already getting booted out of this house, so it's not even much of a threat anymore, is it?

"Fine." I jab the remote at the TV and pause it. "What does She Who Shall Not Be Named want?"

"For you to call her."

"Fine," I say. "I'll call her tomorrow, after work."

Aunt Sarah tips her head my way and levels me with a stare. "Call her tonight."

I groan. "I'm not in the mood tonight. Tomorrow I'll already be tired and sore, and probably cranky, from my first day doing god-knows-what down by the river." I stretch my head back and let it rest against the top of the cushion. "Perfect timing to call my mother."

"She said today, Liv. It sounded important."

I laugh. "Right, because we all know how much important news she always has to share during her quarterly check-in calls." I pull my hair out of my ponytail and shake my fingers through it as the loose brown curls fall around my shoulders. I look like my mother; probably another reason why I'm so terrified to end up like her. I do my best impression, with exaggerated enthusiasm and her signature tongue-click after each sentence. I stretch out my fingers and put my imaginary phone to my ear. "Have you been watching *The Bachelor,* did you see who he picked?" *Click.* "And did I tell you I'm not eating eggs, or carbs, or foods that start with a G anymore?" *Click.* "Not anything white either." *Click.* "You *know* what white foods do to your body, don't you?" *Click.*

I hang up my imaginary phone on my thigh. Aunt Sarah's judging brown eyes are right—I'm being such a bitch right now. *Takes one to raise one.* I turn the movie back on, and my voice is almost a whisper. "I'll take my chances that it can wait until tomorrow."

Chapter Five

OLIVIA

I hate these khaki shorts more than anything I've ever hated before. Why did I trust Aunt Sarah to buy me shorts? How do I not own khaki shorts? And better question, where do girls find these cute little khaki shorts that *don't* look ridiculous? The pair Aunt Sarah bought me at the mall have long square pockets that bunch at my hips, and they're super long. Like nun-shorts long.

"I figured there was probably a length requirement of some sort." There is very little sympathy in Aunt Sarah's voice when I sulk around the living room, moaning about how I don't have time to get anything else before my first day at River Depot.

"No length requirement. Just khaki." I drop onto the couch and moan when my shorts only ride up to mid-thigh. "The girl at the front desk was practically showing cheek." Which is a bit of an exaggeration, but she definitely did *not* have camp-counselor shorts on. I don't need to show cheek, but I wouldn't mind a little thigh.

"Would it make you feel better if I dropped you off?" Aunt Sarah asks.

"Riding my bike is the least of my problems at this point."

My bigger problem is that I didn't think this whole thing through. In my panic over not having a summer job, I somehow managed to get one that I'm going to be horrible at. How did I go from sitting at a desk, writing editorials about local events and sorting through photos and fetching coffee and lunch, to working at River Depot? I mean, "River" is *in the name*. And it's not like I can't swim or anything. I grew up in a beach town—they basically just throw you in the lake when you're born—but I've never been big into outdoorsy things. River Depot is basically nestled in the very spot I usually avoid. And the thought of complete failure—even at a job I'm not excited about—is making me want to crawl back under the covers. I don't know how to prepare for this. Last night I googled "tips for working outdoors" and "surviving your first wilderness job" (a little dramatic, yes, but still semi-accurate). Nothing helpful. I should have found a job as a camp counselor, because *that's* a job a lot of people are willing to give you advice on.

"They make tick spray, right?" I say absentmindedly as Aunt Sarah shoves her wallet into the brown leather laptop bag hanging on her hip.

"I . . . don't think so?" I'm not sure why I'm asking Aunt Sarah, she's not outdoorsy either. The Henry women have a long, robust history of thriving indoors.

"Do you have water shoes?" I ask.

"No, but you can order a pair."

I nod. Maybe it will be a few days before they trust me putting in canoes. Maybe the river won't be as squishy as I remember it being as a kid. *Was that even the same river?* What if I fall in? Surely they'll waive the khaki shorts rule if it's your first day and you fall in the water or something. They're not going to make me work in soaking wet shorts. Ellis seemed reasonable, though it also didn't feel like he was head honcho. Of course he was important enough to interview and hire me. *Crap. What if this whole thing is just some sort of prank?* Would they really put a teenager in charge of hiring people? Maybe that's why I got such a strange look from Aiden. I fell for it.

Stop it, Olivia.

I take a deep breath and untuck my red shirt. I've spent the last thirty minutes tucking it in. And then out. And then in. I hate the first day. Of anything. I hate not knowing what I'm supposed to do, or where to go, or what to expect. I'm not afraid of spiders, or heights, or dying in a plane crash (okay, *maybe* if the turbulence is bad enough), but I am most definitely scared of the unknown. I spent months researching *Lake Lights,* and here I am walking into River Depot with one day's notice and nothing more than a two-minute overview.

At least I'll know Aiden. Sort of. It's better than nothing, and maybe yesterday was a fluke. Everyone has always said how "surprisingly nice" he is. The thought of having someone to talk to, and ask questions, calms me enough to leave my shirt alone. I walk to the kitchen and grab the little pad of paper off of the fridge, and the pen Aunt Sarah always has lying on the butcher block island in the middle of the kitchen.

1. Buy tick spray
2. Order water shoes
3. Pack sunscreen
4. Extra shorts & underwear

Loosen up, Olivia. My mother's voice whispers in my ear like the little devil on my shoulder you see in cartoons. She can tell me herself when I call her this afternoon after my shift. I flick that little guy off my shoulder and tuck my list in my pocket. I'll get Day One over with, and I'll feel better. *You can do this, Olivia. You've got this.*

❧

When I arrive at River Depot the circle drive is still dotted with puddles from last night's rain. Past the building and the little covered walkway where people line up to buy canoe trips, the bike rack sits under a tree, next to an old weathered picnic table, tucked in alongside the woods. You wouldn't notice it if you weren't looking for it, and there's only one other bike sitting there. It's June, so it's still cool in the morning—the air feels light, not yet dragged down by the humidity that will hit by midday when I'll drip with sweat. As I round the front of the building, I can hear the river, the soft tinkling over the rocks, the gentle lapping against the docks that run the length of the property. Maybe working here will be like a spa day, minus the ocean-scented candles and the stress-relief. *Wishful thinking.*

There are five narrow docks, one after the next to my far left, and the huge dock to my right is filled with colorful Adirondacks and round tables with red umbrellas. Red, just like my shirt. Red is totally not my color, but no one is going to notice when I'm wearing these shorts. *Thanks for taking the pressure off, Aunt Sarah.*

Running my hands over the offending beige fabric in a last-ditch attempt to transform them into anything else, I step down onto the gravel. Gone is the peaceful sound of the river, drowned out by every step I take, crunching through the vast expanse of gray stones.

I'm not sure where to go, so I return to the wood stump podium where Ellis interviewed me. A cool breeze sends goose bumps up my legs. This is my favorite part of summer, when the humidity hasn't set in yet and neither have the tourists. In retrospect, this job may be my worst idea ever. Worse than the time I let Emma dye my brown hair red (read: purple) in seventh grade. Because in a few weeks my currently *not*-purple hair will be overtaken by the wet air, and this place will be overrun by tourists. *Terrorists,* we locals call them. A little jab for taking all the best parking spots at local restaurants all summer and tailgating us anywhere the speed limit is under fifty-five. For people who are supposed to be on vacation, terrorists sure do need to *slow down.*

Both of the large garage doors are closed, and no light shines through the slits of glass at the top. *Where is everyone?* The Grill was still dark when I walked by, its wooden shutters closed across both of the small rectangular food windows. I didn't have time to pack a lunch this morning, and I'm sort of excited to have an excuse to eat a corndog and ice cream. With all the boat-hauling I'm going to be doing, I probably won't even have to worry about the possible repercussions daily corndogs could have on these already-heinous shorts. Perhaps this will be the summer I have ice cream cones on the daily.

I kick the gravel and a few pieces skitter into the water, rippling along the edge. One of them skips a few times, leaving little ripples behind it, like the tracks of a water bug.

"Nice," I mutter.

"Hey, New Girl." Behind me, Ellis rounds the building, a small pack of redshirts following behind him. "We meet by the gazebo for morning assignments." He points toward the path leading up toward the building, cutting into the trees. It must wrap around to the little covered area where boaters are checked in. *Morning assignments?* "Thought you were a no-show."

"I'm sorry, I didn't realize." *Crap.* My first day and already I'm "that" employee. Maybe I should have listened to the internet and moved away to one of those all-summer camps, group-shower foot fungus be damned.

"He probably forgot to tell you," the pretty—and very short—black girl standing next to Ellis says with a smile. She's shorter than Emma, who is only 5'3", and I can't help but notice that even *her* shorts are not as long on her as mine are on me.

"No problem, I'll catch you up. Olivia, this is Allison and Avery." He gestures to the girl standing off to his left and the tall blonde next to her, and they each give a little wave. "And this is Alex, Andy, and Aiden." The guys wave and nod.

Avery, Allison, Alex, Andy, and Aiden? What the hell?

"Are you all related?" I suspect the answer is no—aside from Ellis and Aiden none of them look alike at all. Avery has blond hair cropped into a pixie cut, and Allison has long black braids with gold twisted through. They're gathered up in a thick ponytail and swing at her shoulders. Alex is short and stocky, with a mop of messy brown hair, and Andy is a tall, skinny ginger. *Probably not related.* But it's just so strange that everyone who works here has a name that starts with A, like one of those reality-show families that discriminate against twenty-five letters in the alphabet. Everyone except for me and Ellis, of course.

Everyone looks confused. "No, why do you ask?"

"Just—" I feel stupid for even bringing it up. "I know you two are." I nod to Ellis, and Aiden, off to my right, gazing out toward the water with a smug look on his face. *So much for knowing someone, I guess.*

"Nope." Ellis unfolds a paper in his hand, lays it on the stump next to him, and reaches down for a little hammer I hadn't noticed, hanging by a little leather ribbon off of a rusty nail. He pulls a nail out of the top of the stump and slams it into the paper with one quick hit. I flinch a little with the bang. "We go for a certain aesthetic here," Ellis says. "For our visiting friends."

Friends.

"Everyone can take your spots." He points to the girls. "You're in The Grill." The two girls give each other a high-five that rings with familiarity, and head up the stairs. "Andy, you can unload the cages from last night. Your first pickup isn't until ten." Andy nods. "Alex, you're in the gazebo." He turns toward the back of the building, and heads toward the customer—I mean, *visiting friend*—counters, where the river trip sign-ups happen.

"You're on boat duty, New Girl."

"I thought today was orientation?" *We're all just doing our own thing, thrown to the wolves—I mean, visiting friends?*

"For you. Everyone else is old news," Ellis says. "Don't look so scared though—you're with me and Aiden, you'll be fine. You'll be running this place by lunch break."

I nod and smile, relieved I'm not going to be left on my own on my first day. Maybe Ellis—not Aiden—will be my person, my quick friend. There's always one—that person who immediately feels like someone you've known forever—someone you'd tell a secret to immediately after meeting, if they asked.

Unfortunately, Ellis is also a liar. Because within twenty minutes of dispersing everyone to their duties, he disappears with nothing but a "You got this." Which I hope was directed toward Aiden, because I totally do not "got this." I watch Ellis as he leaves, and slowly turn toward Aiden, who has managed to operate in complete silence since introductions. He's almost robotic in his actions, moving canoes from the stacked piles to each dock, then jotting something down on the paper nailed to the stump. Canoe numbers, probably. Ellis showed us the list of today's reservations, and we're basically supposed to queue up all of the equipment for the day, assigning boats to each group and noting the numbers on the paperwork. People are too impatient to wait for us to do paperwork once they get down to the water, Ellis told me.

So I look at the paper on the stump, and pick the first trip that hasn't been checked off. I grab a yellow kayak from the pile, put a life jacket inside, and shove a paddle down into the cavity, jotting down a number for each on the sheet. *Everything* at River Depot has a number on it, so they can track who has returned what. Next to me, Aiden is hauling a canoe down from the rack.

"How's your eye doing?" I say it because I'm nervous. And because I'm stupid around new people. Even though I've seen Aiden around the hallways since elementary school, and at every baseball game I've ever been to, I don't think I've ever actually talked to him one-on-one. New people make me nervous—especially when they seem annoyed by my very existence. But somehow I keep hoping that for some reason he just doesn't recognize me. That outside of school, I must look different. Maybe it's the khakis. Or the lack of makeup. *Yes, of course.* I mentally salute myself for solving the riddle.

"It's fine." Another canoe comes down in a controlled fall.

"I bet you'll have a great scar."

"Yeah, I guess I can check that off the old bucket list," he says.

Okay. This isn't going great.

Before I can think of another benign comment, Aiden turns on me, a light in his eyes that I've yet to see since I got here. His brows twitch up like he's just remembered something exciting.

AIDEN

I know it's not a long-term solution, but I was hoping Olivia and I could just work in silence this morning. But since small talk is inevitable, I figure I might as well steer things into a non-baseball direction. Plus it will give me something to talk about tonight at family dinner.

"Congrats on the big win," I say.

Olivia is looking at me like I'm not speaking English. "Excuse me?"

"My dad told me this morning. He saw it in the paper?" I'm not sure why she's looking at me like she can't believe I'm bringing this up. It's obviously public knowledge if it's in the newspaper. *Does she think I'm going to try to hit her up for money or something?* "I guess my dad and your mom went to school together."

"I don't . . ." She's still staring at me blankly, and maybe she just doesn't want to talk to me. Maybe it's a loyalty thing—me being the guy who ruined her boyfriend's senior baseball season before it even started and all. I'm not sure how I'm the bad guy when *I* had to give up baseball, but whatever. If she can somehow make *my* problems about *her,* then she and Zander must be soul mates.

"It's fine—" I turn toward the garage, ready to grab the first batch of red cushions to be put in the canoes, and feel a hand on my wrist. A grab, a gentle tug, and then it's gone.

"Wait. What *about* my mom?" Olivia asks.

Shit. The way she's looking at me—with eyes that look more scared than excited—there's no way she knows. Now I feel like an ass. But how can she *not?* "Crap. You should talk to your mom. I don't want to—"

"I'm talking to you." Her voice is firm. "So tell me." She crosses her arms over her chest, like she's bracing herself.

"She, um . . . won the lottery. Down in Florida, I guess." Her expression hasn't changed at all—no smile, no screams. Maybe she's in shock. "You're rich!" I say, trying to use the excitement she doesn't have. "Congrats!"

Olivia is just standing there, looking at me with dead eyes. No smile, no tears, no glimmer of excitement. Her cheeks are flushed, almost the color of her shirt now, and she doesn't look happy. She doesn't look like someone whose mom just won $2 million and some change. She actually looks sort of pissed. I mean, it's not move-to-the-Bahamas money, but she'll probably get a new car or house or something out of it. Instead she looks like I just told her I ran over her puppy. *What is wrong with this girl?*

It starts off slowly, almost like she has a weird case of the hiccups, or something stuck in her throat she's trying to clear. One singular laugh, followed by another. Faster and faster, until she's cackling like she's completely lost it. *This girl.* She's bent down, her hands on her knees, like someone winded from running a race. Her shoulders shake as she continues to laugh. Tears are running down her cheeks, but I don't think she's crying. Something catches in her throat, and she snorts mid-laugh. And I can't help it, I laugh too. And when I laugh, she laughs harder. And then I lose it. I don't even know what we're laughing about. I'm laughing at her, because she looks completely ridiculous right now, losing her shit by the boathouse.

When Olivia finally pulls out of her breakdown, two seconds haven't passed before she says, "We shall never speak of this." She holds her hand up dramatically, and I'm not sure if she's joking or serious. Either way, it's hard to argue with, as a guy who doesn't currently want to talk about *anything.* I just nod.

Olivia starts to pull a canoe down from the rack, and I help her, easing the other end down to the ground. I get the next three canoes down from the rack and tell her to get the kayaks and cooler floats that go with it. We don't actually call them cooler floats, because drinking on the river is technically illegal. The paperwork says they're "accessory floats," but we all know what they use them for.

Once our equipment is staged, I walk Olivia through sending the first family of the day out on a trip. We pull each boat down to the docks, pack each with red flotation cushions, and pass out life jackets and height-appropriate oars to the parents and four children. Before they leave, we remind them to look for the giant red sign along the river that says STOP HERE. She pays attention to everything I do, and does it identically, always asking if she did it right, and letting out an excited little squeak with every affirmative nod. Now that I've had a front-row seat to her laugh-fest, and she seems to be happy to be working with me, it's really hard to keep up my plan of not talking to her. Because she doesn't seem anything like Zander. And maybe if we're friends, she'll just keep him away. Maybe that's my best bet anyway; to make her an ally.

After lunch, we'll have our first group demonstrations. This is mandatory for first-time boaters, and it requires one of us to do an overly dramatic flight attendant–style demonstration of life vests and how to hold a paddle properly. Neither of us has done it before, but someone needs to start reading the script to be ready to lead the demonstration. *Not it.*

"I'll tell you what, I'll flip you for it." I pull a quarter out from my pocket and hold it between my fingers in front of me. "Since it seems like good luck runs in your family."

She smiles.

"Heads or tails?" I ask.

OLIVIA

"Heads." I always pick heads. Because my mom always picked tails, claiming it was creepy to bet on a dead president's severed head. *What could be lucky about that?* she said. So I've made it my life's mission to prove her wrong, one coin toss at a time. "Heads, you have to do it and tails, I do," I clarify.

Aiden rests the coin on his thumb and flicks it into the air. He catches it in his hand, closes a fist around it, and looks at me with dramatically wide eyes. "Flip or open?"

"Flip." He's making this fun, and I'm relieved that the last few hours have been tension-free working with him.

Aiden opens his palm and flips the coin onto the back of his left hand. He leaves it covered.

"Come on. Come on," I urge him.

He pulls his hand away, and there is a big beautiful dead-president face looking up at me.

"Yes!" I pump my fist in the air.

"*Now* you're excited?" Aiden shakes his head, a huge smile on his face. "Two million dollars gets nothing, but a coin toss and . . ." He shakes his head and mutters, ". . . you're so weird."

And it should hurt my feelings, but it doesn't sound like an insult the way he says it. It sounds endearing. Have I actually won over Aiden Emerson—Riverton's grumpiest golden boy—with my *weirdness*?

"I've been told I'm delightfully weird," I say.

"Here, it's all yours." He hands me the stack of paddles and I carry them down toward the boats lined up at each dock. Of course eventually I'm going to have to do that first awkward presentation while reading off the script Ellis gave us this morning, but not today. I may be wearing the world's ugliest khaki shorts, and I may have just had a total mental breakdown in front of a really hot guy, but at least I don't have to humiliate myself in front of tourists. It's my lucky day.

Chapter
Six

OLIVIA

"Olivia Henry?" the voice calls out from the deck, and an older man in brown slacks almost stumbles as his feet hit the loose gravel. Before I have a chance to answer, the local TV news van is pulling up in front of the Depot and car doors slam, more feet hitting the deck. *Oh god.*

The man now next to me has his phone held out, probably the way he held his tape recorder out twenty years ago, except now it's just a black-and-green screen. Behind him, Ellis has emerged from the building, looking unnerved.

"Exciting day," the man says, gleaming at me as if I'm the bucket of fried chicken his wife never lets him near. He adjusts his glasses and then his eyes meet mine. "How do you feel about your mother's big win, Olivia?" When I don't say anything, he tries again. "Will you be celebrating with her tonight?"

"She doesn't live here," I say. Not that I would be having dinner with her if she did, but it's the truth. I take a step back and almost trip on the stump podium. "I'm not sure why you're here." Yes, my mother is from Riverton, but she hasn't lived here in years, doesn't live here now, and basically has nothing to do with me. Why am *I* the one being asked questions?

"It's very sweet," the man says, looking at me with soft eyes. "A woman wins the lottery, and all she wants is to win back her daughter." He takes a few more steps toward me, his phone coming at me like a cattle prod. "Quite a story."

"It is," I say. *It is* quite *a story.* "I don't really want to talk about it, I really just found—" But before I can finish my thought, a primped woman in a pencil skirt and a man with thick black glasses are crossing the gravel toward me. A camera hangs at the man's side, dangling from his hand. The woman totters through the gravel, her heels sinking and sliding.

Ellis puts a hand out toward her just as she slips again. "Let me help you there." He gives me an apologetic glance. "Seems like a bit of a liability. We don't want any broken ankles." He wipes sweat off of his forehead and gently touches the front of his hair, which is finally slipping from its perch after all these hours. "I can't be on the news looking like this," he says.

"Olivia!" The woman says my name like I'm a long-lost friend or the waitress at her favorite café, where she gets her coffee for free. She waves her hand at me and for a second I forget that she's actually the hunter and I'm the prey, trapped out here on the gravel, my bike on the other side of the TV and newspaper reporters now advancing on me. *How did this happen? My mom can't even get winning the lottery right.* They should be camped out at her house, not mine.

"Why are you here? My mom lives in Tampa now." *Or Tempe. Or . . . maybe it was Tulsa.* I shake my head. "She doesn't live *here*."

The man shakes his head, "We just interviewed her at her hotel. Lovely woman."

Lovely woman. That's my mother, all right.

"Can we just get a quick clip, maybe ask you a few questions?" the nosy woman asks. Ellis is still escorting her toward me, but she's breaking free, finding her footing in the gravel, picking up speed. I don't have anywhere left to go. Behind me are the kayak racks, the garage bays are on my right, and the river flanks my left.

"I don't . . . I just—" I'm having flashbacks of standing up in sophomore-year speech class, all eyes turned on me as I presented a speech on my family. I made a little tree that plotted everyone out, put in pictures of Aunt Sarah and my Oma, gave Emma and Zander their own honorary branches. I talked about how you *choose* your family. And the entire time I stood there, my stomach was in my throat. I don't have a problem giving prepared speeches, I just don't like to talk about my family. People want to hear about how much you look up to your dad, and why you want to be like your mom. But I don't know who he is, and I don't want to be anything like her. That's not who my family is.

"Olivia." My name rings out again, but not from the direction I'm expecting. It's coming from the river, from Aiden, who is stepping down into a canoe, waving a hand at me as I back-step from the reporters.

What is he doing?

"Olivia." He nods toward the paddle lying on the dock.

I run toward him and grab it. As I step down into the canoe, it tips and bobs under me. Aiden is pushing off with his paddle before my butt even hits the metal seat, and seconds later we're gliding through the water.

"Oh my god." I don't know what else to say.

"You okay?"

"Yeah, that was—" *What was that?*

"Completely unacceptable behavior at work?" he says.

Shit. "Were there customers standing around?" *Am I losing my job on the first day?* "I didn't know—crap."

"I'm kidding, Olivia. Jeez."

"Oh. Right. Obviously," I say, trying to smooth the edge of an emotional breakdown out of my voice.

Our paddles slice through the water, and I wonder where we're headed. Our own pickup location is about two miles down the river at Jasper's Beach, just before the river meets Lake Michigan. *A beautiful, scenic paddle, perfect for beginners and experts alike.*

The silence is making me nervous. "Are you afraid *you'll* get fired? You did steal a canoe *and* an employee while on the clock."

"I didn't steal you." Aiden laughs softly. "And my parents own River Depot."

He's the boss's kid? "Oh . . . that's cool."

"It's not going to be like that," he says.

"Like what?"

"Like I'm going to report back on work at the dinner table."

"Okay," I say.

We keep paddling, the water quiet and calming around us as it laps up against the metal body of our boat. "Thanks for the rescue. That was . . . weird."

"No problem." His voice betrays his lingering curiosity, but he stops there.

I suck at small talk, even though I'm always diving headfirst into it. Because on the one hand, when I've just met someone I don't know what I want to know about them yet. I don't even know where to start. And on the other hand—this is the writer in me—I want to know everything. Because everybody has a million things that make them who they are. If Aiden were a stranger I had been sent to interview by *Lake Lights,* I know exactly what I'd ask him:

What did it feel like to get hit in the face with a line drive?

Why did you quit the team?

What are your plans now?

Tell me about the fight.

Wes Masters, a senior on the team, claims that he saw Aiden and some random guy get into a fistfight behind the Amoco gas station last week. No one else saw it though. But it fits with Aiden's current aesthetic—bruised up, not talking to his friends. Wes is a good guy, I'm not sure why he'd lie.

If I didn't know Aiden it would be easy to pick him apart. But as is, he's my ex-boyfriend's former better-half teammate, and he's sitting quietly behind me. It's weird having someone sitting behind you in complete silence. *I bet there aren't a lot of first dates happening at River Depot—this seating arrangement would be a nightmare.* As we continue down the river, the silence is killing me—all I can think about is what my butt must look like in these atrocious shorts. Or that at any moment he's going to ask me how it's possible to not know your own mother won the lottery. And that's a lot to unpack right now, because I'm still having a hard time wrapping my mind around the fact that my mother won the lottery. I know lotteries are just luck, not merit, but seriously, luck couldn't have picked one of those moms you see in viral stories who donates her own kidney to her kid while going through chemo and working three jobs? *Come on, Luck.*

"Are you and Ellis close?" He doesn't answer right away, and I wonder if it's weird that I asked. "I noticed the last name—he said you're cousins."

"Yeah. We are, actually. We're nine days apart, so we've pretty much been best friends since birth."

"Cousin-twins," I say before thinking, because they do sort of look alike, though Ellis doesn't have the athletic build Aiden does, and Aiden doesn't share Ellis's fabulous hair.

He laughs. "Sort of, yeah."

Around us the trees have turned from oaks to pines. It's the first time I've been down the river—or at least the first time I remember. It's gorgeous. I pause my paddling to look down into the water, so clear it's hard to even tell how deep it is. There are patches of weeds here and there, waving along with the current, but for the most part it's covered in pebbles. Tiny little translucent fish swim in pulsing groups.

In the distance I can make out the faint hum of cars—they must be just on the other side of the trees, on the road that runs along the river.

"You're going to need to focus for a minute." Aiden's voice is teasing and I pull my eyes away from the water to see a concrete structure stretched across the width of the river in front of us. A small opening in the center has a gate overhead that hangs like the blade of a guillotine. "Paddle gently, just make sure we don't clip it."

I dip my paddle back into the water as we slowly ascend. "What is it?"

"No one knows. It just showed up one day."

"Really?"

"No. I'm sorry, I don't know why I said that." He laughs. "I'm nervous."

"Why are *you* nervous?"

"Because you probably hate me, and I don't blame you, but we have to work together all summer, so it would be really great if you didn't." He *sounds* nervous, as the words rush out.

"Why would I hate you?"

"Because I screwed over Zander? Because he probably hates me too?"

"He pretty much does, yes." I keep my eyes on the concrete barrier we're quickly approaching. "But I don't. His problems aren't mine." *Not anymore,* I think. "Plus, you just rescued me. So even if I *did* hate you—which I don't—I'd have to forgive you now. Those are the rules."

"The rules of what?" he asks.

"I don't know—life? Or books, at least."

"I didn't realize books had rules."

"They don't have rules, per se, just expectations. Like, if someone rescues someone, the reader expects that one of three things will happen."

We keep paddling, I don't know that I'm actually helping, but I dip my paddle in anyway, and if it doesn't hit the side of the canoe, I consider it a victory.

"What are the three things?" he says impatiently, as if he's been waiting for this very important information.

"Right. Well, they can become best friends, they can fall in love, *or* . . . they'll end up killing them."

Silence stretches between us, until Aiden's curious voice slices through it. "Which of the three do you think happens for us?"

"We'll have to wait and see, I guess. But I'm really hoping I don't kill you; I look horrible in orange."

☙

I don't know how long we've been out here, but my arm is sore, and there's a little raw spot where a blister is forming on my thumb. My phone is back in my purse, sitting on the floor of the garage. It feels like we just got out on the water, but also it feels like I've seen a million trees, and three different sand dunes that look alike, and around every bend in the river it just opens up to more and more blue ahead of us. It doesn't feel like the river is anywhere close to its end.

"We should probably head back soon," Aiden says, but he doesn't sound very concerned. A perk of being the boss's kid, probably. It's not *his* first day, and I doubt he's getting fired.

I moan, not wanting to think about going back to real life.

He laughs. "Okay, fine. Heads or tails?"

"Heads. Always."

"Okay, heads we go to the right, and I show you the super-secret route through Loon Lake, buying you an extra fifteen minutes."

"And tails?"

"Tails we head back," he says.

I can't stand the idea of going back to face the reporters. To the stares from customers and the A-Team. And soon I'm going to have to think about what the reporter meant when he said he interviewed my mother at her hotel.

I hear a metallic skitter, and Aiden stops paddling for a few strokes.

"Lucky, lucky," he says. "Two for two."

Finally, something goes my way.

෨

One more blister later, we're picking up speed, finally working together and starting to glide smoothly through the water. Loon Lake is spreading out in front of us, tiny and almost perfectly round. It's nothing like the other inland lakes around here that buzz with boats and jet skis; there are no houses, no cabins, no docks. Scrawny, leafless trees are dense around the perimeter. They should be ugly, with their naked gray branches and thin, barkless trunks, but they're strangely beautiful.

"Do you think Ellis knows my name?" I ask. My hands hurt and I'm barely paddling.

Aiden laughs. "Because he calls you New Girl?"

"Yeah. I mean, he *does* know my name, right?"

Aiden's voice is gentle. "He definitely knows your name."

I groan. "*I'm* never going to remember everyone. I don't know how you even manage to hire that many people with A-names."

Aiden laughs and the sound drifts up softly, caught on the wind rushing past us. "I can't decide if I want to tell you or not."

"Tell me what?"

"Promise not to tell Ellis I told you . . ."

"Okay . . ."

"Those are all fake names—Alex, Andy, Allison and Avery—Ellis just wanted to mess with you for being late. Don't tell him I told you though."

"Oh my god, and he seems so nice!" I'm joking of course, but also, what the hell? Day one and already I'm the fresh meat to torment?

"He is, he's just trying to make work fun. He's been telling me for years about the games he makes up for everyone at work—stuff to take their mind off the fact that it's ninety degrees out and they're on the verge of heat stroke."

"Oh god," I mutter. *Is this job really so horrible we have to have games and pranks to distract us from the horror of it?*

Aiden laughs. "Seriously, I've only worked here for a week now, and it's fun. I'm sure you'll have a great summer."

"I thought your parents owned this place. You haven't worked here before?"

"Nah. In the past my summers were busy. This summer's the first time I've had the time to do it," he says.

"Well, I won't tell anyone I know about the name thing, but I can't promise I won't have some fun with it."

"I look forward to it." His voice sounds relaxed now, like the Aiden I expected to work with. The one everyone is always raving about. *He's such a nice guy. Surprisingly nice.* Well, finally, I'm surprised in a good way. Because my mom just won the lottery; I'm on my first canoe trip, with no real destination in mind; and the river is in control. Fate is in control. And I think, for just this summer, I'm going to let it take charge. Let it push me along, like the river's current, through June and July and August. I'm done being the one worrying about everything. It hasn't been working out too great for me, anyway. All of my careful planning, and what did I get: the perfect internship? The perfect boyfriend? A mom who gives a crap? I didn't get any of it. So screw them. And screw plans. This summer, I'm going to do what Emma said, and let loose. I'll let fate decide— one coin flip at a time.

Chapter  Seven

AIDEN

Total trip time: two hours. We missed lunch, and Ellis seemed irritated that we were gone for so long, but he'll get over it. Luckily, The Grill was slow and Beth could come work the launch with him, so things weren't a total disaster when we finally arrived back at the docks. Ellis tried to pull a power play on me and have me work late to make up for my "joy ride" with Olivia, but there was no way I was missing my meeting with Mr. Winters. Not when it's the first time I get to show him some of the pieces I'm working on for my portfolio review.

Even in the summer, when everything is put away and the windows have been closed for weeks, Mr. Winters's classroom smells the same. It's this weird mix of acrylic paint, wet clay, hot glue—even the paintbrushes have their own special smell that's mixed in. I love the smell of it. In this room I feel like Aiden, not Emerson. I pull a sheet out of my black portfolio and stare at the smudged lines of charcoal. That's what life looks like most of the time now—like a smudged charcoal drawing—soft around the edges, blurry and unfocused.

I knew I could get here before Mr. Winters and his door would be open. It always is. His is one of the few classrooms that open up into the open-air courtyard. The school is set up like a horseshoe, with a narrow opening at the back of the building—where the loading area for the stage is—that opens up to the courtyard. It's common knowledge amongst the art students that Winters leaves his door unlocked. I heard a rumor once that it was so students could sleep in the little back supply room if they needed somewhere to go. Some say it's because Winters slept there when he and his wife were separated and he just got in the habit of leaving it unlocked. Luckily for him, the students love him and no one would ever turn him in to the principal, but you'd think they'd catch on after senior prank every year. Don't they wonder how everyone gets in the school? Maybe they think it's one of the coaches who are equally loose with access to the gym—half of the baseball team has a key to get into the weight room.

I've taken art classes with Winters since I was a sophomore, but this is the first time I've ever come through the back door. On a Wednesday, in June. *Talk about going the extra mile.* Winters uses the art room as his personal studio through the summer, so even though school is out, there's a canvas splashed with bright colors set up on a big easel at one end of the room, next to a desk full of paints and other supplies. Winters opens the door with a clumsy shuffle, a cardboard box cradled in his arms. It's overflowing with . . . random-ness. I can make out huge striped feathers, and scraps of fabric, and there are a few books stacked on the top. Supplies. There's an entire wall of the room that's dedicated to random artifacts. Under brightly colored letters that say INSPIRATION is a long table full of baskets, bins, and jars. Everything from feathers and pinecones to dried lotus pods used for stamping and old glass bottles for their textures on clay. He sets the box down on the table clumsily and pushes his glasses up on his nose.

"Aiden!" I'm sitting at one of the two-person stations, and he claps a hand against my shoulder and shakes me a little. Mr. Winters reminds me of my grandpa, with his thin wire-rimmed glasses and curly gray hair that hangs longer around his neck. "How's it going?"

Even without saying it, I know he's asking about *everything*. About my art project, but also about me. He's the only person outside of my family that I've told about my vision problems. I had to, to convince him to give me a crack at the senior art intensive. Because I'm already two months past the normal deadline.

I let out a long rush of air, and decide it's easiest to start with the uncomfortable stuff. "Same. Still no license." I nod toward the door, where the bike he can't see is leaned up against the building. "But I'm good."

"Good, good." He pulls his glasses off of his face, sets them on the table, and rubs the bridge of his nose. "And your portfolio? You feeling good about it so far?" He's letting me submit my port-folio late, but I still have to go through the same process as other students—a blind jury of teachers that doesn't include Winters. Blind, as in they don't know whose art is whose. Not blind like me.

That way, Winters can help us all while still being impartial. Someone doesn't get in just because he's invested a ton of time into them.

I pull the zipper back on my portfolio and start pulling things out. I spread out a few pieces of paper on the table in front of us—a charcoal drawing of a loon, a sketch of the river, and my pastel drawing of the sunset, looking down from the dunes—my secret spot. I have more, but these are my favorites so far.

Winters pushes papers around, pulling them in front of him then pushing them back. Tipping up the paper to get a better look. He's been appraising everything for at least five minutes before he breaks the silence. "These are all wonderful, Aiden. You know I've always thought you had a lot of talent for art."

There's a "but" hanging in the air. I'm tempted to say it, but I also don't want to know. *They're wonderful. Isn't that enough?* I can't help myself—after years of being coached, I'm a sucker to know what I've done wrong and how I fix it. "But?"

Winters laughs and shakes his head. "There's just something missing. A spark."

"A spark?" This makes me ache for baseball. The objectiveness of it. A strike is a strike. And sure, you can bitch about the ump, but if you throw a good pitch, 99 percent of umps are calling it. And no one's judging your pitch on the feeling you put behind it, or if it has "spark" or not.

"I know, it's the worst kind of feedback. They're all just lacking any sort of—and I hate this phrase, I really do—but they're lacking any kind of feeling. They're . . . flat." He says the last word like it came to him in a dream and he's finally put the word to what he's been thinking for ages.

Flat.

"So . . ." I'm waiting for him to tell me how to fix it.

"So maybe you haven't found your thing yet," he says.

I found my thing when I was eight. My thing was baseball. This is supposed to be my new thing. I can feel the heat rising up in my chest as frustration starts to take over.

"Keep working on these, but I also think you should check out ArtPrize and get some new ideas."

I nod, because I'll do whatever it takes to make sure I end up in this program and have something to look forward to my senior year.

Including finding a way to get to ArtPrize, a huge city-wide art contest ninety minutes north of us. I haven't been in years, not since I got busier in the summer with baseball and my parents couldn't drag me around with them. My mom loves arts and crafts shows. I remember it being a lot of paintings in hotels, and weird stuff like giant yarn murals. And as much as I'm enjoying the bicycle lifestyle, a hundred-mile ride isn't exactly practical. Not unless I want to leave on day one of the event and arrive on day four. Which I don't. *No excuses.* "I'll definitely check it out," I say.

I'll figure it out. I always do.

OLIVIA

I never realized how many things you could make with cherries. There is a sea of round, red cherry faces staring out at me from bottles of salad dressing, bags of dried fruit, barbeque sauce, jars of jam, and an entire shelf of glass-bottled sodas. There's a rack of stuffed cherry faces next to me, their shiny black eyes staring down from a gigantic display. I tear my eyes away when I hear Emma's voice.

"Lunchtime," she sing-songs, as she unties her white apron and deposits it on a hook outside of the double doors I assume lead to the kitchen. She has a foil-wrapped something in each hand.

"Are we not eating here?"

"Outside," she says quietly—almost eerily quiet for Emma—as I follow her through the glass doors and into the parking lot. "It's old-people dinner time."

I follow her to a red picnic table under a red and white awning. When it comes to businesses that use entirely too much red, I wonder which came first, The Cherry Pit or River Depot. Emma sets a foil-wrapped log in front of me, and opens hers. She takes a giant bite and makes a satisfied noise. "There is something so amazing about cherries in chicken salad."

I eye the silver roll in front of me. "Do they make anything here that doesn't have cherries in it?"

She stops chewing to think for a second. "The potato salad," she says with a smile, then gets serious. "Have you talked to your mom yet?"

I let out a little grunt. "Not yet. I had a revelation today though. After the reporter ambush." I texted Emma on my bathroom break after Aiden and I returned from our canoe trip. She got the short version, which included my mom's stroke of luck and the reporter ambush, but I sort of glossed over everything else.

"Spill." She makes a little waving motion with her hand. "And quickly, because I have the world's shortest break."

"You'll love this, actually." I start to unwrap the sandwich, but

I'm not actually hungry, even though I missed lunch and it's close to dinner. Which is very unlike me. "I decided that since playing things fast and loose has worked so well for my mother recently, I'm going to do the same."

"You're going to ditch your kid to find yourself?"

I roll my eyes. "I'm not going to stress this summer. I'm going to let fate make all of my decisions." I reach into my purse and pull out two glossy red dice. "For example . . . evens, I text Ellis back and tell him I'll hang out with my new coworkers tonight—"

"Definitely un-Olivia-like," Emma says around a giant bite of sandwich.

"Odds, I get to stay home and recover from my first—and probably only—paparazzi incident."

"Damn paps," Emma mutters. "But they did get you alone in a canoe with Aiden Emerson, so . . ."

Ignoring her attempt to goad me into talking about Aiden, I shake the cubes in my hands and let them drop on the table.

Emma looks at the dice and laughs. "Oh man, I love this idea so much."

I groan. "You would."

"I actually just had an amazing idea." Emma's eyes light up and I'm not sure I want to know what has her looking so excited. "*This* is your essay."

"What?"

"Write about your summer of taking chances. How letting fate decide made you less uptight and got you over the breakup of your one true love—" Emma rolls her eyes, but she's smiling.

"I'm *not* uptight."

"Like when someone starts running a mile every day, or stops eating meat, or something, and then writes about how it changed their outlook on life, or whatever . . ."

"That's . . ." I want to tell Emma that this is a horrible idea, like most of her ideas, but I can't. ". . . Sort of perfect."

"I wish you'd give me more credit for being the genius that I am." Emma takes another bite of her wrap and smiles. "This is going to be so much fun."

God, I hope she's right.

AIDEN

It's weird how much one change in your life can crash into every other part, like a highway pileup. My crappy vision means I can't play baseball, which means I'm avoiding most of my friends, which means I'm home most nights, because I can't drive anywhere else. Except eating dinner with my parents every Wednesday night probably shouldn't be described in terms of injuries and fatalities. My parents don't suck. My dad can be really intense, but mostly he's just a really passionate, enthusiastic person. People like to cast him in the role of the overbearing wannabe-coach dad, but I always got that he was just as invested as me. He was never dragging me out of bed and out onto the field, but he *was* building me my own practice mound in our backyard and driving me to clinics on the weekends and camps in the summer. I'd rather have a dad who pushes me and dreams big with me than one who doesn't care at all.

But this last month it's become apparent that after thousands of games and hundreds of tournaments, baseball was definitely our thing. The thing we did together and talked about together, and dreamed about. And without it, I'm not quite sure how Dad and I fit anymore. I kind of wish we could just rewind it all and go back to the days of hammers and drills and weekend projects together.

"How was work? I heard you helped out the Henry girl." Dad nods to Mom. "Joanie's daughter."

Mom cuts a piece of broccoli with her fork. "She's working at the Depot?"

"I stopped by to meet her this afternoon after that incident I told you about," Dad says to Mom. "Good kid, actually. Not what I expected when Ellis told me he hired her."

"What did you expect?" It's not that I care what they think about her, so much as it's weird that Dad sounds like he's talking about some kind of pseudo-delinquent, which seems like the opposite of the Olivia who was clearly trying to do everything perfect on her first day.

Mom scrapes her fork around her plate, pushing the tiny remnants of broccoli and potato together. *Yuck.* It's utterly unholy to mix food like that.

"Well, just with her mom being the way she was, I was expecting something else," Dad says.

I nod, because I'm not sure what to say. And she surprised me too. Zander has never been one of my favorite people. He has this way of being friendly to you while at the same time making you feel like you're not quite worth his time. I don't even know how to describe it, there's just something off about him. For me, at least. No one else seems to have a problem with the guy. "It turned out okay. The reporters were gone when we got back."

"Well if they come back, call me." He shoves a forkful of meatloaf into his mouth and talks around it. "They shouldn't be harassing her like that, she's a kid."

I nod. Part of me wants to tell Dad about the canoe trip, and how Olivia didn't know about her mom winning *the freaking lottery,* but I don't really want to see my mom's eyes light up the way I know they would if I mentioned the same girl more than once at dinner. *Maybe you can meet a nice girl now.* That's what I've heard ever since I quit, like it's the one bright spot of this whole situation. Except I'm not trading in baseball for a girlfriend. A girlfriend isn't going to help me focus on these art projects, or make me feel like I still know who I am. And it's not like I haven't gone out with girls, but I'm not bringing them home.

"Do you think I can get my car back soon?"

Mom sighs. "Let's wait until your next appointment with Dr. Shah, okay?" She picks up her plate, sets her fork and knife on top, and walks to the kitchen. Like this is the end of the discussion, and she can just casually excuse herself.

"That's not for another eight weeks. How am I supposed to survive an entire summer without my car? The last month has been hellish." I tear my roll in half, even though I don't want it. "And I feel like my vision's getting better. It seems like it." I close one eye, and then the other, watching my dad's face fade away.

Even a room away, with her back to me, I can tell that Mom is sighing. "I know, but Dr. Shah said that might happen. That you'd get used to your decreased vision." She turns from her spot at the sink. "Right?"

"Maybe we can make an appointment?" I plead.

Dad stops his fork just short of his mouth. "Six months, Aiden. The treatments take time. Just give it time." It's ironic, coming from my dad, the world's least patient person.

"How am I supposed to get around all summer?" It's not like I live in some big city. It's a three-mile ride just to get to work every day. Which is fine, but other than that, I'm pretty much screwed. There are no buses in beach towns. No subways, no trains, no ride-shares.

"We'll take you places." Dad looks serious, like he's fully committed to carting his seventeen-year-old son around like I'm still twelve.

I laugh. Because my parents are never around. Dad is running between the Depot and his newest project—a riverboat he bought and is turning into a down-river snack station (until he can convince the town that what it *really* needs is a bar on the river). It's a huge project: flipping the old boat, and clearing the land he bought along the river, where he'll dock it and have parking and another small building. *They'll have to rename this river someday.* That's what Dad always says when he's talking about his plans. He's hardly ever at River Depot—Ellis is practically running the place—so the idea that he's going to drive me *anywhere* is ridiculous. And a few years ago my mom would have been all over this, but now she's no better. She's the new president of the Riverton Transformation Committee. They're working to turn Riverton's main corridor—an ugly set of peach-tiled buildings with teal awnings—into a more appealing entrance to the downtown area. She spends most of her time working with architects and designers to draw up plans for refacing buildings, proposing ideas for businesses that can move into the empty spaces, and going to meetings where people yell about not wanting to spend money. *You have to spend it to make it.* That's what Mom says to the angry local people who call our house at any hour they please.

"Whatever." I could argue but it's no use, I'm not going to be driving my car anytime soon. The keys hang on a hook next to the door, taunting me with their silver gleam. It's not even that I'm one of those guys obsessed with his actual car—an old hand-me-down Honda from my sisters. I just can't stand being trapped here.

When I get the text message from Ellis after dinner, wanting me to hang out with the crew from work, so I can get to know everyone, my first thought is to say no. The only reason I don't is because I need to get out of my house. Luckily, River Depot is one of the few places I can still get to.

Chapter Eight

I'm not sure what I'm doing here. I should be at home, figuring out how to stay in Riverton when Aunt Sarah leaves or planning out what I'm going to say to my mother when I finally work up the nerve to track her down. Except I'm pretty sure that second part is the whole reason Ellis invited me tonight. *You look like you're about to flip a car or something,* he said, as I finished stacking the kayaks at the end of my shift, after Aiden and I returned from our two-hour escape-via-canoe. My arms are still a little shaky from the long day of lifting and pulling and rowing—I don't think there's any car-flipping in my near future.

He was right though. If I weren't on my bike, my bathing suit riding up under my sundress as I pedal, I'd be trying to hunt down my mother. I'd be showing up to whatever hotel she's allegedly at and spilling my guts about how messed up it is that she gets to win the lottery after years of being a shit mom and doing everything wrong. I'd cry and leave my heart lying on the carpet of some hotel, and she'd just stand there. Cool and calm. No, confronting my mother never ends with anything but me being frustrated and her looking like she's won. Won what, I don't know. Certainly not me.

A group outing after the first day of work—when I barely even know anyone's name, thanks to my midday escape and Ellis's prank—really isn't my thing. Big groups of new people, late-night outings I know nothing about—not my usual. But the dice I rolled at The Cherry Pit said differently. Odd numbers, I would have stayed home. Curled up in bed, cracked a book, and eventually fallen asleep to the sounds of *Catastophic Love* seeping out of my little bedside speaker. By now my sheets would be sprinkled with slice-and-bake cookie crumbs.

But here I am, thanks to lucky number eight. When I got home, I had put together my arsenal of taking chances. An old deck of cards Aunt Sarah keeps in a cabinet over the refrigerator, next to her bottles of wine and a cup full of old corks; and the pair of dice that are now in the beach bag that's slung over my shoulder, dangling dangerously close to my feet as I pedal along the county road that leads to River Depot. There's a Magic 8-Ball on my desk now—it used to be Aunt Sarah's, and I had to dig it out of the closet where we keep all of our board games. If Emma saw my new collection, she'd say even my plans for giving up control are too organized and neurotic.

River Depot is still open—the double doors to the gift shop and general store are still flung wide, the concession stand is still bustling with activity, kids and adults clutching ice cream cones. But everything on the waterfront is shut down. Ellis said canoers can't be trusted to get back by dusk, so thanks to their ineptitude, we don't ever work the boats past seven o'clock. Yet here we are at eight o'clock, back at work, while a different crew handles the night crowd.

When I pull in, Aiden is walking away from the parking lot, toward the back of the building, and I follow. I don't want him to feel like I'm chasing him, so I don't rush. By the time I turn the corner, he's talking to the tall blonde whom Ellis introduced as Avery. There's a tattoo trailing up the inside of her forearm. I nod at Aiden as I approach, and get a warm smile. But instead of talking to him, I turn to Avery.

"We didn't really get to meet this morning." I stick my hand out. "I'm Olivia, but you can call me Liv. What was your name?"

Next to her, Aiden smirks.

She smiles. "I'm Beth."

"Oh." I feign confusion, and her eyes widen in realization. "I sort of remember it being Allison or Avery, or Addison, or something." I raise my brows and smile.

"Busted," she mutters.

"And on my first day," I chide.

"Sorry, Ellis put us up to it." She smiles sweetly. "We never would have remembered all of those names, anyway."

"Well now that I know your name, I have to know what your tattoo says." I point at her forearm, where a delicate trail of black script runs from wrist to elbow.

"It's a line from a Frost poem." She glances down at it like she needs to check that it's still there. "But you can barely read it." Then, just as she turns to walk toward the others, standing by the river, she adds, "freshman year," with a dramatic shake of her head, as if that's enough of an explanation. *Don't judge, Olivia, you let dice tell you what you were doing tonight.*

Aiden steps forward when she leaves. He nods at the girl Beth is approaching. *Allison.* She's short and athletic-looking, and her braids aren't gathered in a ponytail now, like they were this morning. In this light I can see the little glints of gold that are woven in.

"And Allison is Jaz," Aiden says. "Jasmine, but Ellis says everybody calls her Jaz. The two of them go to Western but are home for the summer."

"And Adam?" He's standing near Ellis, by the river, both of them with paddles in their hands.

"That's Troy," Aiden says.

From the back, Troy and Zander could be twins. They have the same athletic build, the same blond hair cut short. I half expect it to be Zander when he turns around, but Troy doesn't actually look anything like Zander. His face is rounder, the skin along his cheeks slightly scarred from acne. And he's missing the blue eyes. Aiden and I wave when Troy catches us pointing at him.

Ellis motions me and Aiden over, and then the whole group is moving, shuffling away from the boathouse, through the wooded area and back toward the river. We bypass the main launch and go down a little path two hundred feet or so to the left, until I can see the shiny water glinting through the trees. There's no dock here, just a cleared patch along the bank where three canoes are pulled half out of the water, paddles piled up on the grass in front of them. Beth picks up a paddle and steps into the middle canoe. The boat barely rocks as she steps in, like she's light as a feather and not this towering skyscraper of a girl. Troy follows behind her, guiding the back of the boat into the water as he steps in.

Ellis is holding a paddle and waves me over. He places it in my hand, like he's not sure I'll take it, and nods toward the front of the canoe. I sling my bag into the middle of the boat and immediately regret it. I gave the "don't leave anything sitting in your canoe if it's not in a plastic bag" speech at least twenty times today. *Crap.* I twist suddenly, sending the canoe jarring to one side, as I try to reach for the bag. Ellis laughs.

"It's fine, Olivia"—he must see the panic in my face—"we just say that for liability. As long as you don't tip, it'll be fine."

I smile before turning back toward the river. The boat jerks a little as the back plops into the water, and I brace myself with the paddle stretched across me.

I expect to push out into the water, but I'm just sitting here. I turn to find Ellis still on shore, squatting with one hand on the canoe, keeping me from drifting away. He nods at Aiden, who is walking over with a paddle.

"I guess we're official canoe partners now." Aiden smiles.

Jaz steps into the front of the last canoe and Ellis sits down behind her, pushing them out into the water.

Aiden steps into the canoe, and he's not nearly as graceful as Beth—we lurch to the left and then bob to the right, swaying gently side to side until we're gliding out into the center of the river. We're headed straight for the opposite shore, until I feel us come to a hard stop as the front swings unexpectedly to the left. We're perfectly lined down the middle of the river now, Beth and Troy up ahead, and Ellis and Jaz alongside us. It's unnerving, being in front and not being able to anticipate the motions of the canoe. If I knew how to steer—if I knew how to even hold a paddle properly—I could be in the back. I could be in control.

"How do you even do that?" There's a sort of awe in my voice that was unintentional, though totally warranted.

"Just think of your paddle like a rudder. From there it should be pretty instinctual."

It's also really weird having a conversation with someone behind me, because I don't even know if he's being serious. "Instinctual to anyone who has . . . used a rudder?"

Aiden laughs, and I swear the whole canoe sort of vibrates under me. "How could you grow up in Riverton—with the lake, and the river—and make it this long without canoeing? That's the kind of avoidance that takes actual effort."

"I think I canoed once when I was nine," I correct him. "My Aunt Sarah isn't much of an outdoor person. . . . None of my family is."

"What kind of person is she?"

"The board-games-and-movies-until-midnight kind." *The popcorn-for-dinner-on-Friday-nights kind.*

"And Zander's never taken you?"

"Nope."

"You don't have to paddle if you don't want to. You should just enjoy the scenery, if you've never been on the river before."

I do what he says and set the wood across my lap. "I saw the river this afternoon, remember?"

"Not like this." He says it ominously, as if at some point it's going to open up like something out of a fairytale, and the swirling cyclone of the river will just suck us down into a vortex of talking rabbits and unicorns. In a fairytale we'd either be transported somewhere magically wonderful, or to the complete opposite. *What is my magical place?* I hate that the first thing that pops into my head is Zander. Or, more accurately, Zander and the lake house. That is probably one of my favorite places. And I can't help but wonder what everyone there is doing right now. If anyone wishes they would see me in a few weeks at Fourth of July.

The thought of it squeezes my heart a little—I always loved Fourth of July with Zander and his family. Watching the fireworks at this little beach in town with an old lighthouse, and setting off sparklers on his parents' beach blanket. When we were finally together, kissing through the finale. This will be my first Fourth of July without him. The first one I can remember, at least. I'm not sure how I'm going to handle it—I have a feeling that when the fireworks explode, my heart will too.

Aiden's voice brings me out of my demented daydream of rabbit-filled vortices and ex-boyfriends. "Do you always ride your bike? You don't have a car?"

"I don't," I say.

"You live nearby, then?"

"Not too far, I'm downtown. It's doable." It's going to be much worse when July and August hit and the humidity makes the ride feel twice as long.

"Maybe your mom will buy you one."

"I hope not." There's a long silence and I'm surprised Aiden isn't grilling me, trying to pry apart my relationship with my mother, see how it all fits together. People are fascinated by dysfunctional families. It's like everyone wants to dissect you and see what screwed you up so bad. Not so they can fix it, just so they don't do the same. They want to look at you in all of your screwed-up glory and be glad they aren't you. "I don't want anything from her. She's never given me anything, and now I don't want anything."

I probably wouldn't have said it if I had been looking at him. But I said it to the river. To the tall grasses growing alongside the water, creeping into the shallow water. To the dunes that are starting to jut up behind them, growing up up up, taller and taller with each stroke of the paddle.

"Badass," Aiden mutters, and I'm not sure if he's talking about me, or the fact that it feels as if we've been transported to some other place. We're farther down the river than this afternoon—we forked left instead of right this time. The dunes are looming over us on either side now, and it's like we're in another country, another time, another reality.

The sky is darkening and the sun has slipped behind the dunes, out of sight, leaving a warm glow over the crest of sand. The river narrows, and the two other boats aren't far ahead of us. It feels like everyone is charging forward, faster and faster, and I'm not sure if we're racing one another, or something else, but then I see it. The dunes slope down, down, down, fading back into dune grass and then to sand. We come through a last bend, and the sky opens up. The sun is just creeping down below the water, and it looks like there's a fire burning below the blue expanse of the lake.

"Holy crap," I say.

"Aren't you glad you're a boater now?"

The way the river is angled, cutting into beach, running parallel to the lake shore, it feels like we're paddling right into the blaze. It's nothing like seeing the sun set from on land. "How have I never seen this before?"

"Hanging around with the wrong people, I guess."

I laugh, because he's right. "What beach is this?"

"I'm not sure what it's called. It doesn't have public access, you have to hike through the state park to get to it."

"Ah."

"I'm guessing you don't hike either?"

"Not unless you count the summer after sixth grade, when my Oma made us trek around her subdivision every morning with a bunch of other grandmothers."

Aiden laughs. "I don't."

"If I'd known this is what I was missing, maybe I would have." The earlier parts of the river were full of rocky shores and little crops of dune grass spreading down into the water, but now the river is cutting through nothing but sand, the water getting deeper and darker. Ahead of us, I can see the mouth of Lake Michigan, and beyond it a curved bay, with giant dunes at the peak.

"Now we both get a rest." Having Aiden behind me is like having an invisible narrator the whole trip.

Tonight was the first thing I officially put in the hands of fate, and I can't wait to use this in my essay. I'm making a mental note of the colors and the way it feels to be this close to everything.

I peek back at Aiden, careful not to tip myself like last time, and his paddle is across his lap. We're still moving—picking up speed, actually. It's sort of soothing moving along like this with no effort. But it also makes me just a little nervous. It must show on my face, because Aiden smiles and tips his head up ahead. "The current's going to pick up until we're sucked out."

"*Sucked* out?" I don't like the sound of that. *Maybe I should have worn a life jacket.* We tell all the tourists that they have to wear life jackets, but no one was, so I didn't either. *Do we even have one of those red cushions in here?* I slide my paddle beside me and rest my hands on either side of the boat. If something happens, I'll be no help with it anyway.

"*Sucked* was a little dramatic. Don't panic."

There are waves up ahead of us, slicing in different directions, with little white peaks like on top of my Oma's lemon meringue pie. It doesn't look conducive to boating, but Beth and Troy just crossed through unscathed, and Ellis doesn't seem to be panicking in front of us. He's sitting with his paddle across his lap, like I was before Aiden made his poor word choice. I focus on the red sky instead of the water, and it's hard not to relax. A few more feet and I'll leave the river behind me for the second time today. I'm starting to rethink where my favorite place is.

AIDEN

"Is this a private beach?" Olivia glances up toward the massive, cotton-candy-colored houses set on top of the bluff just north of us as she asks Jaz, who is pulling a towel out of her tote bag. Olivia looks nervous. She always looks kind of nervous, like she's waiting for something to go wrong. Or she's trying to anticipate what she should do in any given situation.

Jaz shrugs. "I think so."

"We've only been arrested once," Ellis chimes in.

Olivia's head snaps to me. She doesn't trust Ellis anymore—not after what I told her about the A-names—but he doesn't know that. So I decide to play along. "It wasn't a big deal." I shrug. "Twenty hours of community service actually goes by pretty fast."

Ellis looks over at Beth and Troy, who are grabbing bags out of the canoes, and I wink at Olivia.

She smiles, then smooths her expression and her voice is serious. "Tell me about it." She pulls the strap of her bag over her head and drops it in the sand. "And those orange suits are pretty itchy, right?"

Her voice is deadpan, her face serious, and oh my god, she just walks away. Ellis looks at her in shock, her back to us as she saunters down the beach toward Beth, who is spreading a blanket out on the sand.

Ellis turns to me like I have the answer, and I just shrug. *Serves him right.*

OLIVIA

I'm sitting on the blanket when Ellis and Aiden come over. Jaz is in water up to her shoulders, her hair now wound into a braided knot atop her head. Beth is shimmying her shorts off, about to follow. Ellis pulls his t-shirt over his head and he and Troy race toward the water, charging through the shallow waves, their knees jabbing high like an army tire drill.

Aiden sinks down next to me, and the blanket shifts. He leans forward, his elbows resting on his bent knees, and his eyes are fixed on the water, like he can see something out there that I can't. He looks out at the water the way Zander used to stare at a football game on the TV. He looks focused, content. And while he appraises the water, I check him over. The little white bandage by his eye is gone since yesterday. There's yellowing across the top of his cheekbone, but the bruising is almost gone too. He's wearing a navy blue baseball t-shirt I recognize from Zander's own wardrobe and a pair of khaki shorts. *Why do khaki shorts look good on everyone but me?* I'm sitting on a beach blanket with *Aiden Emerson.* Former baseball star. Current king of the rumor mill. Coworker. Owner of the greenest eyes I've ever seen. I read once that green eyes are actually the most rare, and they only seem common because most people confuse hazel with green. But Aiden's are definitely green, and it makes him seem even more mystical. *Get a grip, Olivia. He's a guy, not a unicorn.*

"What's up, Olivia?" The way he says it—the hint of amusement—I know I've been caught.

He smiles and his teeth are straight and perfect, except for one on either side that's twisted just a bit. It almost looks purposeful in a way, the perfect symmetry of the imperfection. His brown hair shines gold in the light, and it brushes across his forehead.

I'm trying not to stare, but his head cocks toward me and his eyes are sweeping over *me* now. Not in a creepy way, like guys who blatantly check out your ass, but in a very thoughtful way, like when I'm thinking about how to turn someone into a character in a story. I always try to find a flaw about them—something small and special that makes them unique, like Aiden's oddly beautiful crooked teeth. I wonder what *my* flaw is—what would make Aiden stop for just a second longer.

"Sorry, bad habit," I say, looking away.

It's probably the freckles. I have these three rogue freckles on my otherwise pale right cheek, and they make a nearly perfect right triangle. Emma measured them last year for our geometry homework, and hasn't shut up about it ever since. I honestly never really thought of them before, but now I feel like they jump right off of my face any time I look in the mirror.

Aiden looks back out at the water, and I pull my worn blue Moleskine out of my bag. It's always in there—ever since Aunt Sarah gave it to me last Christmas—but I love it so much I don't even write in it that much. I feel like I have to save it for only the most special of ideas. *And* I use it if I'm going to be writing in public. Because there's something much more legitimate about writing in a Moleskine than one of the ratty old school notebooks I would use at home. I had planned to use it at *Lake Lights* this summer, when I was out on assignment, taking notes on events and writing down names. Where would I be right now if I were working at *Lake Lights*? *Probably not sitting on the beach next to Aiden Emerson.*

"You draw?" The way Aiden's voice hitches up, I know what answer he's hoping for.

"No." I tap the page with my pen, unsure if I'm going to tell him what I actually use the notebook for. There's something weird about telling people you write. Because they automatically assume you want to share it with them. It's like opening this door into your heart and inviting people to walk in and poke around. Even though I want to be published someday. Even though I post short stories online, and I've submitted them to contests—I hate sharing. *Especially* in person. But I don't have anything here that Aiden can see, anyway, and I really want to jot down some notes about the river at sunset for my essay. "I write."

"Poetry?"

I laugh. "No, why would you guess that?"

He smiles and shrugs. "I don't know, you seem the type."

"What type is that?"

"The type with angsty drama?"

I set the journal down next to me and twist to face him. "I don't have angsty drama."

"You have mom drama."

"Okay, I'll give you that one. Me and my mama drama." I laugh at my own joke, and immediately regret it. *God, I'm a dork.*

Aiden laughs.

"But I don't write poetry. I'm not that cool." I tap my pen again. "I write stories and stuff."

"What kind of stories?"

Here we go. *Kissing stories.*

I look away from him, back out to the water, and try to think about how to explain to him that I write a lot of things, but usually the one thing they have in common is that there's a love story. Even when I try not to, it's always there. But I don't write the trashy stuff Aunt Sarah likes to read, and that's what people always think of. I sigh, and reluctantly look back at him. "The kind with words? And a beginning, middle, and end." I give him a nervous smile.

"What *kind* of stories, Olivia?"

I laugh. "Love stories, mostly."

"That makes sense too, I guess." He looks back out at the water and I wonder what he means by that. *What makes me the type of person who writes love stories?* If he only knew how completely un-qualified I am at the moment . . .

AIDEN

"Do *you* draw?" Olivia asks.

She's changing the subject, which is fine, because I don't need to talk about her romance novels. That could get . . . weird. My mom used to have them around in the summer at the beach. My dad's swimsuit magazine had nothing on Mom's books. *Thrusting* and *quivering* and . . . ugh. If Mom only knew the things I saw on those two pages when I was twelve.

"Yeah, and I paint." I pick up a handful of sand, because it makes me nervous to say it out loud. Because there's nothing concrete to declare me an artist. It's just something I've always done. My label as a pitcher was everywhere. It was on the programs they handed out at baseball games, and in newspapers, and on my awards. I never felt like I was pretending in baseball. But being an artist? Something feels so intangible about that label. Like I'm not allowed to just give it to myself. I feel like I need it though. For someone to slap a label on me so I can know what I am now.

Olivia's face twists up in surprise. *"Really?"*

I don't like the tone of her voice, the utter shock I can hear in it. "Yes. *Really.*"

Her face drops. *Why do I have to be so damn self-conscious about this?*

"I just didn't know that. I don't know why I would though." She turns back toward the water and her voice is softer. "Sorry."

We're like mirror images, the two of us sitting with our arms wrapped around our knees, facing out toward the water. *The jerk and the new girl.* It's going to be a long summer if she's afraid to talk to me.

"You want to come with me?" I nod up toward the dunes that climb out of the grass behind us. "I have some prep to do for a project."

"Um." She looks around herself, like she's not sure she's the one I'm actually talking to.

"Do you want someone else to come with us?" I'd like to think she isn't scared to walk off with me, not after we spent so much time together today, but she doesn't know me that well, I suppose.

She looks surprised. "No, it's not that." She shakes her head. "I've just got this thing . . ." She reaches in her bag and pulls out a quarter.

I laugh. "So this is a thing, huh?" I wonder if it has anything to do with our coin toss this afternoon.

"It is," she says. "It's a new thing. A sort of . . . personal experiment . . . for an essay I'm writing." She says it tentatively, like she's hesitant to even share this much.

"Okay, so heads . . ."

"Heads, I go with you. Tails"—her eyes look out to the water—"I stay here alone, watching Troy and Beth make out. Feeling extremely uncomfortable." She laughs, but she sounds nervous.

"That's hard to compete with, I can see why you're leaving it up to chance." I'm just teasing her, but I see a flicker of something on her face and she drops the coin onto the blanket and laughs.

"You're right, let's go."

I make sure Olivia puts her sandals on—the dune grass can be like razor blades if you catch it just right—and she slings her bag over her shoulder and follows me. Ellis catches my eye as we're leaving and I point up to the tree-covered dunes behind us. He returns my gesture with a salute and a smile.

I love the way climbing through the shifting sand makes my legs burn. My summer is usually one long training session, but I haven't been running in the morning like I normally would.

We're only halfway there when Olivia seems to be getting winded. Her face is bright red, and though she isn't gasping for air, it seems like her breath whistles in and out.

"Are you okay?"

"My asthma isn't great in the heat," she says.

Crap. "We can turn around, it's not a big deal."

"It's fine, I'll be fine." She smiles like she's trying to reassure me, but she's still sort of wheezing. "How much further is it?"

"We're about halfway."

"Okay." She nods and lets out a big rush of air as she says what sounds like, "Let's do this."

I shouldn't laugh, but I do, because she looks desperate to be done with this and I probably should have warned her about the climbing. "We're getting close, I swear."

She lets out a little grunt of gratitude, like she needs to save her energy for hiking, not talking, and I laugh again. "You and Zander don't hike?"

"No."

"And you don't canoe, or kayak?" I hold up a branch that's hanging across our sandy route of ascent, and she passes under.

"Nope."

"What do you do?"

"I don't know, just normal couple stuff, I guess." She takes a deep breath and pushes herself up over a little log that's blocking our path. "We went to the movies and hung out at his house, and . . . I don't know . . . *indoor* stuff." I can't tell if she sounds sad, or if it's just a product of her exhaustion.

"Huh."

"This is the kind of stuff *you* do with all of your girlfriends?"

"*All* of my girlfriends?" I laugh. I haven't *had* a girlfriend. Not really. I've made out with girls, and I've gone to the movies with girls. I've had dates to dances and girls I've flirted with at parties. I had a girlfriend in eighth grade, before you actually did anything with them. But I've never had anyone I would have called a real girlfriend. Someone I spent all of my free time with, or whose parents I knew, or who came to all of my games. I guess baseball was my girlfriend. Or Ellis. I stifle a laugh. *God, I can't wait to tell him* that *revelation.*

As we near the top of the little dune, the trees start to thin out and the pink sky pokes through. Our trip back, going downhill, will be faster, but I still need to keep this quick, before darkness catches up with us.

At the top of the hill there's a flat area, a ten-by-ten plot of sand surrounded by trees and dune grass. I love this spot, the way the sandy paths crisscross through the dune grass below, like tiny ant trails, and you can see the lake stretch out from north to south, going on endlessly into the distance. People don't realize how big Lake Michigan is. How much it looks like the ocean, but lacks its salty water and carnivorous creatures. The sand is less coarse, and there are no shells, only rocks, but it's big and beautiful and not to be underestimated. Tourists are always thrown by how big and impressive the lake is. And even though Olivia has lived here forever, she has the same look on her face—like she's seeing it for the first time. Or maybe just seeing it through different eyes.

Olivia's hands are on her hips and she's slightly hunched forward, catching her breath. "Wow. This is . . . incredible."

"Worth it?" I bump her elbow with mine, and she almost topples over, like her legs are rubber. They probably are. I put my hand on her arm to steady her. "You gonna make it?"

She looks at me and smiles, and then she sinks down into the sand, looking out across the water. "Worth it. And yes."

She's already pulled out her little notebook again, and sets it on her knees.

My mom's camera is tucked into the bag hanging across my back, and I pull it out and loop it around my neck before pulling a water bottle out. I hold it out to Olivia. "It's warm. Sorry."

She takes it and smiles. "Thanks." Her eyes fall on the camera. "You're into photography too?"

"I'm actually a pretty horrible photographer. I'm just taking some reference photos so I can paint it back home."

She hands the water bottle back to me and I take a drink. "I didn't know that was a thing," she says.

"You thought every painting ever painted was done while someone sat in that very spot?" I've probably used up my sarcasm quota with Olivia today, but I can't help myself.

"Yes." She gives me an exaggerated smile. "Like in a movie. A man in a little chair with an easel in front of him. In a beret." She laughs. "I guess I just never thought of it, period. You think about the book on the shelf . . . not the writer sitting at their desk."

"—*Or* on a dune."

"Or on a dune."

"I actually have a spot in the dunes where I've been doing a lot of my drawing lately."

She nods like she's not sure what she's supposed to say to me. She fidgets with the pen that's pinched between her knuckles. "Maybe you could show me sometime? I'm sort of lacking inspiration these days."

"You'd probably need to flip for it, or something?"

She smiles. "Probably."

"It's a hike," I warn. "Not as bad as this one, but still."

"I can handle that." She laughs. "I'll just pack my inhaler so I don't die."

O L I V I A

When I was eight, a body washed up on shore at one of the beaches just north of us. I was living with my mom, and I remember her reading the newspaper article out loud at the little table in our kitchen, like she was the narrator of a gruesome movie. Gasping at the descriptions, the way the body had been affected by its time in the water. *No limbs*. That's all I could think about. This stump of a person lying on the beach. How close someone would have gotten before realizing what it was. God, I still get goose bumps thinking about it. I refused to go in the lake that entire summer. Even the next summer, every time anything touched me I was sure it was a severed limb or something. Usually it was just a floating stick, or a stray plastic bag, or something completely innocuous. I was always sure nothing would freak me out more than that.

But when "Skinny dip!" comes screaming out of Beth's mouth—like a knife through the night air—I'm not sure which is worse: the prospect of there being a body in the lake, or *my* naked body being in the lake. The beach is never pitch black. That's what they don't tell you in books and movies. The moon lights up the lake like a spotlight overhead, and washes the color out of everything like an old black-and-white movie. Best-case scenario, the whiteness of my yet-to-be-tanned skin blinds everyone. Worst case—I sneak a glance at Aiden, but he hasn't moved off of his spot on the blanket. Since trekking back from the dunes, we've returned to our original spot on the beach. He's stretched out on the blanket, his eyes closed, and I'm lying on my stomach, sketching a picture of the beach, so I can prove to him how artistically inept I am. Every few minutes he'll open an eye and sneak a peek at it. When he hears the s-word, his eyes open.

The coin is still lying on the blanket and I pick it up, rubbing it between my fingers.

"Whatcha got there?"

Instinctually, I grip the metal tighter between my fingers.

"Olivia?"

I open my palm, revealing the shiny circle that's forcing me out of my safe little world this summer.

I take a deep breath and drop the quarter into my other palm. "Heads, we climb the dune again." I let out a nervous laugh. "Tails . . . we skinny dip—" It doesn't even sound right coming out of my mouth. Like that time my Oma announced we were having a "circle jerk" at a family picnic, when my aunts and cousins and I were sitting with her in a circle of lawn chairs. She was . . . slightly confused about the term. *Gross.*

Aiden's eyes are on the coin as I flip it above our heads and it comes back to rest in my hand. I turn it onto the back of my palm and hold it there, not wanting to see what my fate is. I look out at the water and back at my hand and let out a shallow breath. *Here we go.*

Aiden's voice cuts into the quiet night air before I have a chance to reveal it. "It's too cold for that shit." He stands up and pulls his shirt over his head, revealing an eyeful of skin. "Let's just swim. Save the skinny-dipping for after the Fourth when it isn't a polar bear swim." Aiden reaches his hand down and I take it before he hoists me up. "You in?"

The coin is still sandwiched between my hands. I reveal the shining bird and smile. "I'm in."

AIDEN

We're canoeing along the shoreline, in water so shallow we're likely to run ourselves ashore. I didn't think about having to break against the river's current on my own. Not that Olivia isn't *in* the canoe, but at this point her paddle in the water would probably hurt more than help. I didn't really think through this whole canoeing-in-the-dark business. Everything is hazy, and it's hard to tell how far we actually are from shore, or one another. It's a sobering reminder of what it would be like behind the wheel of my car. I'm staying close behind Ellis, tighter than I usually would, so I can let him and the light he has affixed to the bow of his boat lead us through the dark.

When we reach the river, we bank the boats on the shore and flip them over so we can carry them. Ellis parked a pickup down the dirt access road, and it's better than canoeing all the way back upstream, but it's also a pretty long walk to make it from the river to the little road.

"I'm glad we're not canoeing the whole way back in the dark." Olivia lets out a little grunt as we step over a log that lies across the path. "But this canoe is so much heavier than I expected."

"We carry canoes all day."

"We *drag* canoes." She laughs. "And that's ten feet." She takes a deep breath. "This is . . . more."

We're about twenty feet from where the truck is parked along the dirt road. Ahead of us, Ellis and Troy are pushing the first canoe up onto the metal brace in the back.

I only have twenty more feet to propose the idea that has been forming in my brain all night. "I have a proposition for you."

"I'm pretty committed to not skinny-dipping until the Fourth of July. You said it yourself." She laughs, and she doesn't sound nervous this time.

"You don't have a car," I say.

"This is true."

"But I do."

"Okay . . ." Her voice is questioning, confused.

"What if you borrowed my car for the summer?"

"That sounds . . . like a strange arrangement. Why would you loan me your car? What are you going to drive?"

"Well, I'd loan it to you, because I can't drive it right now anyway. And because I was thinking you could maybe help me out by driving me places once in a while." I hate how douchey this sounds when I say it out loud. It sounded so much better in my head.

"I sort of thought the whole bike-riding thing was just a statement."

"Of what?" I ask.

"I don't know . . . your resistance to what's expected?"

"I like that." I laugh, because it's a much cooler explanation than the truth. "But I'm not that creative."

She's quiet, and I think maybe it was a horrible idea to bring this up after one evening hanging out together. But all I can think about is ArtPrize, and how I need to get there. And Olivia's fun to hang out with—she keeps things interesting; I wouldn't mind being trapped in a car with her for a few hours. I'm actually kind of excited at the idea of getting to check out everything at ArtPrize with her.

"What if we started with a trial run? Would you want to go to ArtPrize with me this weekend? You can test-drive my car, and I can test my theories about your artistic eye."

We've finally reached the truck, and I take a few steps back, inching my hands up the body of the canoe. "You can let go." Olivia moves aside, and I hoist the metal body up onto the braces, next to the others.

Olivia slips her hand into her bag and pulls a coin out. It's a penny, and she has some trouble balancing it on her thumb. It flips into the air, and comes back down with a soft skitter on the gravel. "Crap," she mutters.

I turn my phone's flashlight on, and we squat down, looking for the coin. "This may be a sign," she says.

"Found it!" I spot the copper next to a back tire, and Olivia follows my flashlight and squats down to examine it. I can't make out what it is.

"You're in luck," she says. "I have zero plans this weekend, and I've always heard ArtPrize is pretty cool." She picks up the penny. "And our friend Abe—I mean President Lincoln," she adds in a reverent tone, "says I'm going."

I laugh at her last-minute show of respect for her penny, and a wave of calm comes over me as I tackle this one problem. Maybe she won't go for my idea all summer, but at least I'll have this one weekend. Despite everything, maybe the summer fates are on my side. Maybe I have that one thing going for me.

Olivia

Aunt Sarah's official stance on the whole lottery fiasco is that she didn't know about it. I texted her after work yesterday, and she said we'd talk about it last night and figure everything out. I don't know what *everything* is, but last night I left before she got home, and this morning she had left for work by the time I got up. So when I get home from work, and her car is in the driveway earlier than usual, I know it's because we have to talk.

But then I see the car parked along the street. I don't have to see the out-of-state plates to know who it belongs to. It's little and red, just like every car my mom has ever owned, except that this one is shiny and new, not dull and old like the others before. I'm floored my mother surfaced this quickly. It's been just over twenty-four hours since the reporters showed up at River Depot. Prompt and punctual isn't what I'm used to from my mother. I'm used to elementary school lunch bills so overdue that all the lunch ladies would give me was a stupid PB&J instead of hot lunch. Presents shipped three days after Christmas, sent straight from Amazon, unwrapped.

I don't want to go inside, but when I finally do, Aunt Sarah is standing in the kitchen, her back against the refrigerator. Across from her, my mom looks nothing like the woman I last saw three years ago. Her shirt is fitted and her shoes match, and she isn't lugging around some weird patchwork satchel that looks like a street vendor stitched it together out of old t-shirts or something. A gray leather purse sits atop the little island, resting against her arm. She looks like a normal adult. The kind that doesn't leave you at your Oma's house when you're seven and then doesn't come back for six months. But she still sounds like my mom when she says, "Hey, kiddo."

Aunt Sarah pushes herself away from the counter like she may need to protect my mother from my response. "I invited your mom over, Liv." She looks guilty as she says it. It's ridiculous that she'd feel responsible for anything my mother does, but then I see the suitcase sitting a few feet away, in the living room.

I don't like where this might be going—or the *size* of that suitcase.

"No." I shake my head like I can will her out of the house. "No, no, no."

"Olivia." Aunt Sarah draws my name out into an exasperated sigh.

"You just won the lottery," I huff. "You can afford a hotel, right?"

My mother rolls her eyes but she doesn't look amused. "Yes, Olivia—"

"She *can*," my aunt cuts in, "but my new job wants me to start earlier than I planned. I'm going to have to leave next week. So your mom's staying *here*. Just to be safe."

My mother gives me a pained smile, like she's trying to look enthused but can't quite pull it off.

"I don't need a babysitter."

Aunt Sarah juts her hip out and crosses her arms. "What time did you get home last night, Liv?"

Crap. "It was—I don't know. It was late. But I told you I was going out with work friends," I say.

My mother laughs, almost imperceptibly, and I shoot her a hard look.

"It's a stopgap, Liv. You get to stay through the summer, and I'll worry less." Aunt Sarah sighs. "The house goes on the market soon. There are going to be showings, and inspections, and all sorts of things you can't handle."

"Can she?" I mutter, a whisper I'm not sure anyone even heard.

"Unless you want to go now?" Aunt Sarah looks a little panicked.

"This would give me some time to settle in though. Find us some-place nice?" She glances at my mother and then at me. "The real estate market is brutal, it could take all summer to find something. They've got me in a hotel . . ."

Aunt Sarah looks stressed, and I feel bad that I've put up such a fight about this. I know she can't help it. I can survive with my mother for a while. I'll be working mostly, anyway. And she's never been much of a mother, so I find it hard to believe that she'll start flexing her muscle now. This could be good practice; I'll be prepared if I'm stuck with a less-than-stellar roommate when I go off to college. Still, I can't help but let out a little huff of air.

"It's fine, we'll be fine." I put my hand on top of Aunt Sarah's on the kitchen island. "Find us someplace nice." I hate seeing her like this—anxious and off-kilter, and so . . . not herself.

Aunt Sarah smiles and lets out a deep breath. "Joanie, you okay with the couch until I leave?"

My mother nods. "Sounds good. I'll just put my things in your room?"

Aunt Sarah nods and starts down the hallway, waving her hand at my mother. "I'll make you some closet space."

Aunt Sarah is halfway down the hallway and my mother is stand-ing next to her suitcase. "Congrats on the big win, by the way." I should stop myself there, but I can't. "I bet it's a huge relief to finally be independently wealthy."

Mom's face falls. "Thanks. I was doing fine though." She pushes the button on her suitcase that lets her pull up the long black handle. "I have a photography business. I do seniors and weddings, and I just started doing some corporate work."

Now it's my turn to be hurt. When I imagine my mother in Tempe or Tampa or wherever it is she currently calls home, it's usually in some sort of dire situation. I imagine it looking a lot like my childhood, the months at a time I would spend with my mother, when we thought things were finally turning around; past-due rent notices tacked to the door, a sparsely furnished apartment. Late nights working odd jobs, while she tries to *find herself.* Thinking that she's just off living a normal life, somewhere that's not here—that she's taking photos of other kids my age, chatting with them and getting to know them, while she captures this pivotal time in their lives—that stings a lot more.

Chapter
Nine

Today we're going to ArtPrize, a big annual art contest in Grand Rapids, ninety minutes north of Riverton. At work, Aiden rambled on about how the whole city is filled with art—soaring murals painted on the sides of ordinary buildings, giant statues rising up out of the river that runs through the city, and pencil drawings as big as a wall of our gym. I didn't realize he was wanting to go so soon, but it's the last weekend of the three-week event, so it's now or never. And we were both magically removed from the work schedule for the weekend after Aiden asked me to come with him. A perk of being the owner's kid (and the owner's kid's driver), I guess. *What did he do to lose his license?*

Aiden is standing against his garage door, looking at his phone, when I come up the driveway on my bike Saturday morning. Aiden's car isn't fancy—it's just a plain black Honda Civic with some rust around the fender and a Riverton Baseball decal across the back window. We're only five minutes from Aiden's house, riding in silence, when he turns down the music. Ever since I told him I'm a writer, he has been obsessed with the idea that I must have some sort of latent artistic talent. "Writers have artistic eyes," he'd said to me in the dunes, as we walked and talked on our way back to the beach. *He's going to be* so *disappointed.*

By the time we reach the tall gray parking garage in the center of downtown Grand Rapids, Aiden has managed to get me to share a lot of random personal stuff. We don't know each other well enough to sit in silence for a ninety-minute drive, and at first it made my palms sweaty on the steering wheel, but mostly it was fun and easy.

"Seriously. Not one?" Aiden was floored that I don't follow *any* sports teams.

"Overrated."

He shakes his head, his eyes on me. "But you come to the baseball games."

"Good eye." I mimic what they always yell on the field as a wild pitch flies in, and force out a laugh. I really don't want to talk about baseball or the reason I was there despite not being a fan.

"Favorite color?" he asks.

"Don't have one."

"You have to," he insists.

"Nope. I don't." I think about telling him that my mom insists on giving me yellow things, and Emma wishes I liked pink. But bringing up my mom feels like too much, too soon. Especially after his front seat to my mama drama last week. "Yours is green." I say it matter-of-factly, waiting for the reaction I know I'm about to get.

"I *told* you." Aiden's hands excitedly thump the dash. "Art eyes."

Anyone who pays attention to Aiden at all could guess his favorite color. His shirt the other night was green, the messenger bag sitting between us is a dark hunter green. The strap of his watch is lime. I'm a little unnerved by the fact that I've noticed this in just the few days I've been around him.

We're quiet the last five minutes of the drive, and it feels like the perfect transition into our day together. I'm still in a bit of denial that *I'm* spending an entire day with Aiden Emerson. But also, he doesn't feel like *that* Aiden anymore. *Emerson.* He is—I know, under the art talk and the easy banter, he's still that same guy I only ever saw from down the length of a hallway, or through a chain-link fence, when he was on display for anyone willing to look. But when I'm with him, he just feels like Aiden. Coworker. Friend (I think). Regular guy. *Hot* guy. And it's clear that the rumors were just that— Aiden isn't turning into some kind of delinquent. Maybe he's just over baseball.

When we exit the garage and step out into the street, there's a sort of electricity in the air, like we've just walked into a carnival. Except that instead of spinning rides and clowns and games that cost too much money, there are three-story paintings, and sculptures leaping from the river, and a legion of food trucks lining the streets. Music seems to be coming from all directions, muddled and soft as it mixes between the tall buildings. The road we're on is shut down, and there are lines of people pulsing in every direction.

Aiden pulls out his phone and starts scrolling down the screen.

"I've made us our own Top Twenty to check out." He holds the phone screen up to me. "The really good stuff."

Aiden told me on the way here that normally the public votes on all of the exhibits—and there are thousands—but voting ended last week, and all of the winners have already been chosen. His list has everyone organized by medium, and as we walk to our first destination, he tells me everything he read about it. What inspired the project, and how the textile elements were all hand-woven from the artist's and his children's clothes, representing the bond of family. Before we even reach the exhibit, I have a vivid mental picture of what I'm about to see. "Wow, you're a total art nerd."

Aiden smiles—his whole face lighting up like it's a compliment—and jabs his head in the direction of a red brick building a block down. "This way."

AIDEN

My plan was to take Olivia to everything on my list, but as we enter the first building I can already tell that it's going to be a lost cause. I knew there was art all over the place, but I underestimated what that actually meant. As we push through the glass doors of our first location, it's a sea of bodies. I look at my paper. "The massive pencil drawing of the Civil War soldiers is supposed to be this way."

"It's ridiculous in here," Olivia says, her voice muddled by the noise surrounding us.

I smack the papers against my leg. "Should we wait?"

Olivia shrugs. "Totally up to you." She smiles. "I'm just the chauffeur."

I laugh. "I did promise you lots of cool stuff though." I jab my head to the right, where I can see an elevator tucked into the corner. "Let's see what else we can find."

We push through the bodies around us and make our way to the shiny silver doors. Four floors up, we're deposited on a floor that's quiet and open, with wood beams and metal crisscrossing overhead. I pull my phone out and load the artist notes for this building so I can check what's on exhibit. As soon as she steps out of the elevator, Olivia is headed toward a giant wall of windows. I'm scrolling down my screen when I hear her. "Aiden!" She's waving her hand behind her. "Check this out."

She's looking out the window, down onto the street, and as I approach I just see the sides of buildings. But down below, in what I'm guessing is usually a parking lot, there's an exhibit. I notice now that there's a white sheet of paper attached to the window, with the exhibit name—"Aerial Splendor"—and artist listed. And in the lot is the biggest chalk drawing I've ever seen. It stretches from corner to corner of the parking lot, which is corded off. It features two giant horses, and even from this distance they're insanely intricate. The scale is incredible. And for the first time in two months I'm not squinting to make out details, or to really see something the way it's supposed to be seen. Maybe this is my problem. It's not that art isn't my thing, I just need a medium that isn't compromised by my vision.

"How do they even do that?" Olivia's voice is full of awe.

"I'm guessing the artist drew it small-scale first, and then transferred it using a grid."

"Wow, that's crazy."

I nod, but I can't take my eyes off of what lies below me. Maybe I need to think outside of my usual 16 × 20 paper. *It's so crazy, it just might work.*

O L I V I A

This is crazy. I just walked through a maze of iridescent curtains. Thousands and thousands of tiny strings, fashioned with mirrored circles and iridescent squares, all hanging down around us like a pulsing, flowing current that we're caught up in. I've never seen art like this—the kind that hangs over you, wraps around you, engulfs all of your senses, and burns itself into your brain. It's intoxicating and transporting—I feel like we're different people in a magical place. That seems to be the norm for places I go with Aiden.

"The artist's guide said to run," Aiden says, and before the words have left his mouth he has me by the hand and the bejeweled pieces are streaking past us like stars outside a spaceship. When we reach the end we're still holding hands, gazing at the iridescent tunnel behind us.

"Sorry," Aiden says, and he drops my hand.

I'm not sure if he's talking about the running or the hand-holding, but I tell him *no problem,* because it isn't. That was amazing.

"The artist's notes are really important with this kind of art," Aiden explains. "They tell you how to interact with it."

There's a reverence in Aiden's voice, and it makes me smile.

The historic hotel we're in has been filled with exhibits, and even though we came for one specific exhibit Aiden had picked out, we've roamed from room to room checking everything out. I shake my head as we push through the gilded revolving doors of the hotel. We've seen exhibits in cafés, museums, and Chinese restaurants. And in alleys and parking lots. The whole city is filled with art, tucked into every crack and corner, plastered on every wall. Even the river that winds through downtown hosts art, with a giant metal serpent plunging in and out of the water.

As we walk down the sidewalk, Aiden's head is tilted up, his eyes fixed on a colorful mural on the side of the building we're approaching. It's shades of orange and coral—rippled pieces that look like fish scales that wrap the entire side of the building—and as we pass it, I can see that it's actually moving. The scales look to each be an individual piece of paper, blowing in the slight breeze.

"I love that," I say, more to myself than anything, because I really do.

"What does it remind you of?"

I think about it for a second, about the colors and the way everything bends and shifts.

Aiden smiles. "There's no wrong answer."

"A giant goldfish," I say, and Aiden lets out a booming laugh that makes the person passing us on the sidewalk jump, which makes me laugh too. "Hey, you said no wrong answers. The colors remind me of those gigantic koi you see in the ponds in fancy gardens."

"That's a good answer." He smiles and we keep walking, crossing a big blue bridge stretching over the river. The metal lattice that crosses over us is smurf-blue and the city is on full display down the riverbank.

"Your turn," I say, nudging him with my elbow.

"For?"

"If I'm forced to analyze art, so are you."

"Okay." He stops and turns back the way we came, looking up at the building behind us. From this distance it looks different. The individual pieces are all meshed together, and I can barely make out that there are a thousand little pieces making it up. "It reminds me of a sunset," Aiden says, his voice thoughtful and almost a little sad. I think about the sunset the other night, the way it felt like the first time I had ever really seen one, how happy it had made me. Seeing the sunset that way feels a little like a present he gave me. "The way it's beautiful, even though it's an ending. It reminds me of oil pastels, the way it all meshes together, one color bleeding into the next." He turns and smiles at me. "Or a goldfish. A massive, building-eating goldfish."

I poke my elbow into him again.

"It's like the Godzilla of goldfish, terrorizing the whole city." He's looking straight ahead, smiling.

"I don't care what you say. I love my city-eating goldfish."

He laughs and looks over at me. "Me too."

The bridge dumps us out onto a sidewalk that winds between office buildings and storefronts, and a block down we cross the street into a small parking lot filled with picnic tables and lined with food trucks.

"You really don't draw or anything?" he asks.

"I really don't. I'm not sure why that's so surprising."

"Because you're a writer. Writers are observers, and so are artists. You've got the perfect eye for art. I'm sure of it." He adjusts the brim of his hat. "We just have to figure out what your thing is."

We stop in front of a bright red truck with a yellow awning and a giant white pig painted on one side. It smells like the ribs my grandpa made when I was little, and there's nothing I want more than to sink my mouth into some gooey barbecue. Nothing except not making a fool of myself with Aiden. Because this may not be a date, but he's still a hot guy. Way too hot to watch barbecue sauce drip down my face.

"Two hot dogs. Chicago-style, please," he says to the middle-aged woman at the window as he pulls money out of his pocket. He looks at me questioningly and I shake my head. I'm suddenly not hungry. We walk as Aiden eats.

We're on a side street and behind us is a two-story monstrosity made of metal. I can't take my eyes off of it.

"What *is* this?" I nod up at the dark brown creature's snout hanging over us on the sidewalk.

"Steam Pig." There's a very noticeable sense of awe in Aiden's voice. "This was one of the featured exhibits they had on the website."

My eyes wander over the creature's riveted snout and its rocket-like legs. There must be at least fifteen feet between me and the metal beast's belly, and another fifteen to the top of his head. "Interesting," I mutter, pulling my eyes back to Aiden, who is looking at this giant chunk of metal like it's the most beautiful thing he's ever seen.

"I bet this was a bitch to put together."

"This took a serious plan," I add, and Aiden nods. "You don't put something like this together on a whim."

"Most art doesn't come together that way. Not for me, at least."

"Me either," I add. "With writing, I mean. I need a plan."

"Maybe someday it will come to us without so much effort—the words and pictures."

"You think?"

He laughs. "Now's not a great time to ask me. I'm not exactly the king of optimism at the moment."

"Yeah, I get that. It's hard when things change. Or when you can't have what you really want."

"It is," he says quietly, and tips his head toward the street. "Let's get going." He reaches for my hand and pulls me behind him for a few steps before he drops it. I follow behind, giving myself a few moments to enjoy the view. Of the city, the art, and Aiden Emerson. All *surprisingly* nice.

$$\backsim$$

Our last stop of the day is an exhibit hosted in an old warehouse building. After a half-mile walk from the center of downtown we stood in line for thirty minutes in the expansive space, before being ushered, in a group of twenty or so, into a small room. We follow the guide into the exhibition room—a large makeshift space with a ceiling half the height of the warehouse. In the pitch black, with temporary walls around us, it feels like we're entering a haunted house and a shiver runs through me. Something grazes my arm and I startle, grabbing toward Aiden and catching a handful of his shirt in my hand. I can feel his hard forearm under my fingertips.

"You okay?" Aiden whispers, his voice amused. I can barely see him, but I feel his breath over me, warm and soft as it brushes across my forehead. He pulls his arm away from me, and I feel like an idiot for clinging on to him like a scared six-year-old.

I *hate* haunted houses.

If you ask me, anyone who likes them is absolutely masochistic. I hate that you can't see the other people, or the ground, or what's coming next. I hate the weird noises and the strange things they touch you with. But this isn't a haunted house. *Get it together, Olivia, you're embarrassing yourself.* A second later, something brushes my back, and Aiden's arm slowly but firmly drapes over my shoulders, his side pressing lightly into mine. He doesn't say anything, just keeps his arm there, his forearm resting on my right shoulder as bodies continue to file in around us, filling the room. It doesn't feel romantic. It just feels . . . comforting. *Surprisingly nice,* I think, and almost laugh out loud, despite the eerie shifting shadows around us.

Aiden is whispering as we continue to shuffle toward the center of the dark square room, explaining what the installation is trying to portray. Soft music plays as lights begin to pop on one by one, throwing patterns across the room. Bodies begin to drop from the ceiling panels, on what look like trapeze and—*Wait. Are they people, or are they puppets?* They look so limp, it's hard to tell. They're wrapped in colorful silk scarves, and I'm sure they're attached somehow, but I can't see anything holding them up. They look like limp bodies descending down into the room over our heads. *People. They're definitely people.*

More lights begin to flash from the perimeter of the room, painting the walls and ceiling with intricate designs. It's mesmerizing, and I can't help but smile up at Aiden, whose eyes are fixed on the performers above us. He smiles, but never takes his eyes off of the bodies that are billowing out of the ceiling like an upside-down clown car.

The performers begin twisting and climbing and flipping on their silky tethers, shouting and singing, their voices spinning around and over me as the lights whirl around the room like a deranged kaleidoscope. As a woman dangles in front of us, I look up at Aiden again and realize how close we've gotten as I twisted and turned to follow the performers. I'm nestled into him, my back almost to his chest. His arm has shifted across my collarbone. I'm not sure if Aiden's fingers are moving on my bare shoulder, or if it's just me, vibrating against him, but I suddenly feel like I might explode. *What are we doing?* All the spots where we touch feel charged. The back of my head rests against his chest as I look up toward the performers overhead. There are two of them, limbs tangled in the silk cords and each other, as they rise and fall with twists of the fabric. My breathing feels slow and heavy as I try to keep myself in check, before I crawl out of my skin.

As the last performers retreat back into the ceiling—the flowing cords of fabric trailing behind them like the tendrils of a jellyfish—the lights slowly come up. Like a dimmer switch, Aiden's arm slowly eases off of my shoulder with the brightening of the lights, and as we begin walking behind the mass of bodies in front of us we're completely silent. The moment right after his arm leaves me, it feels like I lost something, but then his hand finds mine, the way it did at the Steam Pig. Except this time he doesn't pull it away after a few steps. He holds on as we're caught in the current of people around us, slowed to a crawl as we filter out of the small door of the exhibit room and back into the expansive warehouse around it.

When we finally reach the doorway and pour out into the open warehouse, Aiden is holding my hand so tight it should be uncomfortable. Except it's actually sort of amazing. We walk faster, picking up pace until we're almost pulling each other, frantic, as we make our way toward the exit. We're not running, but my breath is catching, caught in my throat, my heart racing right along with me. Aiden makes a sharp left, and I follow one step behind, still connected by our magnetic hands. There's nothing in front of us except for a wide expanse of open concrete, but Aiden's charging ahead with a clear goal in mind. And then I see it, the little red letters overhead, waving us in like the lights on a runway. E-X-I-T.

Aiden shoves the door with his shoulder, and there's more concrete as we enter the small corridor of the stairwell. A flight of gray steps goes down, and there's a metal ladder bolted to the wall, but the little space is empty. Aiden pulls me in behind him and then releases my hand.

He smiles slowly and closes the gap between us. His hand slides along my neck, and he's pressed against me as his lips hit mine. It's soft and warm and effortless. Like the way he pushes us in the canoe, strong, but not rough. Smooth. And I feel it everywhere, vibrating through me like the music in that tiny room, filling all of the gaps that have been left in me lately.

When we leave the stairwell, it's hand in hand. Aiden's thumb rests lightly against my hand, rubbing with each fall of our feet as we cross through the building and out into the afternoon sunshine. We walk down the sidewalk, my hand in his, and it feels like we're walking through a different city. Like the day is brighter, the people around us more alive. It sounds so freaking cliché. But for the first time in weeks, I see the happy smiles of couples and I don't scowl. I don't envision how they'll end; don't wish them to crash and burn in some sort of fiery anger-filled breakup. This is what summer is supposed to feel like—exciting and carefree and new. *Emma would approve.*

Aiden's phone buzzes and he plucks it from his pocket, swiping with one hand while mine dangles in his other. He silently slides his finger across the screen and then drops my hand.

"Everything okay?"

There's a long pause as his fingers slow down and his phone returns to his pocket. "Yeah, fine." But he doesn't sound fine. He doesn't sound like the Aiden who sees sunsets where I see goldfish.

And his hand doesn't find mine again. It goes in his pocket, and we walk in silence. Past a giant, glittering mosaic that he doesn't even give a passing glance. Up the hill, and four blocks over, in silence the whole time. So that's that. A kiss in a stairwell. One kiss, and it's over as quickly as it started. Which is fine. Longer just means harder. Trying harder, falling harder. And I'm taking life less seriously this summer, anyway. Aiden gets in front of me, and his long strides are outpacing me. He's not running, but he might as well be. And I'm done chasing.

Chapter Ten

OLIVIA

When you live in a town as small as Riverton, and work somewhere like River Depot—where everyone is up in your business all the time—it's not hard to know when you're being avoided.

When Aiden's bike was missing from the rack on Monday, I wasn't worried. It's not like seventeen-year-old guys never show up to work late. But when our shift started and I was still standing on the riverbank by myself, something felt off. Then Ellis trotted out from behind the building—his hair not coifed into its usual fauxhawk, his shirt visibly wrinkled. *On his day off.* And I knew. In another town, at another job, maybe I could have made it more than thirty-six hours without suspecting I was being blown off. I could have lived in denial for just a little longer and told myself that it wasn't me. Maybe he got bad news. That his dog died, or his grandma was sick.

Not that I want his grandma to be sick—I'm not horrible—I just don't want it to be me. But I do live in Riverton and work at River Depot, so on Monday I *do* know. *I just don't know why.*

"Did you have fun at ArtPrize?" Ellis says it with a smile, and it's clear he doesn't have an agenda.

"It was fun," I say, picking red cushions out of a canoe and looping them over my arm.

Ellis tells me about his date the night before, with a "gorgeous blond" terrorist named Darren who took him to dinner at an artisan pizza place. About mini-golf, where he won, even though he tried to lose. "Liv, I'm *inconveniently* good at mini-golf."

"Poor baby," I joke.

"We're supposed to go out again on Wednesday," he says, but he doesn't sound excited, he sounds worried.

"Well, he sounds nice," I say.

Ellis nods as he stacks an armful of paddles on the rack.

"What's the problem?"

"The problem is we had the best first date ever, and I have no idea how to follow that up."

Part of me wants to laugh at how much I can relate to this. Aiden and I weren't on a date—I don't think, despite the kiss—but it was a pretty magical day. *Art and music and stairwell kisses?* Maybe it's a good thing we stopped before we started. I'm not sure how we'd go up from there.

"What about bowling," I suggest.

Ellis gives me a disgusted look, like I suggested he go sit in a pile of trash.

"Blacklight bowling?" I offer. "That's kind of retro-cool."

"I don't think we're the bowling type." There's a stretch of silence and then Ellis turns to me. "I thought you wrote love stories. Shouldn't you be good at this sort of thing?" He smiles and goes back to stacking.

"Aiden told you that?" I'm not sure if I'm upset that he told Ellis, or flattered that he was talking about me.

"Is it a secret?"

"No. I mean, I don't go around telling everybody, but it's not a secret. I just—anyway, I'll try to think of something for you."

"Awesome," Ellis says, putting his fist out and then knocking it into mine.

We're lowering a canoe down from the rack after lunch when I finally work up the nerve to ask Ellis what I need to know. "Where's Aiden?" I was going for a casual question, but my voice sounds harsher than I meant—obviously it wasn't Ellis's fault that his cousin is an ass.

"I . . ." He's looking at me like he's not sure what to make of my question. "I'm not sure. He just called this morning and asked me to cover his shift."

"Did he sound sick?" For just a moment I let myself believe it isn't me.

"Not really?"

God, why couldn't he just lie to me?

We lower the canoe to the ground and Ellis nods me over toward the brush, away from the family that is loading in to the right of us. "Is there anything you need to let me know about?"

"Um."

"As your boss—" His voice gets a little deeper, more serious.

"—Is there anything you should let me know about? Anything that . . . could become a problem in the workplace?"

"Like?" I say.

"Like . . . a *relationship*?"

I laugh. "No, there's definitely no *relationship* to report." I'm pretty sure kissing someone and then disappearing the next day is the exact *opposite* of a relationship.

"Excellent." Ellis pretends to wipe sweat off of his brow. "That's the first time I've needed to ask anyone that."

"I think *need* may be a little strong. I just asked if he was sick." My head snaps up. "No one has ever dated here before? Does Beth and Troy trying to eat each other's faces the other night not count?"

"That wasn't at work."

"Aiden and I haven't done anything at work."

Ellis gasps. "You've done something *not* at work?" I don't say anything, and Ellis's voice gets serious again. "This is my first year having to worry about it. My brother was still in charge last summer." He pushes a hand through his fluffy hair, and looks disgusted when he touches it.

I give Ellis an accusing stare. "You're just being nosy."

Ellis snorts and smiles. "Fine, don't tell me . . ."

"Nothing to tell," I say. I sort of hate that it's true. *Almost* true.

Tuesday, Aiden's name is crossed off of the roster next to mine and moved to the concession stand. Apparently smelling like greasy burgers and risking a breakout is preferable to interacting with me. *I hope he can't get the smell out of his hair.* Wednesday I don't have to work, and spend the morning googling my potential new high school and planning how I can make Aiden do *all* the safety demonstrations from now on. I'm not sure why I'm so upset. Maybe because this whole thing didn't seem like that big of a deal until he made it one. And *he* kissed *me*. How am *I* the one being avoided in this situation?

When I finally emerge from my bedroom, I find my mom in the kitchen. She's sitting at the breakfast table, a coffee mug cradled in her hands. "Good morning," she says, as I pad across the tile in my bare feet.

"Morning," I mutter, as I groggily open the refrigerator. My mother and I haven't had to see each other much since she moved in last week. I leave early for work, and she seems to come home late. I don't know what she's even doing while she's in town. I pull a two-liter of pop out of the refrigerator door and set it on the counter. I open the cabinet and fish out my favorite glass, covered in pink and yellow polka dots. It's more suited to orange juice, but we're out.

"Oh, Olivia," my mother says dramatically.

"What?" I set the glass next to the bottle.

"Pop at nine in the morning?" She shakes her head as she takes another sip from her mug. "That's unholy."

"I don't like coffee," I say, though I'm not sure why my mother has decided that my drink choice is a good place to make her first stand as a responsible adult. "And I need caffeine." I start pouring a glass, slowly so it doesn't fizz over the top. My mother gets up from the table and joins me across the island, and as I'm twisting the cap onto the bottle my mother dumps the glass into the sink next to me with a satisfied look on her face.

"No," she says. "There are better options. You'll ruin your kidneys."

I roll my eyes and let out a disgruntled sigh.

"Here," she says, setting a mug in front of me. She opens a cabinet over the refrigerator that I didn't know had anything in it, and plucks out three silver cylinders. "Try one of these," she says, as she sets them in front of me.

I twist the cap off of the first and it comes off with a little pop. The smell of berries fills my nose. It looks like potpourri. "What is this?"

Mom's face twists in confusion. "It's tea. You're looking at it like it's a pile of moon rocks."

"I just thought tea came in bags." I open the second container. It smells spicy, like pepper and something else I can't put my finger on. It doesn't smell like something I'd want to drink. I put the lid back on and open the third. It smells like what I expect tea to smell like . . . sort of earthy and warm; there's just a hint of orange. Mom is next to me, filling a yellow teapot—*I didn't know we had a yellow teapot*—with water. I push the container toward her. "I'll try this one." I suppose if my mother and I are going to live together for the next two months, her being my barista isn't the worst thing that could happen.

She sets the teapot on the stove and turns the silver knob. The burner clicks as the flame flickers to life, and it seems so loud in the silence of the kitchen.

"Aunt Sarah leaves tonight, right?" I know when Aunt Sarah leaves. I already said my goodbyes last night, in case we don't cross paths today before her flight. It just seems like the most innocuous thing we can talk about.

My mom nods. "I'm taking her to the airport this afternoon."

The teapot is softly whistling, and Mom sets a little silver ball in front of me. It's connected to a chain, and full of tiny holes. I give her a questioning look.

She nods to the canister in front of me. "Put that GPA I'm always hearing about to work and fill it up," she says. She sets a little spoon next to it.

I twist open the canister and scoop the tea into one side of the ball, then twist it shut. Mom sets a mug of hot water in front of me and lifts the little silver ball by its chain, lowering it into the mug. She twirls it around in the mug, bobbing it up and down until the water is dark.

"How long do you do it for?" I ask.

She holds the chain out to me and I take it, doing the same motion my mom was. "Just depends how strong you want it," she says. She reaches into the cupboard again and pulls down a little glass jar. "You can add some rock sugar if it's not sweet enough," she says, setting the jar of brown crystals in front of me. "Just play around with it."

I dip the ball a few more times before pulling it out and setting it on the little ceramic spoon rest next to the oven. It's pretty bitter, so I tip in a few sugar crystals and stir it with the spoon. I take another sip, and the hot liquid fills my mouth with delicious flavor. "Mm."

"I knew you'd like it," Mom says, and my first thought is to comment on how there's no way that she'd know. But I don't, because I'm still tired and my tea is delicious, and it's hard to be mean when I know I have to see her every day. I sit down at the little table and we sip from our mugs in silence until Mom finally breaks it. "How was the thing this weekend?"

She doesn't know what a loaded question that is at this point. If she had asked me Sunday, I would have said it was unequivocally one of the coolest things I'd ever done. But after a few days of radio silence, it's starting to lose some of its magic. "It was really cool," I say, finally, because it's true. Even if I went with a jerk, the event was amazing.

Mom nods, and I hope she won't ask me about details. Instead, she looks down at the mug between her hands. "We need teacups," she says. "This is embarrassing."

"I like the mugs," I say, taking another sip.

She laughs, and I don't get it, but I just keep sipping my tea.

∾

Late morning I shove a bottle of water, my notebook, and some fruit into a bag and ride my bike to the state park. I've never been here before but I expected it to be busier for some reason. Maybe because Aiden made it sound like such a hotspot. I'm not entirely sure what I'm doing here. Maybe I secretly hope to run into him. Even though I know he's working today. We were supposed to be off on the same day, but he owes Ellis for Monday.

I'm not brave enough to hike out into the dunes by myself, so I lock my bike up and walk toward the little peninsula that juts out into the tiny lake. I haven't been here since I was a kid. It felt bigger then. I'm not even sure I can call this a lake and not a giant pond—the water is shallow, not deeper than my knees for as far as I can see. A quarter of the lake is engulfed in lily pads. The grassy peninsula that pushes out into the lake is crowned by a giant weeping willow, the branches reflecting in the water all around it. I sit under the tree and toe my shoes off. My notebook on my lap, I stare out across the water.

This stupid unnecessary drama with Aiden has forced me to think about Zander. We broke up two weeks ago, and I made out with a guy in a stairwell that I basically just met—*really met*—last week. It took Zander years of us being friends for him to kiss me. It took Aiden one day alone with me. I'm not sure if that means Aiden is just a ho, or if Zander had to really convince himself over the years that he wanted to be with me.

I've drifted into a hazy state, the kind where you're looking at something but don't really see it anymore, and there are no discernible thoughts in your mind, when my bag buzzes beside me.

Emma:
What happened?

Olivia:
Crap, I'm sorry. Completely spaced.

I was supposed to meet Emma at The Cherry Pit for her lunch break. I check the time and realize I've been sitting here for almost two hours. This lake is like the land of no time. It's probably a good thing I don't spend more time outdoors, or my whole life would just rush past me in a blur of moments I don't even remember.

Olivia:
Still nothing.

Emma:
I can't believe you're this pissed.

Olivia:

This is a completely douche-canoe thing to do. You'd be pissed.

Emma:

True. But you're the girl who just broke up with the 'love of her life.'
Two weeks ago you didn't want anything to do with guys.

Olivia:

And I still don't. Definitely not.

Emma:

Hey, at least if you move, you won't leave a broken-hearted Aiden
Emerson behind. That boy has broken enough lately.

I laugh out loud, and the little girl and her grandpa fishing on the opposite side of my giant tree give me a dirty look, like I'm screaming in the middle of the library. *Newsflash, kiddo: If there were fish in this foot-deep water, you'd see them!* The idea of Aiden Emerson in a puddle of broken-hearted tears because of me is ridiculous. Right up there with me spending my day off sitting in the grass like some nature-crazed lunatic.

Olivia:

Thank god we avoided that.

Emma:

You're a heartbreaker, Olivia Henry

Olivia:

Only on Wednesdays

Another hour passes, and the little girl and her grandpa are gone. Fishless, despite my having been quiet for the rest of my time as their peninsula neighbor. I'm lying in the grass, my clothes soaking up the heat of the afternoon sun, when my phone buzzes. Excitedly, I roll onto my stomach, to see if Emma is getting off of work early. But it isn't Emma. It's a text I've been waiting for, for two weeks now. Except now that it's here, I wish it weren't. Because I don't know what to make of it. And I don't know how I feel about it. But I'm definitely not answering it.

Zander:

I miss you.

After an afternoon of grass-sitting, sun-soaking, and boy-cursing (both new and old), I'm in the kitchen in my ratty old shorts and a tank top when I get a text from Ellis, inviting me to a bonfire. Part of me wants to just hole up in my room and show Aiden that if he wants to avoid me I can avoid him right back. But the other part of me hopes that if I go, he'll be there too. I'd love to see the look on his face when he realizes he'll be trapped in the woods with me, after spending half of the week avoiding me. Still, a very equal part of me loves the idea of just lying on the couch and waiting for Emma to get off of her dinner shift. Except there's a 95 percent chance she's out with Mani before she even thinks to text me. And I don't even blame her.

Throwing myself back onto my bed, I look up at my ceiling, covered in tiny blue clouds and yellow stars. Aunt Sarah and I decorated it the summer I was eight, when I was spending a lot more time at her house on weekends when Oma needed a break, and Aunt Sarah wanted me to have my own room. We made stamps from cut potatoes, and I'd dip each one in paint and send them up the ladder to Aunt Sarah, who would press it onto the white ceiling. Some are light blue and some are dark, because eight-year-old Olivia didn't know anything about consistency. I sort of love that they're all so different.

I let out a deep sigh, because I know what I need to do. The old Magic 8-Ball is still sitting on my desk, and I grab it and sit on the edge of the bed again.

Should I go out tonight? Shake shake shake.

The dark blue liquid sloshes around and the white triangle appears in the window, surrounded by tiny bubbles.

Without a doubt.

I'm starting to think fate has a real problem with homebodies.

Chapter Eleven

AIDEN

"What's the deal with you and her?" Ellis points to Olivia walking up ahead of us with Beth and Jaz, and I smack his hand down.

"Shit. Stop." Not that she's going to see us behind her, but still.

"What?"

"Stop acting like you don't know. That you didn't set this whole thing up. You told me she wasn't coming." I stop and turn toward him. "Tell me you don't know."

"Okay." Ellis shrugs. "I don't know."

"God, you're obnoxious sometimes." Ellis has been this way since we were kids; getting into my business, trying to fix things to the way he sees them. And for some reason the way he sees things is me and

Olivia. Together. There's no other reason that the two of us are *constantly* scheduled for the same days, and always at the docks together. The only others paired up so consistently are Beth and Jaz, and they flat-out beg Ellis to put them together.

"I know you weren't sick and I had to work on my day off," Ellis says. "I know you're avoiding her. And I know you've got a real stick up your ass about something."

I grunt.

"And you're pissy. Like when you were a kid and didn't get what you wanted for Christmas." He kicks a stick that's in his path. "It's like—"

"Don't even say it."

"It's like that year you wanted that ugly green baseball mitt, but your dad got you the navy one instead."

"I wasn't pissy."

"Please. You were the most passive-aggressive ten-year-old ever."

"I screwed up," I say, hoping he knows I'm not talking about the mitt, so I don't have to say it.

"You can't avoid her all summer. It's been hard enough keeping you apart for a few days. The Depot isn't exactly Disney World, I can't keep you on opposite ends of the park."

"It'll blow over," I say, and I'm not sure who I'm trying to convince.

"I hope so. Because if I have to choose between you and her—" His voice is teasing.

I laugh. "Understood."

OLIVIA

It turns out Beth is building a tiny house with her dad in her free time. She pulls the pictures up on her phone and starts sliding through them as we walk.

"The stairs are going to have little cubbies under them," she says as she shows me a photo of the hollow stairs that ascend into the loft over what will eventually be the kitchen. The more I work with Beth, the more I can see her living in some tiny house built on a trailer, with a weird little toilet that doesn't flush and a special window where she grows her own lettuce. It totally fits the I-could-be-happy-anywhere aesthetic she has going on.

"Where do you just hang out?" I tip my head, trying to see what she does in the photo.

"Anywhere. There's a ton of space." She smiles and puts her phone away. "I'll have everyone over once it's done."

Beth tells me her parents have rented a little plot of land near her college, and how it will save her so much money in housing costs and student loans. "I'll just sell it when I graduate," she adds.

I'm not usually jealous of dads—maybe because I've never had one and I don't know what I'm missing—but I'm jealous of Beth's dad. I don't even want a tiny house—with their weird little composting toilets and each space repurposed for four different things—but I wish someone wanted to build one with me.

Ellis said we were going to River Depot's new building—the one they're all referring to as the Annex, since it doesn't have an official name yet. It won't open until next summer. When we get to the right spot along the river, Ellis and Aiden start piling sticks up in a sandy spot away from the frame of the building.

"I thought this was going to be a river boat," I say to Ellis, who has an armful of sticks. "Where's the boat?"

Ellis opens his mouth, but it's Aiden who speaks. "It needs a lot of work, it's getting rehabbed at one of the marinas. They've got it indoors until it's ready to go."

I have more questions, but not for Aiden. "Ah" is all that comes out of my mouth.

Aiden's face drops and I turn to the river, where Beth and Jaz are already sitting on weathered wooden benches. There are two—one on either side of the charred circle of ground—and on either side of those is an old canoe. They're the kind so skinny they seem unlikely to fit an actual person in them. Not like the wide boats the tourists use that seem almost impossible to tip. I sit on the overturned boat and cross my legs in front of me. Ellis is dropping a few larger branches onto the pile, and using a lighter to start tiny fires on the ends of sticks. Some of them don't take off, but others do, and it's sort of magical looking from a distance, all of these tiny sparks of flame suspended in the air, slowly growing and bleeding into one another until they consume the sticks and fill the air with heat and warm light. I'm staring into the fire, letting the dancing light lull me into a daze, when my view is obstructed by the outline of a very annoying boy.

"Come with me?" His voice is hushed and low and he's already got me by the hand, pulling me up off of the canoe.

Aiden tugs me into the woods—out of the glow of the fire and into the darkness of the trees—and I'm having flashbacks of the warehouse and the stairwell, and his hands. His lips. My stomach is twisting into knots at the thought of it. And I hate how good his hand feels around mine right now. The same hand that hasn't even bothered to text me all week. The hand that probably crossed out my name on the assignments board. I pull my hand out of his and it brings us to an abrupt halt, about thirty feet from everyone. Cloaked by the trees and the darkness, and the heaviness hanging around us.

He turns toward me, and he feels uncomfortably close. Closer than he's been since the kiss. "I feel like you're mad."

"I'm not mad—" It's *almost* true. I'm not mad in the same way that Aunt Sarah isn't mad when I forget to take the trash out. I'm not mad, in an "I don't know if I have the right to be mad, but I am anyway" sort of way. "—I'm . . . disappointed, I guess." *For someone who grew up without a real mom, I sure do sound like one right now.*

"I'm sorry." He stubs his toe down into the ground and shuffles pine needles and sand around with the toe of his sandal. "Last weekend at ArtPrize . . . I was out of line. I shouldn't have kissed you. I knew you had a boyfriend, and I shouldn't have been an ass." He shoves his hands down into his pockets and tips his head up toward the sky. "I got caught up in everything. That performance was intense, and it seemed like you were into it too. But I felt like shit about it."

I can't help but let my eyes follow his. The inky sky shows in patches between the trees, and there are little clusters of stars visible, mixed in with clouds so thin they're just barely veiling the little points of light.

Aiden's chest slowly rises as he takes a slow, deep breath and lets it out. "I was hoping if we had some space for a few days, we'd just forget about it and never bring it up again, and we could still be friends and everything, but . . ."

"But I'm mad?"

"Yeah." Aiden is looking at me now—looking me right in the eyes in a way that makes me want to run. "So I'm sorry."

I cock my head to the side and look him in the eyes. "It sounds like you're only sorry because I'm mad."

"I *am* sorry that you're mad."

"But you're not sorry that you kissed me."

"I mean . . ." Aiden hesitates, and glances down quickly, like he's not sure what to say. "I am. But also, you didn't stop me." He stubs his toe into the dirt again. "Why didn't you stop me?"

I laugh a little—I'm nervous, and surprised by the turn this whole conversation has taken. "You should have called me."

"What?"

"After you *kissed me.*" I raise my eyebrows and lean into the scolding-mom vibe I've got going on. "You should have called me. You shouldn't have avoided me like I was some stranger you hooked up with at a party and would never see again." I can't believe I'm saying this out loud, being so honest about what I want from him. Maybe it was all the time we spent together on Saturday, talking about art, and how it made us feel. "*That's* why I'm mad."

"You're not mad about the kiss?"

"Zander and I broke up, Aiden." I don't know why I say it. Why after all of this time it finally feels ready to fall out of my mouth. I'm also not sure why I didn't say it sooner. Maybe it was the text today. The fact that it didn't light me up like I had thought it would. I had been disappointed that the text was from Zander and not Aiden.

His eyes are glowing with a certain heat, but the way he's looking at me, I'm not sure if he's excited or mad.

"We broke up right after school let out," I say.

"You never said anything."

"You never *asked*. I didn't exactly plan for us to be the kissing-in-stairwells kind of coworkers." It sounds ridiculous when I say it out loud. "And I don't go around announcing my personal problems to the world—"

"Only when the news crews show up?"

I laugh. "Right. Only then."

There's a long silence—I can hear the fire popping, the hushed voices in the distance.

Aiden puts his hand on my wrist, and lets his fingers trail down to mine. He leans imperceptibly closer and his voice is soft. "Can I kiss you?"

A million things go through my head—how angry I was at him this week, the text from Zander, and the fact that I could be leaving. I want to kiss Aiden right now—more than anything—but I also remember how I've felt the last few weeks after everything with Zander. The idea of going through that again at the end of summer is crushing. Kissing Aiden is almost certainly the wrong decision. Of course, at one point I thought dating Zander was the *right* decision. My personal judgment obviously can't be trusted.

Aiden must see the doubt on my face. "Shit. You can just say no if you want." He rolls his head back and looks toward the fire in the distance, like he might bolt. I grab his forearm and pull lightly.

"No, I just—"

"I'll tell you what." Aiden puts his hand out and grazes mine with his fingertips, sending a chill through me. "Rock, paper, scissors."

I laugh, and Aiden smiles.

"I guess coin flips are more our thing, aren't they?"

He's right. I pluck a nickel out of my pocket.

Aiden takes the coin out of my hand, running his fingertips along mine again. He's trying to hide a smile, but he can't. What if this doesn't go my way? Will I walk out of these woods and never kiss Aiden Emerson again? *Fate,* please *don't let me down.*

"Heads, we . . ." I can't say the word. It hangs in the charged air between us, but I can't say it while standing this close to him. Aiden raises his eyebrows at me and tries to hide another smile. "Tails, we don't."

The coin flips in the air and as it's about to land in Aiden's hand, he steps forward. The coin falls onto the forest floor and my eyes follow it to the dark ground, and then to Aiden. He shrugs, with a pout that doesn't look at all apologetic. And then his lips are on mine. They're warm and full and soft. His hands settle on my waist, his fingers moving slowly as he pulls me closer, wrapping his hands around toward my back. My head feels foggy, like every thought I've ever had is suddenly spinning in circles there, kicking up dust like tiny tornadoes, spinning and whirring around. *What are we doing?*

I can hear the crackling of the fire in the distance, and footsteps as everyone shuffles around. I shiver and Aiden pulls his mouth from mine. His eyes look clearer now, more like himself and less like the guy who pulled me into the woods.

"We should go back to the fire." He sounds concerned. Probably that this is another pivotal outdoor experience I'm missing.

"It's not my first campfire."

Aiden smiles and my lips are twitchy thinking about more time with him.

"No, but we should still get back. If we're gone too long Ellis will insist we file some sort of paperwork." He rubs his hands down my arms. "And you're cold."

I laugh, but I don't totally agree. I *am* cold, but if it were up to me, we'd stay right here all night, locked together. A little paperwork to feed Ellis's ego seems like a fair trade-off. Wondering if maybe he doesn't feel the same rubs a raw little part of my heart. *Don't get attached, Olivia.* Don't *chase him. This is just fun.*

Aiden takes my hand in his as we walk toward the fire. There are sticks and rough ground and hanging limbs to traverse. I feel like I'm supporting Aiden as much as he's helping me, as we stumble our way along until the glow of the fire penetrates the trees and helps to guide us. Around the fire, everyone has quieted down. *Is it just me, or is everyone staring?* Aiden's hand feels hot around mine. Ellis is sitting on my canoe, and gets up. "Here, you guys take it." He winks when he passes me, and I make a mental note to just volunteer to fill something out for him, so he shuts up about it.

"We were getting sticks for the fire." I don't know why I say it, why I'm so panicked about everyone looking at me, like they know what I just did. That my shirt smells like boy, and my skin is all tingly and hot. Kissing Aiden isn't a crime, but after only kissing Zander, it feels weird. I wonder if it's something you get used to, kissing new people. If someday I'll have kissed too many guys to even remember. The thought is weird and foreign, and it makes me a little uncomfortable.

"Where are they?" Jaz asks.

I'm not sure what she means. "What?"

"The sticks."

I look down at my hands, like I was ever holding any sticks. Everyone laughs, including Aiden next to me, and the sense of dread lifts. We sit on the canoe, and after a few minutes I've even convinced myself that no one is looking at us anymore.

AIDEN

"There's this project I have to do—" Even as I say the words, I'm not sure if I should be. If I should be letting her in like this, laying out the work-in-progress that is my current life. It feels weird wanting to include someone in that. "I might be a little MIA for a while."

Her face drops—but just for a second, like she refuses to let herself be disappointed.

"I was thinking if you wanted to help me . . ."

"What are you doing, exactly?" She sounds nervous, like I'm about to suggest she help me with a bank heist. I know rumors have been flying around about me—our old neighbor stopped me at the grocery store last week and told me all about her son's struggles with alcoholism, and suggested that my (supposed) DUI was a stepping-stone toward worse things to come. I just nodded, because Mrs. Graham is ancient, and it wasn't worth explaining anything to her. I don't really care if people talk about me. But I do care if Olivia thinks I'm some sort of delinquent.

"It's an art project," I tell her.

"An art project?" She doesn't sound interested, she sounds disturbed. Like maybe she'd *prefer* illegal activity.

"It's not a project, not really. It's a three-day epic art . . . adventure."

"Three days of . . . *art*."

I laugh at her reaction to that one word—like it's some kind of torture—and it sounds so loud cutting through the quiet night air around us. "Days, maybe nights. Three days, maybe more. Don't sound *so* excited. This probably isn't the kind of art you're thinking of. We're not going to sit at my house and do oil paintings." I bump my shoulder into hers, and then I stay there, pressed up against her.

"So what *are* we doing?" She says it in almost a whisper, maybe because it is, or maybe because we're so close now, we don't need more than a whisper.

"I can't tell you until I know you're in." I turn toward her, my face a forced mask of composure as I look her right in the eyes. "Are you in, Olivia?"

O L I V I A

Aiden's eyes have drifted past me now. To the sky, probably—it's an amazingly clear night and out here away from everything the sky is lit up. I take a moment to look him over—the broad shoulders, the smooth planes of his chest under his t-shirt, the strong, perfect jaw. *Three nights with Aiden Emerson.* The words sitting on my lips, threatening to plunge off, are "*hell yes.*" I don't say them, because he's still

Aiden Emerson, and I'm still me. This all feels a little like the plot of some nineties teen movie. At the end of night three, I end up a victim of the world's most epic makeover, or deserted on someone's front lawn as I throw paint-filled water balloons at the house of some carefully chosen victim. Probably the principal. I'm taken to jail, and Aiden is never seen again. Not with me, at least.

Maybe he has a superhot popular girlfriend I don't know about? I can see it in my mind—the squishy balloon in my hand, the acrylic paint smearing my arms. I can see the look on my face when my mother—my *legal* guardian—has to pick me up. "I'll think about it," I tell him.

He nods and turns back toward the fire. Jaz is in the middle of a story about an old guy who rented a kayak and stranded himself in the middle of Loon Lake when he lost his paddle. Another renter called in for him and by the time staff showed up in the motor boat, he was hanging off of the back of his kayak, trying to kick his way to shore.

She's gasping through laughter as she recounts the rescue. *So there he was, in his old man button-down shirt, his fishing hat . . . just dangling in the water, clothes and all. He couldn't get into the boat either, we had to sort of slow-drag him to shore with a tow rope. Never stopped smiling. Tipped me five bucks when we got back to the lot. I swear that guy had the time of his life.* Jaz is a theater major and it shows—she tells a story with her entire body.

In one graceful movement, Aiden turns my way and throws his leg over the canoe so that he's facing me, straddling it. He puts his fist in the air in front of me, but he isn't saying anything, he's just looking at me expectantly, like he's waiting for something.

"What's up?"

"Rock-paper-scissors me."

"For what?"

"For my epic art adventure." He raises his brows at me, and there's a hint of a smile pulling at the corner of his mouth. "This is our thing now, right? Letting chance decide?"

Our thing? My stomach flutters at the thought that we're already sharing some sort of secret.

"Fate." I can't help but laugh at him throwing this back at me.

"Is it the same thing?"

I feel like it is. Like whatever fate is, it's decided by chance. Or that chance follows along with fate's plans. Something like that. "I don't know." I shift nervously on the canoe. "I thought you preferred coin tosses though," I tease.

He pats his pockets. "I'm all out. You?"

"Ditto."

"Rock, paper, scissors it is." He shakes his fist in front of me. "I'm willing to take the chance if you are."

"You seem awfully confident. It might not go your way."

"Lady luck owes me," he says.

"Me too."

My eyes meet Aiden's and we pump our fists in the air three times, and let luck and chance and fate decide.

❧

In the light of day, kissing Aiden and agreeing to go on his "epic art adventure" feels less like fate, and more like setting myself up for failure. He still hasn't told me what this epic art adventure actually entails, and I'm not entirely convinced it's a real thing.

Emma is sitting on the floor next to me, leaning against my bed. She's still dressed in her Cherry Pit uniform—the ridiculous, ruffly red dress and white apron with a giant red cherry emblazoned on it—and her long legs are crossed at the ankles. Her ruffled white socks peek out from her white patent shoes. They look like an adult version of what I wore when I was five. Working at The Pit has done wonders for Emma's personal style.

I knock her foot with mine. "Did you have to buy these?"

Emma lets out a little snort. "I doubt you can buy these, they're circa my great-grandma. They're part of the uniform they give you."

"They're *used*?" I shudder thinking about summer after summer of teenage feet shoved into the same pair of shoes.

Emma twists the cap off of one of the cherry sodas she brought from work and hands it to me. "It's like bowling shoes . . . they sprayed them down before I got them. I'm not eating lunch out of them."

"I guess." We both sit in silence, sipping our cherry sodas, leg-to-leg like conjoined twins. If I had to pick someone to be literally connected at the hip with, it would be Emma. I rest my head on her shoulder. I'm just using her shoes as a distraction from what we're actually talking about—the prospect of my epic art adventure with Aiden.

"This isn't that big of a deal. I promise you're overthinking this," she says.

I don't know how to explain to her what it feels like to be left your whole life. Over and over. And just when you think you've found your person—boom. They leave you too.

"This is *Aiden Emerson,* Liv."

"So?"

"So, this is what I was talking about. This is how you're *supposed* to spend your summer." She pats my knee. "Making out with hot guys in stairwells, and going off on epic art adventures, and falling in love." She takes a swig of her soda. "And knowing it's going to end, but not giving a shit, because it's so good while it lasts."

"Is this supposed to be a pep talk?"

"Yeah." She doesn't sound confident. "Yeah, just give me a second to get my thoughts together." She tips the mouth of the pink bottle at me. "You're leaving in a few months."

I reach for the bottle and she passes it to me. The tart cherry soda bubbles in my throat on the way down. "Am I?" I've been holding out hope that Emma could convince her parents that letting me get shipped off for senior year is inhumane. To both of us.

"Ross and Teresa are being completely unreasonable." Her eyes squint in anger. She always calls her parents by their first names when she's mad at them. "They don't want responsibility for another teenager. They still have three left after me, and apparently they're not sure they're going to pull through." Emma rolls her eyes. "What a burden my B+ average must be."

I let out a long sigh, and angrily flick away a chunk of lint from my carpet to distract myself from what Emma is telling me. *Dammit.* "You'll keep trying though?"

"Relentlessly," she says. There's a long stretch of silence before she speaks again. "I hate that you're leaving, but you're probably leaving."

I nod. I can't say the words out loud. *Moving my senior year.*

"I still don't see what this has to do with Aiden."

"My point—" She burps, a loud rumbling noise followed by a dainty laugh. "Is that this is your chance, Liv. A no-strings-attached, just-for-the-summer *fling.*"

Fling. The bottle is cool as I press it against my lips again. No-strings is so not my style. It's my antithesis. I am basically one giant ball of strings and exposed nerves.

"You're living summer by chance, right?" She points to the Magic 8-Ball, resting where I last left it on my desk. "Stop stressing. Let fate decide, and then roll with it." She shakes and throws a pretend set of dice onto the carpet, and laughs. "It's just for the summer, then you'll be out of here. So if it turns out he's a total douche-canoe . . . no big loss. You don't even have to see him in a few months."

"That's true," I say.

"Plus, I've never heard of Aiden having a girlfriend—I bet he's down for a fling. *Especially* this summer."

"Hm."

"And how much more fun will your epic summer essay be, if it includes an epic summer love story?"

I shake my head like my cherry soda has gone bad. "No love."

"Right, no love." Her voice turns from serious to overly sultry. "Just kisses in stairwells and hot sex in . . . canoes."

I almost spit my soda out. "Oh my god, stop. Canoe-sex is not on the table." We both laugh, so hard we can barely breathe.

"Come on Liv, it's like all of the fun, with none of the risk. Two months and you're done."

I hold my bottle up and she clinks it one more time. *Two months and I'm done. With everything, apparently.*

Aiden

I was looking forward to seeing Liv at work, but when I get to the Depot my name isn't on the assignment board. But I'm on the schedule, so I wander around looking for Ellis until Jaz points me toward the little office tucked away behind the corner of the gift shop that displays all of the t-shirts.

Even though the door is open it feels like I should knock, so I do. Ellis's head pops forward.

"Hey. Where am I today?" I ask. "With Olivia on the docks?"

Ellis shakes his head. "Sorry, I meant to write it on the board. Your dad requested you today, said he needed some help at the Annex."

"For how long?"

"All day?" Ellis shrugs. "I don't know, he just asked me to send you over there."

By the time I make my way out of the gift shop, retrieve my bike, and start down the little path that leads to the Annex, I've created the worst-case scenario of spending the day with my dad. Which is that he talks about baseball all day. My dad is the kind of guy who loves to rehash the best moments of life, treating things that happened last year like they're long-ago memories. And I'm not ready to talk about what a "great run" I had playing baseball. Because it just reminds me of how much further I could have gone. Of everything I've lost. And right now, I'm trying to focus on what I have to look forward to. I like my job at River Depot, and I'm excited about the art projects I'm planning for. When I don't think about what I *don't* have, things feel pretty good.

My dad is on the roof of the building when I get there. I stand at the bottom of the ladder and yell up to him. "I thought you hired someone for this."

"Grab that hammer and come on up," Dad says.

I find the hammer lying on the frame of a window, stick it in my pocket, and make my way up the ladder. Dad is perched on a two-by-four, hammering at a row of black shingles in front of him. "What happened to the roofing guys?" I ask, climbing carefully up the long narrow boards and taking my place on the right of my dad.

"Shoddy work," Dad grumbles. "I'm not paying someone to do a job worse than I can do it myself." He hammers in another piece. "So I'm doing it myself."

"In your free time?" I joke, knowing my dad is already spending every minute of daylight here.

Dad grunts. "You remember how to do this?"

I helped Dad roof a small shed two years ago. I'm pretty sure it doesn't make me anything close to an expert—or qualified to do this on a building people will actually see—but I know Dad's going to give me a step-by-step regardless of what I say, so I tell him yes and climb over the roof so I mirror him on the other side.

I start at the corner, hammering in a row of black shingles, and my dad reminds me how to place them and how many nails to put in and tells me it's okay to go slow. Meaning *don't screw this up trying to get out of here.* By the second row I'm in the groove and feeling pretty confident about what I'm doing. And by the fourth row I'm pretty sure my dad isn't going to talk to me the rest of the day. I work my way across the roof and it's slow, hot, and silent. So I didn't need to worry after all.

Chapter
Twelve

This may be the weirdest date I've ever planned.

Actually, it may be the *only* date I've planned. If it's even a date. In retrospect, maybe I should have been clear about that. Inviting someone to an "epic art adventure" is the definition of vague, but Olivia is obviously committed to this idea of letting chance decide, so I needed to lock down a few days with her. I couldn't worry that every time I asked her to do something, I'd need to hope that luck was on my side. There's enough pressure without worrying about that too. And I've been thinking about this ever since ArtPrize—I want to try out some ideas I have, to see if I'm even any good at large-scale art. Just because my vision is too shitty to do the small stuff well, it doesn't mean I'll be good at this.

I carefully place the jar of gunpowder into the cardboard box, alongside the spray paint, twine, and wood stakes. I'm putting the box and the small piece of plywood into the trunk of my car when Olivia comes up the driveway on her bike. She has a backpack that looks so stuffed it may topple her over. I grab it from her as she pulls her arm out of the strap, and set it on the ground. It's not heavy but it looks like she probably had to sit on it to zip it.

"You know we're not leaving the state for the weekend, right?"

She rolls her eyes and pretends to look annoyed. "I don't, actually. I don't know *anything* about what we're doing." She picks the bag up by a strap and sets it in my open trunk, next to the box. "I assume we're driving?"

"We are."

She smiles. "Great, now I know something."

I'm a little nervous she actually did pack thinking I was taking her somewhere that required multiple changes of clothes, and shampoo, and whatever else is now in my trunk. "What's in the bag?"

"Let's see." She looks up, like she can see the list in her head. "My bathing suit, flip-flops, sneakers, a sweatshirt, yoga pants . . ."

"You thought we might do yoga?"

"I thought maybe we'd do something . . . athletic? So far, you seem to be into things that are . . . new to me. So I just came prepared."

"You could have just asked me."

"You could have just told me." She's smiling, like nothing I say can make her regret her packing decision. "And I actually don't have your number."

I hold my hand out and she hands me her phone. I type in my ten digits and a few words, and then hand the phone back to her.

Mine buzzes, and I pull it out of my pocket. I type a reply and put it back just as Olivia pulls hers out. A smile spreads across her face as she reads what I wrote:

Olivia:

Excited for tonight. Can't wait!

Aiden:

You should be, it's going to be awesome.
I hope you brought something you don't mind getting paint on.
Or burning?

Her eyes go wide. "*Burning?*"

I really should have told her what to bring. *Get your head in the game, Emerson.* "Scratch that. Let's focus on the paint."

She's looking at me like she thinks there's a chance I'm taking her somewhere to burn her clothes in some sort of strange ritual, but she's not running yet. Probably because she's wearing sandals, and her running shoes are in the bag. "I can make something work," she says.

"Excellent." I toss my car keys at her and she catches them clumsily. "You can hold on to these from now on."

"Your parents won't think it's weird I have your car?"

I hadn't even thought about it. My grandpa bought it for me when I turned sixteen, and until recently, my parents never really policed it. It is mine, and my responsibility. If I trash it, no one is buying me a new one. "They won't even notice. It just sits in the garage." Even as I say it, I'm only ninety percent sure it's true. It's in its own stall, but that doesn't mean Dad's never going to go in there to get out something random like the lawn chairs that hang on the west wall, or one of our old beach coolers.

"Well, my aunt—and my mom—would ask me a million questions."

"Gotcha. No keys."

Olivia smiles, and shakes the offending pieces of metal. "Are we ready?" She glances at the open trunk, and I slam it shut as I walk to the passenger seat.

"Let's do this."

"Whatever *this* is," she says with a smile.

O L I V I A

I didn't expect that my first time out with Aiden Emerson I'd end up at the old football field behind the middle school. The junior varsity team and the marching band use it, since the high school doesn't have room for a practice field since putting in tennis courts a few years ago. It's tucked behind the red brick school, and you wouldn't even know it was here from the road.

"Just pull right up to the grass," Aiden directs as I drive down the little road that runs behind the building and dead-ends at what used to be a playground, but is now just a sidewalk that leads to an open field.

I do what he says, and drive off of the concrete and right up to the edge of the grass, next to the one set of metal bleachers that runs along the sidelines.

"I didn't bring any cleats," I joke, hoping Aiden will tell me what the hell we're doing here. I wasn't serious about the yoga pants; I *did* bring them, but didn't actually think he was going to take me out to run sprints or something. *At least I remembered my inhaler this time.*

AIDEN

"We're going to make this easy, and go by yards."

Olivia nods, ready for more instructions. I love that she hasn't asked me for details yet, even though it's clear that she's dying to know what we're doing. We're standing along the sidelines, her with a giant spool of string looped over her arm and me with a handful of wooden dowel rods. There's a hammer tucked into my pocket, which is the only thing that feels familiar right now.

"I'll put the stakes out, and you're going to run the string." I show her the sketch I've made of a giant grid, with a line running between each yardline, and another set of lines running every five yards crossways. "We'll do the perimeter first, and then we'll work our way from end to end."

She nods again, like she's ready to be sent to war.

I smile—or maybe it's a smirk. I'm pretty amused by myself right now. "Have you figured it out yet?"

"Honestly?" She looks at me blankly. "The longer we're here, the more confused I am. Running wind-sprints made more sense than this."

I laugh. "You thought my idea of a date was wind-sprints?" I wait for some sort of reaction to me dropping the d-word, and am relieved when she just smiles. I did need help with this, but I wanted *her* help. And if she just broke up with Zander a few weeks ago, I figure we probably need to ease into this whole dating thing anyway. Because I have enough problems with all of the guys on the team without dating Zander's ex being added to the mix. I'm in no rush to parade Olivia around Riverton.

I stick the first stake in the ground and jog to the next corner. Olivia ties the string around the first dowel rod, and then follows behind me. "I also considered some sort of crazy hike up a dune that almost kills me," she yells as I run to the next corner. I'm glad it's a cool afternoon so I'm not covered in sweat. This isn't the fun part though, and I want to do this as quickly as possible. I run from spot to spot, shoving the dowels down into the soft ground. I've finished two rows when I hear Olivia laughing behind me. She's running string down a row and watching me, an amused smile on her face.

"What?" I shout downfield.

Olivia laughs as she comes up the next row. "Nothing," she yells back. "I'm just glad you're the only one doing sprints on this date."

I smile. Because I somehow proved her crazy theory right, and because it turns out I am, officially, on my first date.

O L I V I A

This is not a date.

I mean, it is, but also there should be another word for something as complicated as this. And something as strangely entertaining as this. I guess an epic art adventure was an accurate description after all. It took us over an hour to run string around a section of the field. An hour of Aiden running, and me watching. It's fun, being involved in something Aiden loves so much, and trying something new. This is so unlike the dates Zander and I went on.

Emma was right, we never really did anything together. We were always in his house or his car, or we were at the movies. It's not like Zander didn't want to be seen with me or anything. We went to football games, and his sister's college track meets. We went to dances. But we never had these kinds of days together, when he tried really hard to do something fun with me and show me how cool he was.

And Zander never *taught* me anything. On vacation, he would leave early in the morning to go fishing with his dad, and I wouldn't even know he was gone until I woke hours later for breakfast. I've never fished. Why did he never invite me? Or take me out later, and show me how to cast a line like he could, in one smooth motion, the line flying over his shoulder, out into the water.

But Aiden is running across a field while telling me funny stories, and he's been so patient with me—with my wheeze-filled hiking, and my beginner-level canoeing; even my string skills aren't that great, but he's not stressing about the way some of my lines are slanting toward the sidelines.

After he finished the stakes he took over with the string, running that back and forth too. It was hundreds of feet of him asking me about my Aunt Sarah, as he ran one direction, and telling me embarrassing stories about Ellis as he ran the other. And as he ran, I barked out questions like a coach would. A coach on TV, at least. The kind that rides on the sleds barking things like *Do you want to win or not? Is this as fast as you can go?* while the players shove it across the football field.

"When's your birthday?" I shouted as he ran from the ten-yard line to the thirty with the length of string.

"March twenty-fifth," he replied, not even winded.

"Do you have any siblings?"

"Two," he told me. Both sisters—one in college and the other already graduated and working as a kindergarten teacher in Tennessee. He talked about them for a while, telling me about what they liked and that one was probably going to be engaged soon. Once he's done, the grass is covered in a giant grid of string. We're sitting on the bleachers, looking down at the spidery web we've woven across a third of the football field.

"Have you figured it out yet?" he asks.

I take a drink from the bottle of water I pulled out of my bag-of-preparedness a few minutes ago. "It reminds me of weaving. Do you remember all the weaving we did in Ms. Wilson's class?" Middle school was the last time I took art, back when everyone had to.

I tip my bottle toward Aiden and he smiles and takes it from me, taking a giant drink that wipes out half of the bottle.

I grab at it. "Oh my gosh, you're a fish!"

He laughs and hands it back to me. "It's all the wind-sprints! Is this the only bottle you have in your gigantic bag?"

It's not. But I'm not telling him that, and getting teased about my over-packing again.

"Ms. Wilson was obsessed with that stupid loom. I swear when we weren't there she was weaving those dogs' hair into creepy blankets or something." Aiden scrunches up his nose.

Ms. Wilson had these two horrible poodles that the school let her bring in constantly. All we did in seventh grade art was use her gigantic loom, and draw pictures of those dogs. "It always smelled like ugly poodle in there too."

"Totally." Aiden shakes his head. "Not it though. No weaving."

I shrug. "Then I give up."

Aiden stands up and reaches into his back pocket. His hair is a little sweaty and tousled, and his tan cheeks have pinked up. It reminds me of seeing him on the baseball field. He pulls a piece of paper out of his back pocket before sitting back down. He unfolds it and hands it to me. There's a black-and-white sketch of a bird—a phoenix— with a long tail and outstretched wings. It's simple, just an outline in black pen. And covering the page there's a grid of pencil lines, stretching from edge to edge. I look out at the football field, and back to the paper. "No way."

"Doing it on grass is kind of lame, but I need to practice before anyone lets me near a wall."

"I didn't realize this was the kind of art you did."

Aiden stands up and steps down from the bleacher before reaching his hand back. "Neither did I, but I'm going to give it a shot."

I smile and take his hand, following him down to the grass. Aiden retrieves a box from the trunk and pulls out two cans of spray paint. He holds one out to me. My eyes go wide. "No way. You don't want me near this." I look down at the drawing in my hands and back at him. "This is way too complicated for me."

"You're not drawing the whole thing," Aiden says, and then points to the paper. "You're just drawing one box at a time." His finger is on a section of the bird's wing. Inside the box there are only three lines. "We'll just take it one box at a time." He shakes his can and a smile spreads across his face. I can't help but smile in return. "Ready?"

I let out a long breath and shake my can, my voice teasing. "Don't say I didn't warn you."

~

It turns out I don't suck at drawing lines. It really was as easy as Aiden made it sound. We worked from box to box, each of us taking a row and working side by side from top to bottom so we were never stepping on the wet paint we left behind. It started out slow and with some shaky lines, until I got the hang of using the spray paint; but as I gained confidence I got faster, and even though I'm pretty sure Aiden was hanging back for me, I kept pace with him. When I get to a particularly difficult box, filled with the intersecting lines of the bird's tail feathers, I offer the can back to Aiden, but he waves it off.

"Our fingers are going to be white forever." I look at his solid white fingertip and then hold up my own.

"Probably should have brought gloves," he says apologetically.

"Nah, it's kind of cool. I'll look mysterious, walking around town with one white fingertip."

"They'll think you're a vandal," he says.

"You think?"

Aiden laughs. "No, I don't."

I smack his arm, and the line he's drawing curves off to the side. "Oops!"

Aiden doesn't move his paint can, and I think maybe he's upset, but then he just adds another line and connects everything together. "Fixed it," he says. Then he turns on me and sprays paint across my forearm in one quick movement. "*Now* you look like a vandal."

I gasp, and then lunge at Aiden with my paint-covered finger. Before he can stop me, I wipe it across his cheek. He grabs my wrist and holds it away from his face. "I like it," I say, admiring the white streak that runs across his cheekbone. "It really brightens up your face," I joke.

"I bet it does." He's still holding my wrist and he pulls me closer to him. I'm in front of him, just my arm separating us, the paint can dangling in my other. I look up at him and he smiles. I'm thinking about his lips, and wondering when he's going to kiss me again, when I hear the sound of the spray paint, and feel it tickle my neck. I gasp.

"You didn't," I say, grabbing at my ponytail. The very ends are dusted white. I shake my can at my side and Aiden's hand goes to mine, stopping me.

"Truce."

"You can't call a truce when you're winning." I meet his eyes and he smiles.

"Fine." He drops his spray can and raises his hands like he's surrendering. "You get one more. *Then,* truce."

I reach for his face. "I'm not a monster." I spread a matching streak across his other cheekbone and take a half-step back to admire my work. "There . . . symmetry." Aiden turns his head from side to side, like he's letting me get a good look at my paint job. "Yeah, I like it."

Aiden drops his head to mine and kisses me. Not like our other kisses, feverish and a little desperate. This isn't the kiss of a one-time thing, it's soft and sweet, and holds a promise of more like it to come.

And I probably like it more than I should.

AIDEN

Two hours later, we're standing at the top of the bleachers looking down at our work. It isn't half bad. Standing on the field, I worried our inconsistency with the paint cans would be obvious, but from up here the mistakes aren't noticeable. Next to me, Olivia has her hands on her hips like she's looking down at the world's greatest mural, and not a rough outline.

"This is so cool," she says.

"Wait until it's done."

"It's not?"

"I'll have to come back and fill in color. That part will be a little harder, but now that the outline is done, it should be doable."

"Can I come watch?"

I'm caught off guard that she would want to just sit and watch me do this. It fills a little hole inside of me, knowing someone wants to witness this new thing I'm throwing myself into. That anyone cares about it as much as I do. And I wouldn't have asked her to sit here while I paint, but I'm excited she wants to. Even if it's just out of curiosity.

"Yes," I say, and I pluck the can out of her hand. "You can actually watch me make something tonight, if you want. If you don't have plans." I give her an out, because we've been out here for hours already. And maybe she's not as into this as I am. The art *or* me. I don't know what the time limit is on first dates. "Fair warning though, we're going to be playing with fire."

She claps her hands together like I just told her tomorrow was her birthday or something, then her face gets serious. "Wait. We're not doing any *actual* vandalism, right?"

I laugh. "No, Olivia."

Her face lights up as a smile spreads across her face. "Then I'm in."

I look at the girl standing next to me, her shoulders a little pink from being out in the sun all day, a white streak of paint in her hair, and it's hard to believe that only a few weeks ago so much felt like it was ending this summer. But this is a beginning I can get behind.

I'm in too.

⟿

If we hadn't been in the same car when her mom called, I would have thought Olivia was just trying to get away from me. But even hearing half of the conversation, I can tell that she's doing everything she can to avoid whatever it is her mother wants. Until finally, with a grunt, she tells her she'll be home in ten minutes. And I shouldn't feel as disappointed as I do—because I've already spent most of the day with her—but I can't help but be disappointed that the day is ending sooner than planned.

Olivia sighs as she puts her phone back in the cup holder between us. "I have to go home, my mom is apparently losing her mind," she says. "She took a bunch of stuff off of the walls but now there are holes everywhere." She sighs. "How am I supposed to fix that?"

"Your mom is living with you? I thought you lived with your aunt."

She tells me it's just temporary, and from the annoyance in her voice, it doesn't sound like it's temporary enough.

"You want me to help? We can fix it in five minutes, I swear."

"You don't have to do that, Aiden."

"I don't mind, really."

Olivia smiles. "Awesome, because home projects with my mom was not how I wanted to spend tonight."

She smiles and so do I, and ten minutes later we're pulling into the driveway of a blue house with light gray shutters and an over-grown yard. "They're going to stick one of those shame signs in your yard, you know."

Olivia looks at me like I'm speaking a foreign language. "*Shame signs?*"

"The signs saying you have five days to cut your grass or the city will do it for you."

"Good to know," Olivia mutters. "I'm supposed to be mowing it, and Aunt Sarah would murder me if we had a shame sign in our yard." She rolls her eyes and groans. "But one problem at a time." She pushes her door open and looks back at me as she twists out. "Come meet my mom."

Olivia's mom is basically just an older-looking version of Olivia. Or she's a younger version of her mom, I guess. It sort of makes me wonder about all of that nature versus nurture stuff we've talked about in psychology class, because even though Olivia makes it sound like she hasn't seen much of her mom, they even walk the same. And they both tip their heads to the side and sigh when they get frustrated.

Now that we've made it past the awkward introductions (where Joanie assumed I was Zander and Olivia looked like she was going to throw herself out a window) we're all standing around the kitchen island, squeezing toothpaste into little cups.

"You're sure this is going to work?" Olivia asks.

"We did this in my sisters' dorm rooms every year. Trust me." I take a cup and walk up to one of the walls, smearing some toothpaste on it. "Just smear a little in the hole. It dries white."

Joanie takes a paper cup from me. "I think I can handle this. Thanks, Aiden." She exaggerates my name, like she's trying to prove she knows it. "Olivia, do you think you can make dinner for us? I've been cleaning this place all day and I'm starving."

"We actually had somewhere to go." Olivia's voice sounds disappointed but also unsure.

"We can do the thing another night," I say. "I've probably hijacked you for long enough today."

"Okay," she says, her voice still disappointed. "Or—you could stay and have dinner with us, if you want."

"I make really good tacos," I say. Once we were old enough my mom always had my sisters and I make dinner once a week. Tacos have always been my specialty.

Olivia smiles. "That sounds awesome."

"Zander who?" Joanie yells from the other room, and I laugh. Olivia may not be a big fan, but I'm still glad to have won her mom over. *Who knew toothpaste and tacos could be so helpful?*

Chapter Thirteen

AIDEN

I don't wake up in the morning and think, *Man, my vision is shit.* Maybe I would, if I had a pair of glasses I put on every morning that made my vision *not* shit. But as it is, this is just how I see. It wasn't some dramatic, overnight change; I didn't even realize I had a problem until I ran off the road two months ago, when I mistook a trashcan for a person, and swerved to miss it, plowing into the ditch. That accident got me a bill for body damage that wiped out my birthday money since I was ten, and an appointment with Dr. Shah. And then a follow-up appointment with two others, shots in my eye, and my car keys snatched.

I don't realize how bad my right eye is until I close it. During the day, I notice it the most when I'm trying to read something, like the tiny menu on the back wall of The Grill. Because unlike my phone or our training scripts at work, I can't move that stupid menu any closer to my face.

And since I'm not driving, I feel like I've figured out a workaround with most of my major issues. At restaurants I grab a to-go menu. If I can't read something, I take a photo with my phone and zoom in, and if I think I might know someone but can't quite tell, I just wave. People around town probably think quitting the baseball team has seriously upped my personality, because it's a false alarm 90 percent of the time. Lately, I'm giving out waves like I'm giving out life jackets at the Depot: *to everyone.*

So sometimes I forget. In the light of the day, when I decided I'd bring Olivia out here, I forgot that my depth perception is crap at night. That's what happens when you have one eye that's better than the other, and neither are good. I forgot that I'd be leading her through the woods in the dark, and stumbling as I try to walk at a normal pace without biting it on some gigantic limb hiding at our feet. I forgot that I wouldn't want to carefully traverse the woods, like I would if I was on my own, because I don't want to look like a freak with her. I haven't told Olivia about my eyes for the same reason I haven't told anyone else: I'm not ready for this to be who I am. I'm not ready for this possibly-temporary problem to define me.

I feel like we've been walking through the woods for a short eternity, but at least she's here. On the Fourth of July, she's with me. Even though I told her that this would be better than the overrated fireworks display in town, and her face said that she didn't believe me. I'm not sure if *I* believe me. Hopefully this nighttime obstacle course isn't for nothing.

Olivia

The woods are dark and Aiden's holding my hand, but it's not much help when he's tripping more than I am. The only thing you can hear, other than twigs snapping and bugs and birds and other creepy nighttime forest sounds, is the constant cadence of *shit, shit, shit.*

"Where are we going?" I ask.

"You'll see."

That's been his answer for the last thirty minutes, and I'm not entirely convinced we're not lost. Because I can't figure out what we could possibly be walking toward out here in the middle of the woods. As far as I can tell, we're not walking toward the lake. The river is behind us, and up ahead is . . . just trees. And falling darkness. And sure, I like the outdoors more than I used to—especially when it's with Aiden—but I'm still not looking to just wander around in the forest, admiring the trees. Maybe he had a really awesome date planned, but changed it after I made him fix walls at my house and suffer through a dinner with my mom peppering him with questions. *Bring a boy home, and suddenly my mom wants to be a mom.*

"Almost there," he says.

I'd love to know how he can tell, because the patch of trees we're in now looks just like the patch of trees five minutes ago. And like the first patch, when we stepped out of his car and into the woods. I keep looking for some hidden trail—ribbons tied to trees, or bread-crumbs, or something, but for all I can tell we're just wandering in the dark. I'm half expecting us to emerge from the woods in the exact same spot where we entered. But also, Aiden is holding my hand, and for as long as we're walking, that won't stop. Out here in the dark, surrounded by silence, I'm not thinking about anything but the way this feels. And the little flower of hope blooming in my chest—the one filled with images of the two of us kissing in the woods, under the stars—it reminds me of the old Olivia. The way I hoped—every minute of the day—that a moment with Zander would go differently. Until it finally did. Did I wish that into existence? Make it happen just on sheer hope? What are the chances of doing it twice?

I shake the thought away as I look up at the stars, set against the dark sky like a spray of paint.

"Finally," Aiden mutters, and I want to agree.

There's a break in the trees, and the path begins to thin out. The crunching of our feet quiets as we move from the cover of the trees to an open clearing of rutted dirt and grass. A wall of old brick rises up in front of us. It's the shell of a building, one long wall that turns into another, and a gaping hole where a door used to be. There's no roof, no windows, just the partial remains of four walls.

"Uh . . . *why* are we here?"

"I want to show you something," Aiden says.

"I really hope that's not a euphemism."

He laughs. "Close your eyes."

"Oh god, seriously?"

"Please?" He squeezes my hand as he says it, and my insides turn into a warm puddle. I close my eyes. The ground is clear here, a big patch of weedy ground and hard dirt, and I step carefully as Aiden leads me forward. Forward to what, I don't know. He directs me to step over something, and the ground gets harder under my feet. He tugs me to my left, and lets go of my hand. I miss it, until his hands are on my shoulders, guiding me to where he wants me, rough against my bare skin.

"Okay, give me two minutes?"

I laugh, because I'm nervous. Nervous about what's in front of me, both literally and figuratively. Nervous about who I'll be when I get out of this forest. Who I'll be when Aiden is done with me. Or when I'm done with him.

Something hits the ground, a zipper echoes through the night, much louder than usual, and I can hear Aiden rustling around. Something flutters behind my bare legs, sending a chill up my spine.

"Okay, sit down," he says.

"Right here?"

Aiden laughs. "Right here." He grabs my hand and puts the other on the small of my back, helping me to sit down. I'm not sure why everything feels so much more difficult with your eyes closed, but it does. I feel like I might topple over just trying to lower myself three feet.

I expect to land on the rough ground, but meet soft fabric instead. Aiden sits next to me. I hear another zipper, and then music is filling the air. It's nothing I've ever heard before—a strange mix of strings and brass and electronica. It reminds me of the music at the ArtPrize exhibit, and I half expect to see aerial dancers and strobe lights and theatrics emerge from the trees.

Aiden's voice is soft and he sounds nervous. "Open your eyes."

I hesitate, because I don't know what to expect. I wish I knew what I wanted to see. When I finally do open them, I feel sort of disoriented, like in the two minutes my eyes were closed the last remains of the sunset disappeared and everything was plunged into total darkness. And in the darkness, all I see is a gigantic wall of glowing waves.

"Holy crap." It's like looking out at the lake at night, except that every little peak is glowing a soft blue. And the big brick wall in front of us is filled with wave upon rolling wave. Along the top, little flecks of light fill the sky—glowing stars looking down over the rough waters below.

"You like it?" Aiden says.

I'm so wrapped up in it that I'd forgotten Aiden was right beside me—forgotten that there was anything to look at but this amazing wall of light.

"What is it?"

"Glow in the dark paint, basically."

"And you painted this? All of this?" I ask.

"I started it right after ArtPrize."

"Luckily you were avoiding some girl, and had lots of extra time on your hands," I tease.

He laughs, but he sounds nervous. "Luckily."

"I wish it wasn't out in the woods. I wish everyone could see this." I turn to look at Aiden, and he's already looking at me. "This is amazing. You are . . . incredibly talented."

Aiden leans toward me, and brushes a piece of hair away from my face. His hand feels cool against my warm cheek. He licks his lips, and the anticipation is killing me . . . it's coiling around in my stomach and twisting its way down my legs. It's rooting me in this spot like the old trees looming all around us. Like a wall of this beautiful, disheveled building that's crumbling before us. Just thinking about kissing Aiden makes my lips part. His fingers drift to my cheek, and then to my chin, and trail down my neck. I'm fighting the urge to lean into him like a needy cat who never gets enough attention.

Then his hands are gone. He reaches over to his bag, unzips it, and digs around inside until he pulls out whatever he was looking for. "Just to keep it official," he says, as he pulls out a coin.

"You're carrying around a quarter now, huh?"

"It's become a thing," he says. His lips twitch up into a lopsided smile, and as if they're attached, my own lips follow suit. "Consider me the official keeper of the coin."

"Heads," I say, eager.

"Heads for—?"

I laugh. "My choice." Fate has been good to us, but I don't quite trust her yet. Not with this moment.

Aiden smiles and then tosses the coin high into the air. It settles between us on the red blanket. He's staring at it, but doesn't say anything, so I do. "Heads."

"Your choice."

"My choice," I say, leaning in toward him. I mimic what he did to me, and run my hand over his jaw and down his neck. My fingers trail down his arm and to his fingers. He turns his hand over and captures mine in his, puts our palms together. He's pressing his hand against mine, guiding it toward him.

My hand is on his chest and I can feel his heart there, like a heavy drum, pounding against me. I leave my hand, feeling his chest rise and fall under it. His eyes are fixed on me, and my breath catches in my throat at our closeness. I don't remember moving closer, but we're barely separated now, just our hands pressed between us. Waiting.

"Olivia?"

I make a tiny sound, like a squeak, not a yes.

"You won."

I forgot about the coin toss, forgot that it's all up to me. It's empowering to have him like this, stilled in front of me, waiting for me. I run my hand up his chest and behind his neck. I have to raise up on my knees to meet his face with mine. My lips brush his, and he takes a sharp breath in. *Yes, I like this.* Knowing how much he wants me to kiss him, making him wait for me. But I don't have any control either. On contact, our lips move together, and his hands are at my waist, pulling me closer, until our legs are intertwined and I'm almost on his lap.

"You're mean," he says, as his lips move to my ear, then my neck. It tickles, and I roll my head away, directing him back to my lips. Behind him the waves glow, casting us in a soft blue shadow. We kiss for what feels like forever, but also not long enough at all, until our lips are swollen and we're lying on the blanket, pressed up against each other. My tank top is riding up around my ribcage, and my hands are under Aiden's shirt, and I'm starting to think we've been kissing too long; that if we don't stop now, we won't ever.

As if it has a direct line to my brain, Aiden's pocket starts ringing—a bouncy sound I recognize as an alarm—and he pulls away. He takes his phone out, swipes the screen, and returns it to his pocket. He sits up and pulls me along with him, pulling my shirt down and sweeping away a chunk of hair that's come loose from my ponytail. "Sorry, but we don't want to miss this." He stands up and puts his hand out. "One last thing." He hoists me up and we walk through the trees, away from his beautiful wall. The ground gets sandier as we go, and soon the forest empties out into tall swaths of grass. I hear the first explosion just as the edge of the dune comes into sight. "Hurry!" Aiden pulls me, and we're running, clearing the last few trees and bushes, our hands still intertwined. I hear another explosion and turn toward the sound on my right, just as a sparkling gold firework bursts in the sky. Then another goes off on my left. We come to a stop at the edge of the bluff, the sand and dune-grass sloping down in front of us until it disappears into the blackness of the lake.

Wow.

"Best spot," Aiden says, wrapping his arms around me and pulling me back into his chest. He points to the left—"The Riverton fireworks"—and to the right—"and those are South Hills."

"I thought fireworks were overrated," I say.

"I thought you didn't like 'outdoorsy stuff.'"

"I like it with you."

Aiden is rubbing a little circle into my arm as explosions go off all around us, reflecting in the waters of the lake and leaving white trails of smoke like chandeliers in the dark sky above. "Ditto."

A shiver runs through me, and a realization explodes inside me—I'm falling for Aiden Emerson.

⁊

It's dark out here, perfect for looking at the stars. Especially on a night like this, when the only clouds are in tiny, thin little strips that stretch across the sky like white gauze. We're lying on the blanket, my bare feet hanging over the edge into the hard dirt. There's a soft glow from the wall I've lovingly dubbed "the ruins," but otherwise it's black and still all around us. We both took about a million pictures of his mural, trying to capture the magic of it, but probably failing.

"Why'd you quit?" I hope I'm not going to ruin our perfect night with my curiosity, but it's like this is the one piece of Aiden that is missing from his story. "Was it your dad?"

He shifts a little and looks at me, obviously surprised.

Crap. "He's just really . . . *intense.*"

"Yeah, but he's not like that all the time."

"Sorry," I say.

"It's fine."

I can feel a tenseness radiating off of Aiden as we lie in the silence, close but not touching.

"I can't play because my vision is screwed up," he says, his voice hesitant.

"Because you got hit."

"No." He rolls onto his side and props himself on one elbow, facing me. "I got *hit* because my vision is screwed up. I have an eye thing."

"An eye *thing*?"

"Saying I have an eye disease sounds gross. Like pus is going to start oozing out or something." His face scrunches up like even he's grossed out by the idea. "But yeah, I have an eye disease that's making my vision shit."

"Wow." I should probably say something more profound, but I don't know what.

"Yeah."

The only thing I know about eye diseases is that my Oma is always complaining about her cataracts, even though they were supposed to get cut out a few years ago. And my neighbor used to have a little yippy dog with some sort of *eye thing*. She told me after I mentioned that the dog had the weirdest opaque eye color. *Not an eye color, just diseased,* she'd said.

"But you don't wear glasses."

"Glasses fix the lens of your eye. It's the back of my eye—my retina—that's messed up. Glasses won't help."

"You know a lot about eyes?"

"I do now," Aiden says. "More than I used to, at least."

"Can they cut it out?"

"No, it's not like that. It's only my eye in there, it's just not doing what it's supposed to. It's more like there's arthritis in my eye; like my eye is attacking itself so it's swelling up in there." He pushes a hand through his hair, like this whole conversation is stressing him out.

"Is it bad?"

"It's not good." He rolls onto his back, so I do too. "I'm probably not going blind though. Not anytime soon."

I hadn't even thought about that being a possibility. "That's good."

"I've been getting shots. That's why I had the black eye a while back. I thought I could keep playing."

I shudder. "I can't imagine getting a shot in your eye."

"Honestly, it's not as bad as you'd think. You can't see it coming at you, and they numb it first. Plus it's not nearly as bad as taking a baseball to the face." He's tapping his hands next to him on the blanket. "But yeah, it's creepy. My mom can't watch." Our fingers touch between us, and he runs his fingertips up and down the length of mine. It's distracting, and I can't help but think that's probably intentional.

"So that's why I'm your summer chauffeur?"

"When you say it like that it sounds really shitty." He fidgets. "I thought you had a boyfriend, and I wanted to hang out with you . . . but I also needed a ride . . ."

"It's fine, I loved going to ArtPrize. And your car will come in handy for my cross-country road trip next month."

His head pops up. "Really?"

I laugh and poke him with my arm. "No." I feel like I owe him something for his confession, so I blurt out the worst problem I can think of. "My mom's trying to be a mom again, and it's really weird."

"I caught on to that." We both laugh, and it bounces off of the bricks around us and settles into the darkness.

I think about telling him that I'm moving at the end of summer. I *should* tell him. Except the words feel stuck in my throat. Eight more weeks with Aiden doesn't feel like nearly enough, and the thought of it grips my chest and squeezes. I like the Olivia I am with him. And I can't help but think how different things would be if *he* was the one I had met years ago. *Why did we have to meet the summer before I move away?* I tuck the thought away and force myself to just focus on this moment, lying next to him, feeling like we have so much ahead of us. Tomorrow I'll worry about how I'm going to stay—or how to tell him I'm leaving.

Chapter Fourteen

AIDEN

"Are we there yet? Are we there yet? Are we—" Olivia's voice is teasing and excited.

I poke her in the back with my paddle. "We're close."

"You said that at the last turn in the river," she says. "I'm starting to think you don't actually know how to get to your secret art spot."

"What if it's so super-secret I can only get there by accident?" I promised Olivia that I'd show her my art spot in the dunes, and today I'm finally doing it. She's in front of me, paddling in a way that's actually helping us get somewhere, which is a fun change from the first trips we took together. When I spot the crescent of sand that dips into the shore and leads the way to my favorite spot, I point my paddle toward the bank.

Olivia squeals, and I'm a little nervous that this trip is going to be a total letdown after what she's built up in her head. I think she might have envisioned a unicorn up there, or something. I get out and pull the canoe out of the water, helping Olivia walk up to the bow and out onto the sand. Unlike the other spots I've taken her to, this hike is short; through a patch of trees and then up one dune that slopes gently upward.

"Is it just me, or am I getting better at this?" she asks as we get near the top.

"You're so excited about this, I'm actually having second thoughts about showing you," I say.

She stops where she is and smacks my arm. "Aiden Emerson, you better not be a pony-promiser."

"A . . . what?"

"It's someone who breaks promises," she says, taking a few more steps. "When I was a kid we used to get those sweepstakes forms— you know, the ones you get in the mail—and I'd peel off all of the little magazine stickers and send them back in, and my mom would always say that *when* we won, I could get a pony." She laughs but it sounds kind of sad. "So I always thought getting a pony was actually this inevitable thing, until I got older and realized that a million other people were entering that stupid contest. And that— you know—we were *never* going to win." She looks at me sternly. "Pony promises."

"In that case I think I should probably be up front, and tell you there is absolutely, positively, no pony waiting for you up there." I laugh, and she stops to smack my arm again. I grab her hand and pull her more quickly, until we're trudging through the sand in a slow-motion run. When I can see the top I bring us to a stop and lower my voice. "Are you ready for this?"

"I think so," she whispers, and I push her up the last few feet, until she's standing in my favorite spot. She looks at me and smiles, and now—at the top of this hill overlooking everything—she has officially invaded every part of my life.

Olivia

I'm not sure what's wrong with our real estate agent, but she seems determined to have me out of bed by eight on the weekends, regardless of my work schedule. The last three weeks it's been a steady stream of home-gawkers milling through our house on weekend mornings. It's really throwing off my routine, which now includes morning tea. So I'm not surprised when Mom says, "We gotta get out of here," but I am surprised when she tosses me her car keys and says we're going to the weekend market on the bluff. My options are limited, so we take our mugs of tea with us and drive the five minutes to Riverton's little downtown shopping area.

Vendors are set up on the bluff that runs along one side of the town, overlooking the buildings below it and the lake in the distance. The area is split in half by a giant set of brick steps that lead to the shops and restaurants that lie below. On one side of the stairs the market features little tents full of local fruits and veggies, each with a banner displaying the local farm of origin; on the other, antiques fill tables and tents, old pieces of rusted metal and colorful glass spilling out of each little nook.

I stop at the very first booth we see and trade two dollars for a little paper box full of fresh raspberries. Mom picks a berry out of my box and after some grumbling from me about her stealing the food I bought with my hard-earned summer cash, we wander through booths. Antiques really aren't my thing. Most of the time it just looks like old junk to me. What am I going to do with old farm tools, or eighty-five blue mason jars? Mom spends a lot longer in each booth, moving things around, inspecting items, and wondering out loud what things were used for, and asking the seller if she can't figure it out. I do a quick walk through each space, and if nothing bright and shiny catches my eye, I move on.

So I'm about four booths ahead of my mom when I see the little pile of teacups. There's a whole stack of them, all white with different colored designs in pink, yellow, green, and blue, with little trails of gold or silver wrapping round their rims and handles. I pick one up, running my fingers over the floral pattern painted across it. I wave a hand at my mother, directing her to my booth like an air traffic controller.

"What did you find?" my mother says excitedly as she joins me in the booth.

I hold up one of the teacups. "Check it out."

"Oh, Livi, we have to get them, they're gorgeous," she says, picking one of them up and turning it in her hands, examining the fine details like I did. My mother hasn't called me Livi in years, not since before I lived with Oma. But now doesn't seem like the time to argue; we've come to a peaceful ceasefire the last few weeks since Aunt Sarah's been gone.

I pick up one of the cups and check the little white sticker on the bottom. "Yikes. They're twelve dollars."

"These are old, they have real gold plating," she says, her voice reverent. "Just pick out your favorite."

I only make ten dollars an hour at River Depot, and ever since I started I can't buy anything without thinking about how many canoes I had to drag around to pay for it. And this seems like too many for a cup. I put the teacup back down. "It's okay, my mug is fine."

Mom shakes her head. "Don't be silly. We *need* teacups. And I'm *independently wealthy* now," she says, using my words. "Just pick out your two favorites and I'll pick out a few too."

I run a finger along the rim of a teacup. *Am I going to let my mother buy me something?*

She picks up two cups, a yellow and a green, both with silver rims and handles, and I pick a matching pair that are pink with gold. In the grand scheme of life, my mother owes me a lot of presents, so this is like back pay. *Don't overthink it, Olivia.* I set my teacups in front of the seller, next to my mother's, and she hands him a few bills.

He's handing her change when she says, "Aiden seems nice." It's been a few weeks since she met him, and it's the first time she's brought him up.

"He is," I say, taking the little brown bag of teacups when the man holds them out to me.

"That's good."

I expect her to keep peppering me with questions like Aunt Sarah would, but we just keep walking from booth to booth. At the end of the bluff Mom spends way too long sifting through vintage camera equipment. She tells me about the old camera body she's buying, and how film is actually making a resurgence. About how she's shooting a couple of weddings with film. And I realize this must be why she gets home so late on the weekends.

Before I know it it's ten o'clock, and we're able to go back to the house. We wash the teacups and put them in the cupboard next to the canisters and the little jar of rock sugar. And even though they don't all match, they actually look really pretty together in our cupboard.

AIDEN

My parents finally noticed that my car was missing. I knew it would be those damn lawn chairs that gave me away. I had gotten a text from my mom while Olivia and I were out. She was irate, thinking I was driving around town half-blind. When I got home Dad smacked the table, telling my mom, "Yes! I *told* you I saw it at the grocery store last week!" He pointed at my mother and whooped like he'd just won some sort of exciting contest. But once she knew I wasn't using my car as a weapon of mass destruction, all my mother wanted to know was why I was at the grocery store with a girl. And her reaction was exactly what I expected.

So now I'm in the car that started this whole mess, sitting next to Olivia in the parking lot of the state park. A double kayak is strapped to the roof. I'm about to push my door open when I spit out what I've been thinking about for the last five minutes. "My mom wanted me to invite you over for dinner."

"Why?"

"Why?" Nervous laughter wants to bubble up and I choke it down. I was hoping this wouldn't be awkward, but it's as bad as I imagined. "I don't know, because she's heard me talking about you." I pull at the baseball cap I'm wearing. "And she likes to feed people. I swear, it's like one of the great joys of her life." I wish Olivia would say something so I could shut up. "She still makes me breakfast every morning."

"Seriously?" Olivia is looking at me like I just sprouted a third arm and she doesn't know what to make of it.

Just shut up, Aiden. "Yeah. I mean, only when I'm around, obviously."

"God, it must be awesome being a boy. No one has made me breakfast since I was . . . nine." Even though the words sound judgmental, Olivia doesn't. She sounds disappointed. She's also just sitting there, behind the wheel of my car, looking at me like *she's* the one waiting for something.

"So . . ." I drum my hands on the dash. ". . . Food at my house . . . that sounds good? Or horrible?" I adjust my hat again. "Or I can just leave and pretend this never happened."

She laughs. "When?"

"We always do family dinner on Wednesdays. Maybe next week?"

She nods, and I feel like I can breathe again. *This dating stuff is more stressful than the bottom of the ninth.*

Chapter
Fifteen

OLIVIA

Aiden is late, so I'm sitting on one of the rusty old canoes behind River Depot, scrolling through photos on my phone. When I make it past the photos of me and Aiden out on the lake, and me and Emma in our red uniforms, and the glowing ruins, there's a photo of me and Zander. Just a selfie, taken after a baseball game. It feels like a century ago that I was sitting on his bed, suggesting I move in with him senior year. The thought makes me realize that I may not even see him before I move. *How weird is that, having loved someone for so long, and then they just drift away into the ether?*

It makes me want to text him. To tell him all of the things I've been thinking about the last month—how much of a mistake we were. But when I think about texting him, I just jot it down in a note on my phone. Because I don't need to open that door.

When Aiden and Ellis come around the corner, I'm just finishing a note. Aiden is smiling as he run-walks down the hill toward me, barreling ahead in an almost uncontrolled way. He kisses me on the lips and then pulls me behind him toward the river, only pausing for a second. At the river, we come to a stop, still hand in hand.

Even though we've been hanging out—and kissing—for weeks now, it's the first time he's kissed me in front of anyone. And my face must show it, because he looks at Ellis and then me. "What?" He shrugs and smiles, his eyebrows pulled together in confusion and amusement.

"Nothing." I smile, and shake my head, because it feels like we might have just had a very official couple-making moment. *Did we?* When Zander and I got together we had a talk. A really awkward talk that was way too long and was all my fault. Because I needed to know that we were making the jump from friends to a couple. That something *official* had happened when he kissed me that day. I needed confirmation that I wasn't going to show up to school in two days and find him making out with some other girl in the hallway. But there's nothing that makes me want to interrogate Aiden or ask him for a label. A tiny little voice in the back of my head reminds me that we don't need one anyway, because I'm leaving in four weeks.

Unless something changes.

It's the first time I've really let myself think what could keep me here. *A miracle.* Maybe Aunt Sarah won't like Arizona. Our house has only had a few showings—it's small and the bathroom still has old pink tiles everywhere, and there's almost no backyard, so maybe it won't sell. Maybe she'll hate her job. The last time I talked to her, she sounded more stressed than usual. Mom said that in her own time in Arizona people weren't as friendly there. I didn't think much of it, because Mom is either in love with someplace or thinks it's the seventh circle of hell. There's no in-between. But maybe she's right, maybe Aunt Sarah's not just stressed, maybe she's lonely. And that brings up a little twinge of guilt in me, too. Can I just ditch Aunt Sarah in a new state and stay here?

I'm sitting in the canoe, and I can't even remember walking away from the building or getting in. But now I'm paddling. I've gotten better, thanks to Aiden. He doesn't tell me *You don't* have *to paddle if you don't want* nearly as often as when I started. I thought he was just being nice then, but now I know it was because I was slowing us down, dragging my paddle like a limp noodle along the canoe. Tonight we're headed back to our beach and we're all camping out. I'm a little nervous about staying in a tent with Aiden, but we're also going to be tent-to-tent with Ellis and Jaz—who are very much not a couple—so I think it's probably not going to turn into some wild party out in the woods. I catch a glimpse of the blue cooler up ahead. *Hopefully.* As long as things don't get out of hand with the cooler full of beer that Ellis loaded into his canoe. I haven't drank since Emma got me tipsy on two glasses of champagne at her cousin's wedding last summer.

By the time we get to the beach the sun is setting, and as we walk off of the sand and into the trees behind it the orange of the sky seeps in through the cracks and washes everything in sepia.

Aiden puts a hand on my shoulder. "Let's set up the tent before it gets dark?"

I nod, and follow him toward an open patch of ground where the stubby grass spreads out into a wide half-circle before bleeding into sandy patches along the tree line.

Aiden points toward the flattest patch, almost entirely covered in grass. "Here."

Ellis yells at us from near the bluff. "You're doing that crap already? Don't tell me you're already one of those couples that holes up by yourselves. Are you going to be in your tent the whole time?"

Couple.

Did Aiden say something to him, or is this just Ellis teasing us like usual? I don't know if hearing that word should make my heart soar, or sink down into my stomach, but right now it's doing a little of both. It feels like it may rip right through my chest in its commotion.

"Nah, man. I just don't want to get stuck with that crap spot over there." Aiden nods over to the spot left next to us, where Ellis and Jaz will have to put their tents.

So, we're *not* a couple? God, maybe we should have had the talk. *You're leaving, Olivia.* I have to remind myself it's a moot point. I'm not going to wish for bad things for Aunt Sarah, and I'm not going to be around for a long-term relationship. I'm not getting too attached. It makes me a little sad that I won't get to do boyfriend-girlfriend stuff with Aiden though. There won't be a first Christmas, with over-thought presents, or Valentine's Day. I bet Aiden would give really thoughtful gifts—things that have meaning and significance, or something he made himself. But we won't make it to Labor Day, let alone Christmas.

Unless.

Maybe I really can get Emma's parents on board. Maybe if I offered to watch the twins whenever, and Aunt Sarah paid for all of my food, and I somehow got a car, so they didn't have to worry about taking me places.

"Olivia?" Aiden pulls on the pole in my hand and I let go. "What are you thinking about?"

"Carpooling."

He laughs, and threads the pole into the edge of the blue mesh. "Of course you are."

I smile and tell him what he's told me so many times. "I'm weird."

"Yeah." He adjusts the pole and the front of our tent takes shape. "Are you nervous about what I told you? Because it's not like I'm never going to drive again." He doesn't sound as comfortable talking about this as he did at the ruins. "So you don't have to worry about chauffeuring me around forever."

"No, I was thinking about how I was going to get around senior year when I don't have a car." I pick up the next pole and hand it to him.

"I'll drive you to school and stuff."

"Yeah?" I probably shouldn't be surprised by Aiden's kindness, but I am.

"Sure. You have good taste in music, and you smell nice." He smiles. "You're welcome in my car anytime."

I scrunch my nose up. "I definitely smell better than your car."

"Hey." He shoots me a hurt look. "It's really aired out now that I don't have smelly cleats in there. By the start of school I bet it will smell like . . . you." He smiles and laughs. "Silver lining, huh?"

"You don't think you're going to miss it?"

"The smell of feet?" He shakes his head. "No."

He walks past me and bends down to get the next section of tent. I reach out to smack his back as he walks by, but he moves and I hit his butt.

Oh god. Maybe I can pretend like it didn't happen. Maybe he won't notice. "The baseball, not the smell."

"I mean, I don't really have a choice."

My nerves start to settle.

"I probably *will* miss all the guys smacking my butt after the game though." He gives me the tiniest wink and smiles. "Luckily it seems like you're volunteering to fill that void in my life."

AIDEN

Olivia looks mortified, and she isn't making eye contact with me. "But you said your vision's going to be better by the time school starts. That gives you six months before practice even starts." Her eyes dart between me and the tent, and she's really cute when she's trying to act like she didn't just smack my ass.

"Just pretending it never happened?" I tease.

"Yep."

I laugh. "The thing is, my vision could go to hell again. Dr. Shah said flare-ups are common and I'll probably be dealing with them for years." I put my hand out and Olivia hands me the last tent pole. "It's not fair to anybody if I take a spot and then can't deliver for half of the season."

"But maybe you could."

"But *probably* I couldn't." I'm trying not to be annoyed, but I hate that she brought this up. "I quit, Liv." *And I don't want to quit again.* Does she think she's dating Emerson the baseball star? Is everyone going to forever see me as that guy, even when I'm so far from it? *Are* we dating?

"Sorry." She sounds like she means it, and it takes some of the sting out of my voice.

"It's fine."

"Can we just pretend it didn't happen?"

I smile. "Kind of like the butt smack?"

"No, I've decided that was kind of fun." She smiles, but she still looks shy about it.

I laugh, and pat my butt dramatically. "Anytime, Liv. Anytime."

She waves a hand at me to stop, and laughs. "You're weird."

"Only with you."

Olivia

Ellis might be right. We might be one of "those" antisocial couples now. Even if we're not an *actual* couple. But either way, we're paired off, sitting on the beach together, a line of empty glass bottles nestled into the sand between us.

Aiden puts the brown glass to his lips. "What's the weirdest thing you've ever written?"

"The *weirdest*?" I shake my head.

"Yeah. I've drawn some pretty weird things over the years. I went through a phase where I only drew fingers. I'd draw pages and pages of them. My sisters thought it was super creepy."

"That *is* weird. Why fingers?"

Aiden shrugs and smiles. "We had to draw them in art class one day and I was just really good at drawing fingers."

I know what I should say, but I don't want to. Because for all of Aiden's little comments about being weird, I'm not quite ready to embrace that just yet. Of course, there's a little—slightly drunker—voice in my head that tells me not to care. The one that's always reminding me that this is just for the summer. I don't need to impress him, or make myself something I'm not. Aiden never makes me feel like I need to, anyway.

"I wrote a short story once—early middle school, maybe—about a girl whose mom gets turned into a dog, and then she takes her mom-dog to the pound." I cover my face with both hands and let out a strangled groan. "I never finished it. Which was probably good, because it could have gotten pretty dark." I take a drink from the little pink bottle covered in strawberries. "I was working through some things."

"Obviously." Aiden laughs and I don't know if it's him, or my impending departure, but it feels good to just be myself. To not feel like I have to try too hard to be a certain way, a certain kind of person.

Zander didn't even know that I hated his cologne. *Hated* it. I loved the way he smelled right out of the shower—the freshness of his shampoo, the coolness of his soap. He *loved* that cologne. So much that he wore it to the Christmas dance last year, even though I told him it gave me a headache. We danced to this song about running away to Paris, and he kissed me in the middle of the courtyard, and it should have felt really special, but all I felt was annoyed. And nauseous. When we got back to his house I took two Tylenol, and then I took his stupid cologne.

I can't help but think of all of the other ways he never listened to me, never cared. All the times I didn't say anything because more than anything I wanted him to want me. I wanted to belong—with him, with his family. I pull out my phone and I start typing. I've thought of a million different things I could say to Zander to tell him how shitty he made me feel sometimes, but at this moment I can't stop myself. So I tell him about the cologne. I tell him that it's in his closet, hidden behind the boxes of comic books he pulls out every summer when his mom has a garage sale and he debates selling them. I don't know why I'm suddenly so mad about Zander. Maybe because it feels like I wasted so much time being *that,* when I could have been *this.*

I don't care if you wear it now, I type.

As I'm about to hit send, Aiden's voice distracts me. "Who are you texting?"

Duh, Olivia. Hot guy. On the beach. Put your phone away. I click send and slip my phone back into my shorts pocket. It feels good, like I've taken another step toward closure. It also feels like nothing. The feel of the cool air brushing across my hot face overshadows everything else. It's all I can feel, all I want to feel. Except for maybe Aiden's lips. So I lean over, and I do what I'm thinking about. Because I've waited long enough for this, and now I don't have any time to waste.

⁂

Ellis decides if we won't come to him, he'll come to us. The number of bottles between me and Aiden has doubled, and so has the number of bodies in the sand.

"Stars are kind of underwhelming," Ellis says from where he's wedged in between me and Aiden. Jaz is on the other side of me. We have miles of deserted beach and all four of us are squished into this tiny square of sand, body-to-body. "Don't you think? I mean . . . I don't get the appeal. They're just . . . so far away."

I laugh. Only Ellis would be underwhelmed by a celestial wonder that took billions of years to form.

"Hell. No." Jaz twists next to me, like she's trying to see Ellis over me, and she sounds personally affronted. "Stars are crazy romantic. Like, show-me-a-sky-full-of-stars-and-I'm-taking-my-shirt-off levels of romantic."

We all laugh, and I half expect Jaz to start stripping down, but she just lies back down and lets out an exasperated sigh.

"I can't see the stars anymore." Aiden sounds a little sad, and I'm tempted to reach over Ellis and pretend he isn't there. "It's all muddy, like they're hiding behind a curtain. Or it's like I'm seeing stars on top of stars on top of stars." He sighs. "Too many stars."

"No such thing," Jaz mumbles.

"Sorry, bud." Ellis sounds almost as sad as Aiden. "Getting old is hard." Ellis laughs and throws his empty bottle behind him in the sand. A little spray of liquid showers over us.

"Shut up, you're nine days older than me," Aiden fires back.

"Yeah, but *you* see worse than Grandpa Tate, so . . ."

I tense up—I hate that Ellis is picking on Aiden right now, when he's sharing something that he obviously doesn't talk about much. Aiden laughs, and I relax a little. *Boys are so weird.*

Next to me, Jaz is shifting around. She jabs me with her elbow and when she sits up, she's in only her bra. She wiggles her shorts off and stands. "I'm going in," she says, already barreling toward the water. It's a still night, the kind where the water shimmers like a pane of black glass in the moonlight. Ellis is up next, stripping off his shirt and sandals and t-shirt until he's just a blur of underwear tripping toward the water.

Bathing suits and underwear are basically the same thing. Somewhere deep in my brain, I know this. They cover the same parts—hell, my underwear covers *more* than some of my bathing suits. So why does it feel like I'm about to get naked in front of Aiden? It's just the two of us left on the sand, but we have a gaping hole between us now, where Ellis's body used to be. Aiden turns his head to me and reaches for my hand. "You wanna swim?"

There's no pressure behind the words, no note of irritation at the idea that I may not want to. And I really wish we were alone, because lying this close to him in the sand, our fingers barely touching, I want to pull his shirt off myself. Feel the warm skin underneath, touch mine to his. But not with an audience. So instead I sit up and I pull my shirt over my head. My bra isn't the prettiest one I own, but it's black and covers everything important. Aiden pulls his shirt off while I stand and push my shorts down to my ankles, kicking them off along with my flip-flops.

I sprint for the water as soon as my foot is free of my sandal and don't slow down until the water is to my knees. I'm up to my waist, my blue underwear just under the water's dark surface, when I look back to Aiden. He tosses his phone on top of the pile of his clothes, and strides toward the water in nothing but his underwear. My eyes need a distraction, because I can't stand here and watch Aiden's slow strut out into the water like this. I look back out toward deeper water, where

Ellis and Jaz have found the sand bar, and are once again in knee-deep waters. I'm thinking about how good the cool water feels against my sticky, overheated skin when I feel arms wrap around me from behind.

It's the first time we've been skin-to-skin like this—his chest to my back, his arms pressed against mine—and I wish we didn't have an audience. Ellis glances at us, then plunges back into the water, and part of me wishes he would swim all the way back to shore, and just disappear, like some sort of freshwater merman. I feel tense under Aiden's touch, not because I don't want it, but because I feel like we're in an endlessly awkward situation as the only couple. We don't even have Beth and Troy here to paw all over each other as a diversion. Aiden's breath is hot against my ear when he whispers, "Turn around."

I do what he says, and then we're chest to chest. Just for a second, before he turns and the water rushes around me as he plunges underwater. His arms rise up out of the water and grab at me, so I take them, realizing he wants me up on his shoulders. *Oh god.* I take hold of his hands and pick my feet up, letting him back into me until my legs are over him. His hands move from my hands to my legs as he rises up out of the water. I sway a little, and then steady myself when his hands come back up to meet mine.

"You good?" he asks, letting go of my hands as I rise up into the night air.

"Yeah, it's—" But before I can get the words out, Aiden is sinking under me and I'm falling back into the water. I come up with a gasp. "Aiden Emerson!" I push the wet hair out of my face and look around for Aiden but he's nowhere. I think about the dark water and the beers he drank, and something inside of me sinks. "Aiden?" I'm trying to keep the panic out of my voice, but Ellis must hear it, because he's swimming toward me. We know better than to swim in the dark, especially out here, where we're away from everything, totally at the mercy of the darkness. Ellis has closed the gap by half when I feel a flutter against my legs, and then Aiden rises out of the water behind me, wrapping his arms around my waist and pulling me toward him. I give him a little jab with my elbow. "You scared me."

"Sorry," he says, just as his lips fall on the bare skin of my neck. "You looked hot, like you needed to cool off."

Ellis mutters something and swims back toward Jaz and the sand bar.

I laugh and turn back toward Aiden. I loop my arms around his neck and he picks me up by my hips until I wrap my legs around his waist. Everyone else is still in the water, but in the dark, with Aiden's arms around me and the water covering us, I can't make myself care anymore. The strawberry wine is still warming my stomach, but being this close to Aiden is its own kind of intoxication. When I press my lips to his, I'm not thinking about anything but the way it feels to be wrapped around him like this.

⁊

Hours later, when our skin is wrinkled and the drinks have worn off, Aiden's face is against mine on the soft blanket. The vinyl tent is sticky and noisy, and we only brought one blanket, so we're lying on it. It's July, and hot even at night, but I feel strange and exposed, curled up with nothing on top of me. I still have my damp bra and underwear on, because it's too awkward figuring out how to take it off. "It's really hot in here," I huff.

Aiden makes a little snorting sound. "No comment."

"You don't think it's a million degrees in here?"

"I think I'm not commenting, because the only suggestions to *fix* that problem will make me sound like a creeper."

Oh. "Right."

In the corner of the tent, where my clothes lay in a crumpled pile, my phone buzzes. *What time is it?* It has to be one, maybe two in the morning. Aiden reaches over and passes it to me. It buzzes twice more, as I slide the screen open. Three new texts.

From Zander.

I roll onto my back, so Aiden isn't looking over my shoulder, and I open the box.

Zander:

Are you drunk?

Where are you?

Drunk? I look at the text I sent him a few hours ago. *Oh god.* It's missing two words, and three more are misspelled. *I drunk-texted Zander.* I reply, because I can't have him blowing up my phone all night.

Olivia:

I'm camping. And no.

Zander:

Bullshit. You don't camp.

Olivia:

No, WE don't camp

I don't know what has come over me, but I feel the uncontrollable urge to show Zander how little he knows about me. How everything he *thinks* he knows is wrong. I open my notes, and copy and paste all the little rants I've been saving. All of the snarky little jabs I convinced myself not to send.

The words form a giant bubble that snakes down page after page along my screen. Aiden clears his throat, and I shake off the urge to read through the message one more time before sending. My finger hovers and I do it. I hit send. There's a sort of exhilaration that sweeps over me as my finger makes contact with that little blue button. And it's immediately followed by an all-consuming wave of panic and regret. *Oh my god. What did I do?*

"Everything good?" Aiden asks.

My first thought is that he knows what I've done. That he read every word as I scrolled through. But he's still lying on his back. No, it's just what a nice guy says when you get an unexpected text at 2 a.m. Because this is when bad things happen. *You lose fifty IQ points when the sun goes down; that's when bad decisions happen.* That's what my mom said to me on my sixteenth birthday, when she was giving me an uncharacteristically motherly pep talk about keeping my pants on. She was barely older than that when she got pregnant, so the sentiment wasn't lost on me. But I'm not her. She *is* right though—bad decisions happen when the sun goes down. Like that text.

"Yeah, everything's fine."

I stare at the screen a few minutes longer, but it's just my message staring back at me. There's no reply. And finally, it feels over.

Chapter
Sixteen

Aiden still owes me night three of our epic art adventure, and no matter how much I beg, he won't tell me what it is. Even though I take every opportunity to harass him about it.

"Just tell me what it is," I whisper, as I wrap my arms around his chest. *Click. Click.* "Fasten all three of the buckles," I say to the group of boaters in front of us. Aiden and I never could decide who would do the live demonstrations, so we entertain ourselves by doing them together. Aiden stands straight faced in front of me, doing his best mannequin impression. "I know it's more comfortable but don't skip the bottom buckle," I say, fastening the last buckle of Aiden's life vest. We rotate who has to be the dummy. I circle around Aiden and face him. "Then tighten all of the

straps," I say, pulling on the first of three. "Not too tight," I tell the boaters.

I pull the last two straps of Aiden's vest a little too tightly and whisper, *"I'll get it out of you eventually. I have ways."* I pick up the paddle—the next part of the demonstration—and smack it into my palm. Finally Aiden cracks a smile, and I win. I almost always win. Except for the time Aiden covertly tickled me while putting on my life jacket. *That* was cheating.

Aiden

It's one of the few days Olivia and I don't work together. Ellis almost always schedules us together, but today it's just Beth and me working the dock, and a crapload of boaters. Olivia stopped by for lunch at The Grill, and after work I'm headed to her house to do some prep work for my next project. The final hour of my shift goes by as slowly as the river.

"Hey, Emerson!"

I'm just leaving River Depot, walking from the gift shop entrance to my bike, when I hear him. His voice takes me back to every baseball field I've stood on since I was ten. He's wearing a baseball t-shirt and hat. I'm half surprised he didn't show up in his cleats and pads, just to rub it in a little more. I slow down as I cross onto the grass, and he steps out of the parking lot. *Is Zander here to see me, or Olivia? Has word finally gotten around about us?* Obviously it was going to happen, I just hoped we'd have a few more weeks before we had to worry about going back to school and dealing with everyone. Maybe I secretly hoped Zander would just stay up north indefinitely.

"Hey, man." I'm hoping if I pretend he doesn't hate my guts, that maybe he won't. "If you're looking for Liv, she's not working today."

He comes to a full stop in front of me and his brows quirk up. *"Liv?"*

I can tell by the surprise in his voice that this isn't why he came. But now I've opened the door, and it feels like I might as well just swing it wide open and pray that the hurricane doesn't take the whole house with it.

"Listen, we've never been friends, but I don't want it to turn into a thing, so . . ." I'm not sure why I feel like I'm doing something wrong. She's his *ex*-girlfriend. And in a small town, if no one dated anyone's ex, everyone would be single after fifth grade. ". . . We're together. Just so you know."

"Together?" He shakes his head at me as if I've said something ridiculous.

"You know what the word means, Zander." I'm not sticking around to hash out the details of our relationship, so I turn back toward the little picnic area where my bike is still waiting for me. I let out a deep breath and a certain lightness comes over me. It feels good to say it out loud. *Together.* I pull out my phone so I can give Liv a heads up before I get to her house, just in case Zander is planning to turn this into some sort of drama.

Behind me, Zander's voice cuts through the parking lot, low and biting. "You think a summer hookup is going to last long distance?"

He lets out an indignant huff. "We were together for two years and I wasn't sure it would work."

Long distance. The words rub around in my brain and make everything hurt.

"Don't you have enough to worry about, Emerson?" Zander's face twists with pity, like I've lost a limb and it's lying right next to me on the gravel, and I'm bleeding out as I watch. Like my life is such a mess. "Let me worry about Olivia."

"Your *ex*-girlfriend?" I want to tell him Olivia can worry about herself. That she doesn't need a babysitter, or a dad, or a shitty boyfriend. But I'm not going to get into it with Zander; not here. Not when Olivia is waiting for me, and we—apparently—have things to talk about. "Whatever."

"There's no way she picks you," he says as I walk away.

In my head, I just keep going. Or maybe I calmly tell him that it isn't a competition, because he's out of the picture. He and Olivia are old news. But in real life, I mutter *fuck you,* and throw my middle finger up over my head as I walk away. By the time I reach my bike my face is hot and my chest is tight. It's a twenty-minute ride to Olivia's house, and I'm torn between pedaling faster than I ever have and just cruising along. Because I don't think good things are happening when I get there.

Long distance.

The two words are on an endless loop in my head, and there's nothing to distract me. There's also no way to put those two words into any sort of scenario that sounds good. By the time I get to her house, they barely sound like words anymore, they're just a buzz in my brain like the whir of my gears. Olivia is sitting on the cement step of her porch in her paint-streaked yoga pants, and her hair is up in a messy ponytail. Sometimes it's hard to remember she's even the same girl I saw around school with Zander. My car is parked on the street, left from yesterday.

She's looking down at her phone and when she sees me a smile spreads across her face. She bounces upright, and then two steps forward, until I come to a stop in front of her. I stand, but don't get off of my bike.

I don't know how to make small talk right now, so I just spit it out. "You're leaving?"

She looks down at her feet and chews on her lip. "Not until the end of August."

"That's in a few weeks, Olivia."

"The summer's gone by really fast." Her voice is soft and sad but I'm too mad to let it slow me down.

"Were you going to *tell* me? Or were you just going to disappear into the night?" I think about what she told me about Zander, about their sudden breakup and his escape up north for the summer. *Has this whole thing with us just been some sort of weird revenge? She can't do it to Zander, so I'm a good enough substitute? Any guy's broken heart will do?*

"I was, I just didn't know when. Or how." She touches my handlebars and leaves her hand there.

"But you told Zander."

"*Zander* told you I was leaving?" I don't love how she seems to be thinking about this fact, like she wants to ask me something but can't find the words.

"I just saw him at River Depot," I offer up, before she asks.

"What was he doing at River Depot?"

"I don't know, Olivia, that isn't the point. The point is that he knew you were leaving and I didn't."

She shakes her head. "I told him right after it happened. When we were still together. That's the *only* reason he knows." She's looking at me like that's a good excuse. Like it's obvious, and how could I have missed it. I hate that the word that made me feel so hopeful—*together*—now feels weaponized.

"So why didn't you tell me, now that *we're* together?" Even as I say it, it's dawning on me that maybe we're not actually together. Maybe that's the whole problem here. And the look of surprise on her face tells me that I'm probably right. *How did I get this all so wrong?*

"I was going to tell you. Time sort of got away from me, I guess, and then I was trying to figure out how to fix it."

"You didn't think I'd want to help with that?"

Her face is blank, like it wasn't a thought she ever entertained. And even though I feel like everything I thought about this relationship is now wrong, I still can't help but try to fix this. "What about Emma?"

"Her parents don't want another teenager in the house."

"Do you have any other friends who would let you stay?"

"I tried," she says.

"Maybe we could change their minds?"

"I don't think you actually want that." She raises her eyebrows and twists her mouth up, like I should know why. And then I remember who her other friend is.

"Zander?"

"We never actually asked his parents . . . that's when we broke up," she says. "Of course, I don't think that option is on the table now, anyway."

Hell, no. "Could you stay with your mom?"

She shakes her head. "She's just helping Aunt Sarah out for the summer, she doesn't live here."

"But maybe she could stay—you said she's pretty flighty anyway . . ."

"Yes, but . . ."

"You'll at least try?"

She doesn't say anything, just looks to the side, to the row of bushes that run between her garage and the next, and sighs.

OLIVIA

I'll talk to her. Maybe I should have just said it. But I'm *not* going to stay with my mom. I get that Aiden wants to fix this, but I've exhausted all of my options. My stuff is already half-packed—my books line a wall, stacked in boxes and wrapped in old clothes I should have thrown out but used as packing peanuts instead. There's a note lying on my dresser about my scheduled orientation at my new high school, three weeks from today. Two days before my senior year starts. But Aiden looked so sad, and if I had just said it, maybe he would have stayed. Maybe he wouldn't have stormed off and left.

Or maybe he would have; maybe he was always going to. I try to shake away the thought, but it won't leave. It pokes at me all afternoon and into the evening. And at nine o'clock when I get the text from Zander asking if he can see me tomorrow, I can't think of a reason to say no.

⁓

I have weeks before I leave, but everything in my room is already sectioned off into areas. Under my window, clothes are in stacks, and in a box next to my bathroom door my lotions and flat-iron and every bottle of hotel shampoo I've ever taken greet me each morning. It's not that I want to leave now—I'm not in any kind of rush—I just don't want to be packing this stuff last minute. I don't want to forget anything either. And it gives me something to do when I'm at home, other than just sitting here, thinking about what I can't change. Because leaving is inevitable.

When Emma plops down onto the old beanbag in the corner of my room after her shift, she isn't amused by the prospect of my seeing Zander. "It's a horrible idea, Liv."

She's right, that's what I've been thinking ever since he texted me. What a dumb idea it is to meet Zander. But at the same time, it seems ridiculous not to see him before I leave. We've been friends since we were kids, and I'm just going to move cross-country without giving us a chance to talk? So I decided it's only fair that I treat this decision like I have the rest of the summer.

"I'm going to decide the same way I decide everything," I say.

"With logic and reason?" Emma is curled up on the beanbag in her Cherry Pit dress, and she looks like she might just take a nap.

I pull the coin out of my pocket. Coin flips have started to feel like my thing with Aiden, and it feels weird to use one for *this*.

"Sorry, I was thinking of someone else." Emma shakes her head and rolls her eyes. "With a coin flip. Obviously."

"Heads, I meet him tomorrow," I say.

"And tails, you find Aiden and you fix this."

"He left." I flip the coin on my thumb and catch it in my hand. "I'm not chasing after him." The words send a little ache through me. *Another boy to chase; another person walking away.*

"I mean," Emma shoves a hand into the beanbag, pushing it under her butt, "you sort of gave him a reason."

"*You* were the one who pitched the summer fling idea!" I launch a bed pillow at her. "No strings! Nothing but fun!" I throw her words back at her. "Now *I'm* the bad guy?"

"That's when I didn't know Aiden Emerson was *totally* into you. Like *in it to win it* into you."

I smash my face into the bed and pretend to scream. It doesn't matter if I want Aiden, because I can't have him now. I never could. This is pointless to debate because it's already over, anyway. He's gone, I'm leaving, and according to the shiny president in my palm, tomorrow I'll talk to Zander.

Chapter

Seventeen

I regret the results of the coin flip almost immediately, but now I'm here, and Zander is walking toward me, almost jogging across the dirt parking lot. He's tan. Maybe more tan than I've ever seen him, his skin a deep brown thanks to the last six weeks on the lake. His hair is a little fluffy, the way he lets it get in the summer, when it's growing out from the late winter buzzcut he kicks off every baseball season with. I hate his hair buzzed, but he hates the way long hair feels under his helmet. I don't feel the anger I thought I would. The hurt is back. The little jab of pain under my ribs that reminds me that one of my best friends is gone.

Zander nods behind me and squints, as if something's hurting his eyes. "Is that Emerson's?"

"Hi to you too." Until this morning, I'd completely forgotten that my only option to get here on time was driving Aiden's car. I'll take it back tonight, after his shift at River Depot; it seems sort of questionable to have it when I'm pretty sure he's done with me.

Zander raises his brows at me, like he's waiting.

"Yeah. I'm borrowing it."

"It's that serious? That you're driving his car around?"

I don't answer. I don't even know the answer. I told myself it wasn't serious, that I wouldn't let it be, because I was leaving, but it felt serious when he left yesterday. It felt like I hurt him—badly. But then he left, and he hurt me, too.

"To get back at me?" Zander asks.

I laugh. This isn't how I thought our first meeting was going to go. I should be the one grilling *him*. "I didn't even tell you about it, so how would it be getting back at you?"

He rolls his eyes and shakes his head. "I need to talk to you. Leave your bag in the car?"

"Why?"

"Because I'm taking you fishing," he says.

For the first time, I notice that Zander has his dad's truck. The little metal fishing boat they haven't used in a million years is on the trailer behind it.

"Zander, if this is about that stupid text I sent you—"

"Just come, Liv. I want to talk to you. The worms and fish and shit will just make it less awful. For both of us."

⌒

Zander dumps the little boat into the water, and while he parks the truck I hold onto the shiny yellow rope and make sure it doesn't float off. I tie the rope to the dock and get into the boat so that I'm ready to go when Zander returns. When he steps down into the boat he's smiling, but we don't talk. He pushes us off from the dock and starts up the little black motor, kicking up a dark cloud of dirt that plumes out around the boat, like we're floating on a billowy brown cloud. Soon, we're at the center of the little lake, the only spot deep enough that you can't see clear to the bottom. My seat is so close to the front that I have no choice but to sit facing Zander. He's looping a wriggling brown worm around a hook, and we still aren't talking. I used to think that meant something about us; that being able to sit in silence was somehow evidence of our close relationship, but now it feels awkward. When he has the worm twisted and knotted around the sharp metal, he holds the handle out to me.

I shake my head. "You can do it."

"I can show you how."

Realization smacks me in the head, the way I wish I could smack Zander with the pole he's holding out to me. "Zander, I don't *actually* want to fish."

"But you said—"

"It was just an example. A dumb example," I say.

"It made me feel like shit."

That was sort of the point. "Breaking up isn't supposed to be fun. Losing your best friend doesn't feel great either."

"I didn't think you hating me would hurt this bad," he says, his eyes dropping from me to the bottom of the boat.

"Did you think it would be a good time? Were you looking forward to it?"

"I thought you were leaving, Olivia. We're seventeen, you think a cross-country long-distance relationship in our senior year was going to work?"

I don't say anything, because it's clear that he didn't, and I did. If he had asked me two months ago, I would have said absolutely. Absolutely, Zander and I could survive a long-distance relationship for *one* year. That's all it would have been, one year until college. One year until all of our plans would kick into gear. How could two people who'd known each other as long as we had not make it work? And if we couldn't, then how could anyone?

"I didn't tell my parents right away," he says.

What? "Why not?"

"At first I just couldn't figure out a way to do it. They would have had a million questions, you know?"

"You didn't want to tell your mom what an ass you were?"

"I mean . . . yeah. I felt really guilty at first. Because I wanted to have a good senior year, I didn't want to be missing my girlfriend who was a thousand miles away."

I want to be mad, but I get this. I get not wanting to be attached to someone who is clear across the country. Except unlike Aiden and I, Zander and I were already attached.

"But then once I was up north, it felt like a normal summer. You're not usually up there, you know?" He shrugs. "And every time someone would ask me about senior year, I'd imagine you there. I couldn't think of senior year without you, Liv."

"But I'm *not* going to be there, Zander. I'm going to be in Arizona, across the country, just like you didn't want."

"What if you *weren't* moving to Arizona?" he asks.

"Then none of this would have happened?" I say, exasperated.

"I love you, and—"

I shake my head. "No."

"No?"

"No, you don't love me." My skin is hot, and I swear to god, I'm about to dive out of this boat and swim back to shore. If I thought I had any chance of making it, I would.

"I talked to my parents," he says.

"Good." I was starting to worry I would have to march over to the Belles and tell them myself. Did Zander think they wouldn't notice when I went MIA for the entire summer?

"You can stay with us."

Wait, what? "Your parents are going to let your ex-girlfriend live at your house senior year?"

He doesn't say anything, but his eyes drift out to the water.

Oh my god. "They *still* don't know?" I drop my chin to my chest and roll my head around, like maybe if I work the stress out of my neck, I can work out this mess he's made too. "Zander—"

"If you stay, it doesn't matter. We'll finish senior year together, and we'll go to college, and it will be just like we planned. I didn't tell them because it doesn't matter. We can just pretend like it didn't happen. It shouldn't have happened."

I don't say anything, because none of it sounds real.

Zander's voice is soft when it cuts through the silence. "Couples break up and get back together all the time, Liv."

I could stay in Riverton. I could have the life I always wanted—
Zander, our perfect life, his perfect family. But this summer isn't that
easy to forget. And I don't know if Zander is perfect for me anymore.
Or maybe it's just that I'm not the same person I was two months
ago. Because I can't see myself in those dreams anymore.

❧

I've come to this park at least once a week since I met Aiden, but
I've never sat out on the lake. The water isn't as blue as the big lake;
it's more of a greenish brown—but not in a gross way—and it ripples
toward the shore, like someone just skipped a giant pebble across it.
The lily pads are in full bloom, little spots of pink dotting the shoreline. If it weren't for my ex-boyfriend sitting across from me, this
would be an idyllic setting.

Zander doesn't say anything as he sets a pole in front of me, laying
it across the boat. Or as he casts his line out, slow and exaggerated
in his movements, like a video tutorial with no words. He's facing
the water, and I pick up the other pole and do the same. Pressing in
the lever, placing my thumb over the thin plastic line, letting it go
when the pole crosses in front of my head. My line flings out over
the water—not nearly as far as his—and lands with a tiny splash.
I keep my eyes on the little white and red circle bobbing in the
water where my line disappeared. If I have to be out here, at least
I don't have to look at Zander.

We sit in the boat for hours—until my stomach grumbles in anger and the water flattens like glass. It's not until Zander opens the
little white Styrofoam dish he's been using to replenish our hooks

with—the two of us engaging in a completely silent performance of poles and worms and lines flying out into the water—that we both realize we'll have to go back at some point.

"I get that maybe I wasn't the best boyfriend." He reels in the last of his line and tucks the rod into the boat. "But I do love you. Just think about it, okay?" He chews on his lip, and I smack his knee.

"Stop that." I hate when he chews on his lip. It makes them rough and horrible. *But you're not kissing him anymore.* He would though. If I wanted him to, he'd kiss me. He's begging me to take him back, telling me how much he wants me. He wants me to live with him this year. And I love the way this feels, him finally wanting me so much more than I want him. I wish I could care more.

"It's your best option, right? Your only option?"

"Maybe not." Zander has made a good point. It's only a year. And I can't spend a whole year at his house pretending to be his girlfriend, but maybe I can survive a year with someone else. "My mom is in town. It's a long story—"

"And you'd actually live with her?"

"I am, right now. It's not horrible." It's weird, trying to convince Zander that living with my mother wouldn't be so bad. But really, this summer has been tolerable. She's stayed out of my way, mostly. But she's not staying, so I don't know why I'm trying to convince anyone it's an option.

"Why the change of heart? Is it Emerson? You'd stay with her for him?"

"I was going to stay for you."

"That's different," he says.

"You do know I have friends, right? Emma isn't exactly thrilled about senior year without *her* best friend. She wasn't quite as quick to abandon me, you know? And yes, there's Aiden." *Maybe.*

Zander doesn't say anything, he's just looking out at the water, resigned. Maybe, like me, he's thinking about all of the things I have in my life now that aren't him.

"Are you going to tell your parents?" I ask.

His face looks pained. "Do I have to?"

"Yes. You do."

There's a long stretch of silence. Zander pulls up the anchor and starts the engine. The smell of gasoline fills the air as it rumbles to life and bubbles kick up around it. We're slowing down, drifting toward the shore, when he speaks again. "You're really dating him?"

I don't really have it in me to admit to my ex-boyfriend that I may have been dumped (again) just yesterday. "I really am."

"He's off the rails, Liv. You want to be part of his meltdown?"

"You're seriously going to give me dating advice? That was all start-of-summer rumors, anyway. He's just going through some stuff. Cut him some slack."

Zander grunts. "For torching my senior season before it even starts? Not likely."

"He can't help it. He'd play if he could."

"So why doesn't he?"

I shake my head. "He just can't, okay? Give him a break." If I'm not going to be here senior year, maybe I can at least make Aiden's a little easier.

"Tell me, and I will."

AIDEN

I hate waiting rooms. Especially Dr. Shah's, because it's basically a giant rectangular senior center. Except there's no bingo or crafts. There *are* sugar-free cookies. The three women sitting across from me all have matching gray hair with tight curls and those solid-colored pants that people over seventy are required to wear. They must be in their eighties—I'm bringing down the median age big-time. And they all give me these judgy old-people glances, staring at my shaking foot like "Just wait, kid, someday *you'll* be old. Then you'll have a *reason* to be so fidgety." And I get it, things suck when you get old. But also, my vision has been fucking horrible.

Not that I want to get into a "whose vision is worse" showdown with a geriatric, but seriously. I'm just glad I can see the judgy old man across from me giving me his smug look. It's not that I want to fit in somewhere as unimpressive as this, but come on. Doesn't he know I'm his people? My mom pats my knee, like the bouncing is bothering her too.

"Mr. Emerson?" A woman in Pepto-pink scrubs is looking expectantly into the sea of old people, her gaze scanning from one side of the room to the other. I don't react right away, because no one ever calls me mister. I'm guessing she didn't notice my age, because she looks surprised when I pop up. And a little sad. "This way," she says. Her nametag says Angela, and she leads me and Mom past the half-circle reception desk and down a long hallway. She's walking so slow I have to force myself not to run her over. A side-effect of being a herder of old people, I suppose. "Have a seat." Angela nods to the big black leather chair.

I was never nervous at the eye doctor before, but now the place basically gives me sweaty palms upon arrival. Mom takes a seat in a chair across from me, under the white rectangle that will display my eye test. Angela sets my folder on the desk.

"I'll be right back," she says.

Mom sets her purse on the chair next to her, and rubs her hands together, which she does when she's nervous. Even though they keep it about ninety degrees in here. She lets out a long stream of air that's almost a whistle. "You feel good?"

I laugh, because she's making it sound like I've been training for this. Like it's a big game I've been putting in extra hours for. "I feel nauseous."

She purses her lips like that's not what she wanted to hear. "Is Olivia coming to dinner?'

The question catches me off guard. Yesterday wasn't great, and I don't even know where Olivia and I stand at the moment. But we should probably figure it out before I subject her to a family dinner. She didn't seem thrilled about it to start with, so I doubt she's going to be interested in coming now. "She can't make it this week, but maybe next week?" I can work with a week.

Mom looks disappointed but smiles anyway. "Sounds good, hon."

Angela returns in all of her Pepto glory, and sits on the little spinning stool next to me.

I feel like I'm about to take a test I didn't study for. One based entirely on luck. I should have told Olivia about my appointment; maybe she'd be here and we'd be talking through what happened. *People do that in waiting rooms and exam rooms, right?*

"Let's see how things are doing." Angela hands me the black plastic spoon and I put it in front of my eye. The lights flick off, and a giant black E is illuminated in front of me.

Yes. I can do this. But the letter doesn't stay, it scrolls down, further and further, until it looks as if a newspaper is being held against the wall. I can tell there are letters there . . . I can see the white spaces, the blur of dark ink. I blink a few times and fidget in my chair, like shifting two centimeters to the right or left might make a difference. I open my eye as wide as I can, and then squint. My eyes probably just need a minute to adjust to the dark.

"Let's try the next one." The blurry black cluster disappears and is replaced by a slightly larger cloud of black. A tiny surge of hope starts to rise up in me. I can make out some peaks on this line.

"M . . . wait, no, N." I shift again. "P. Or R . . ."

"Let's see if the next one is better," Angela says.

Shit. What am I at now? 20/30? 20/40? I squint at the bright white square on the wall and wet my lips. It's suffocating in this room.

I try to focus. "Five—"

"It's just letters, Aiden."

Fuck.

"S. P. Or . . . R, maybe. Yeah, R. S, P, R . . ." The letters are right there. I can see them, make out the gaps, but I can't focus on any of them. I dart my eye around to see if it helps. I read online that sometimes with retinal damage, focusing on something off to the side can help. I look toward the last letter, hoping it brings the first into focus, but it's like trying to make out someone's face in your peripheral vision. I can see that it's there, I just can't identify it.

"Let's bump it up a little." The screen scrolls again, and it might as well be my car up there, rolling away from me. Out of sight. "Can you read anything on this line?"

The letters are bigger now, more distinct. They're not crisp, but I can definitely read them. I take a deep breath and start listing them off. "M. R. S." *Only three letters?*

"Great job, Aiden. How about this line." She clicks the button and the screen changes. And my stomach drops. It's all blurry again. I stare at the screen, blinking and swallowing and shifting in my chair, until Angela finally turns the screen off.

Fuck. I mutter it under my breath, but she must hear me, because she's looking at me like I'm a five-year-old who just found out his puppy died or something. She rolls her stool closer to me. "You actually did a lot better than last time, Aiden. You're up to 20/70 in your right eye."

I hate that she's smiling at me like there's something to celebrate here. She's right, it's a huge improvement over 20/200. *Congratulations, Aiden, you're not legally blind at seventeen anymore!* I bet they make banners for that; I'll have to remember to swing by the giant party store on the way home. Oh, except I still *can't drive.*

Just to add insult to injury, she puts drops in both eyes and then ushers me back into another waiting room. I pull out my phone, even though I know in five minutes I won't be able to read it, and I send Olivia a text. I hate how yesterday went down.

Aiden:

I'm sorry

My vision blurs out before I get a response. Thirty minutes later, when I've been moved into another exam room, my screen is still sporting a single bubble. *Come on, Olivia.* I fire off one more text, unable to even read it on my own screen.

Aiden:
Having a shitty day. How are you?

But even when I leave in my green Ray Bans an hour later with a new prescription in hand, there's no reply.
This day fucking sucks.

Chapter
Eighteen

OLIVIA

My ninth-grade English teacher, Mrs. Tedrowe, always said the tricky thing about personal essays is making them personal, but also universal. In theory, when teens—and especially the judges—are reading my essay, they should be nodding along. My favorite essays are usually ones that make me feel validated in some way. When Zander and I broke up, it made me think about this piece I had read at least a year before about a girl who married her high school sweetheart. Their story reminded me of Zander and me—childhood friends, entwined in each other's families—but at the time, the rest didn't ring true. Five years after getting married they were divorced. Because they weren't the same people anymore. I didn't get it then, but I get it now. I've changed so much this summer already. And I didn't realize until it was over that even when we were together, we didn't fit. But middle-school Olivia couldn't let go of the idea of Zander.

So I hope that my story of living my summer by chance will ring true to people, even if it isn't something they'd ever consider doing. Because the more I think about it all, the more I realize it wasn't just the coin flips that pushed me out of my comfort zone; it was Aiden. Making me want to do new things, showing me that I could.

He's coming over after work, and I'm excited to tell him about the idea I have. I've printed off an ArtPrize application for him. I even emailed a few venues, to see if I could find him a spot this early for next year. Something to look forward to all year seems needed right now.

It's an "I'm sorry" for—everything. A white flag that I hope will at least mean he won't hate me when I leave.

AIDEN

Zander texting me isn't the weirdest thing to ever happen. We practiced together for an hour before school every Monday and Wednesday for most of the last three years. He obviously has my number. But when his name pops up on my screen, just a few days after he tells me to back off of his ex-girlfriend, I know it's not because I'm a few minutes late to the gym.

Zander:

Can we talk? Field at 4:30?

I stare at the message, wondering why he needs to meet me at the baseball field to beat his chest about Olivia again. Obviously he can do that anywhere. And she and I haven't actually smoothed things over, so maybe there's nothing to even get into it over. Except that she's meeting me tonight, after work, so I can show her the plans for my newest project. *And* apologize for walking off the other day, but I'm luring her with the project. Maybe she's rethought living with her mom, or doing the long-distance thing, or maybe somehow, miraculously, she's not leaving at all. I don't know what I expect to be different, I'm just hoping something is. So I text Zander back, because if she does stay by some strange act of fate, then I'm hoping he won't make my life miserable.

Aiden:

Out of work at 5:00

Zander:

See you then

The afternoon is chaotic, filled with screaming toddlers that refuse to climb into inner-tubes and a disgruntled canoer who cut his foot in the river. I'm not sure how it's our fault he got out of the canoe, or that he didn't wear the suggested water shoes, but the way he told it, we're all lucky he didn't bleed out in his canoe. Ellis told him we'd consider his suggestion of adding first aid kits to the canoes next season. Then he mouthed "bite me" as he walked away. But the last thing he saw as he climbed the stairs was Ellis's smiling face.

And it was the last thing I saw too, before I made my way toward my bike and rode to the high school, still in my red River Depot t-shirt. It's a solid twenty-minute ride, so I'm going to be late, and halfway there my phone starts exploding with notifications; probably Zander thinking I'm not coming.

When I pull into the parking lot behind the high school, where the baseball fields are, the first thing I notice is how many cars are there. It's not enough for a big event, but there are at least eight cars, which is more than you see at the high school in the middle of the summer unless there's an event. As I cut through the parking lot and onto the grass leading up to the baseball field, I realize there *is* an event taking place, because I recognize some of these cars. I've hit them with foul balls, and piled into them for tournaments. And when I'm close enough to see into the dugout, I know I'm right. Because at least half of the baseball team is here.

My first thought is that Zander brought everyone to beat me up, like some retro movie set in a town that isn't Riverton. That shit doesn't happen in a town where you've gone to school with everyone since basically kindergarten. It's like six degrees of Kevin Bacon around here; even if you don't know someone, you know their cousin, or their boyfriend, or your dad went to school with theirs. *Six degrees of Riverton.*

So I know I'm not actually getting jumped on the baseball field, I just don't know what *is* happening. Quitting right before summer break, it's been easy to dodge these guys, but now they're all in front of me. Zander is leaning against the fence outside the dugout, and when I push the little gate open on the visitors' side and step out onto the field, he doesn't move right away. I'm halfway to home base before he pushes himself away from the fence. A few other guys are out on the field, messing around, throwing grounders; Mani is kicking third base like he's making sure it didn't get soft over the summer.

"Man," I say, trying to sound like I'm not nervous as I approach the dugout. "The whole team is concerned about Olivia and me." I shove my hands down into my pockets.

Mani's head pops up from where he's standing by third. "No way," he mutters.

Zander looks annoyed that I said her name, but quickly softens his face. "Not about her." He tosses me the ball he's holding. "We're here to help."

I clench the ball in my fist, and instinctually, I start rolling it around, feeling the laces under my fingertips. "With what?"

Zander throws a hand behind him and clangs the dugout fence. "Throw it out here," he says. A helmet hurdles over the fence, and I realize for the first time that Zander's wearing his shin guards. It's what I expect to see him in on the baseball field, but this isn't a game, or a practice. He picks up the helmet and thrusts it in my direction. It's not actually a helmet though, it's a face mask. I've seen them online before but never in person. It's like a wire cage that goes over your face, with straps that wrap behind your head. It looks a little like something a killer would be wearing in a horror movie, and they're mostly used for players recovering from some sort of facial injury.

I shake my head as Zander thrusts it at me again. "I don't need this," I say, irritated. "Give it to your pitcher." I look at the bench where Callahan, my backup, must be feeling like total crap right about now.

"You don't have to let one hit ruin everything," Zander says, the mask still in his hand. "Get up there." He nods to the mound behind me. "And let us help."

"You can't help me with this."

"We can, just let us practice with you, help you shake it off. We'll have you back in no—"

"I don't *want* you to help with this," I say, leveling him with a stare I hope will shut him up.

He looks confused. "But Olivia made it sound like—"

"Like what?" I spit at him. "When did you talk to Olivia?"

Zander rolls his eyes. "Relax. She turned down my offer to move in, so don't get your panties in a bunch."

I'm not sure when I tune Zander out, but before he decides to drag me back onto the mound, I practically run back to my bike. And as I leave, my friends are shouting my name like it's a curse word, and it feels like the last day of school all over. Like I'm back to square one.

O L I V I A

We don't usually spend time at my house, but when I see Aiden from my window I text him to just come in. He hasn't been to my house since that first time a few weeks ago, and he wasn't in my room then. But my mom's gone for the day and Aiden knows I'm leaving, so when I poke my head out of the door and wave him back, I'm not as nervous about it.

"Hey," I say, from my desk chair. Usually I'd sit on my bed, but the last talk I had with a guy while on a bed didn't turn out that well.

Aiden's eyes scan the room, stopping on my piles of boxes and little piles of clothes and picture frames that are in the process of being packed, and then they land on me. "Why were you talking to Zander about me?"

I'm caught off guard by the question. I didn't expect to talk about Zander. "I—I was just trying to help."

"By going out with your ex?"

"No, of course not. That's not what happened. We didn't *go out*." But even as I say it, I'm not entirely sure it's the truth. I was mad that Aiden left, and anyone who saw us definitely would have *assumed* it was a date. "I was just trying to help."

"By telling him my problems? Problems I would tell people *myself*, if I wanted to?"

It doesn't sound great when he says it like that, but it's also not how it actually went down. "That's not what happened, Aiden."

"I don't believe you, Olivia."

I want to tell him that he can, that he should, but I'm not sure that it's true. I'm not sure what is true anymore.

"You've kept me at arm's length from the start," he says, his voice tight. "I've never met Emma."

"You're in the same class; you've *met* Emma." I say it gently.

He shakes his head at me, his eyes squinted in disbelief. "I've never met Emma as your best friend. We've never hung out with her. You've never introduced me to your aunt, or anyone."

"You met my mom."

Aiden snorts. "Under duress. While I was helping you do housework."

I put my hands on my hips. "I never made you do that. I told you you didn't have to."

"But I *wanted* to, Olivia. That's the difference. I *wanted* to be with you."

"I haven't met your family either." But as soon as the excuse slips past my lips I wish I could yank it back.

"Not because you weren't invited."

I want an excuse but I don't have one. He's right, I was only half into this. He showed me every nook and cranny of himself.

"I get it; you went into this knowing it wasn't going to last. You were planning on quitting this before it even started."

I swallow back the guilt rising up in my throat.

He turns away from me and takes two steps toward the door. But instead of leaving, he turns back. "You're not the only one who lost something. You're not the only one who needed an escape this summer." He pushes a hand through his hair. "And you took one more thing from me." He shakes his head and his eyes squint at me like I'm too bright to look at. "It was so fucking selfish."

I look down at my hands, at the pile of papers they're sitting on. I didn't feel selfish this summer. Aiden felt like something I was owed, like my reward for all of the crap. And I never once considered that he wanted me this way. That he'd be this upset about my leaving.

"Did you ever think this could work?"

I can hear us ending. *This* is the explosion I always expected. "I don't know." He looks disgusted with me, but it's true. And when he walks out of my room, I know it's over.

Chapter
Nineteen

AIDEN

I wonder what it is about fire that's so cathartic. If it's the heat, or the color, or the little snaps as anything in its path is destroyed. I've been waiting all summer for this; to feel this way. As I strike the match, it feels like the last three months have been building up to this. The night I drove off the road. *Snap.* The diagnosis I initially ignored. *Snap.* The ball that smashed into my face. *Snap.* The look on Coach M's face when I walked out of his office. *Snap.* Letting go of all of the plans I had made. *Snap.* And now Olivia. Olivia treating me like a summer project, Olivia leaving, Olivia talking to Zander. *Snap. Snap. Snap.*

I put the match to the soft cloth and watch it sizzle and snap, just like my life. As the fire climbs up the makeshift fuse and reaches the vinyl-coated paper, the gunpowder pops and crackles as the orange glow consumes the thin trails of powder that make up the bird's tail, rising up to its breast and across its outstretched wings. The final flames consume the phoenix, and I feel a little better. Just a little. I still feel empty, but some of the anger is gone—captured on paper for the portfolio committee.

OLIVIA

Two weeks before we move, Aunt Sarah comes home for the weekend. There are still no offers on the house, and apparently Aunt Sarah thinks she can work some sort of real estate witchcraft that we cannot. *I hope she packed* all *of her best candles.* My mother and I are in the kitchen, drinking our tea, when she walks through the door in a hurried fluster, muttering something about goddamn toll roads as she rolls her tiny suitcase behind her.

When she sees us on either side of the little bistro table, the whirring wheels come to a stop. She lets out a sigh that sounds a lot like "Hello," but has the tone of "What the hell."

Aunt Sarah rolls through the kitchen and pulls out a chair, lowering herself into it as if she walked here from the airport.

"You look destroyed," I say, taking another sip of my tea. "What time was your flight?"

Aunt Sarah lets out a little huff. "Too early. We took off just before midnight. I slept through the flight but the ride from the airport was brutal."

Mom is stirring her coffee, watching us as if we're a new TV show she's heard a lot about but hasn't seen before.

I push myself away from the table. "You want tea?" I take a teacup out of the cupboard and set it on the counter.

Aunt Sarah eyes the piece of pink-and-gold china. "We have teacups?"

"We do now," Mom says, dipping her bag into her cup again. She looks nervous.

"We bought them at the weekend antique market downtown." I take the yellow teapot off of the burner and pour steaming water into the little cup. "We have Berry Blossom, black . . ." I rummage through the little tins. "And plain old herbal."

Aunt Sarah shakes her head. "Coffee. I need the hard stuff. Lots of it."

"The hazelnut stuff?" I pull the canister out of the cupboard and shake it.

"You know it." Aunt Sarah sets her head on the table, and then, as if she had forgotten she was there, her head pops up and turns toward my mother. Her voice is soft but I can still hear her. "How's it going?"

Mom looks down at her teacup and nods her head, almost imperceptibly. "It's good. We're doing good."

Aunt Sarah turns on me next. "And you? How is your summer going? I haven't heard much from you." She sounds disappointed and I make a mental note to text her more often with updates. I've just been so swept up this summer.

"It's been good."

"Your job is still going okay?"

I nod. "Yeah, I like it."

Mom takes a sip of her tea and grunts.

"What?" Aunt Sarah says. "Did something happen at work?"

"No," I say, at the same time that my mother mutters, "Ask her about her boyfriend."

"Something happened with Zander?"

My stomach sinks. *Oh my god, I completely forgot to tell her about Zander. This is awkward.*

"Well . . ." I'm having a hard time figuring out if I start with the new boy or the old boy. The good news, or the bad news. Is it even bad news, anymore, what happened with me and Zander? Are Aiden and I even worth mentioning, now that we broke up our non-relationship? *Is there anything in my life that isn't a question anymore?* It doesn't seem like it.

I set the cup of coffee down in front of Aunt Sarah, and lean against the butcher-block island. "Zander and I broke up."

Aunt Sarah lets out a little gasp. "Oh, Liv, I'm sorry." She sounds like she means it.

"It's okay. Honestly, I'm over it. It was . . . months ago."

Her face twists in confusion. "Months?"

I nod. "First day of summer, when I suggested I could stay at his house senior year."

Her face is soft and sympathetic. "I'm sorry, sweetie."

"It's fine." And I really mean it when I say it. Zander and I weren't right. We weren't wrong, but there was something missing there, something I didn't even realize until it was over. Until I could see it from the outside; all of the holes and gaps where we didn't quite fit together. "Honestly." I take a sip of my tea. "I'm sorry I didn't tell you. I didn't think it was going to stick at first. You know, it seemed like a fight. Then I got . . . distracted."

Aunt Sarah nods.

I focus on my socks—white with little purple unicorns on them—while I figure out how to share the rest. "Then I met someone at River Depot," I continue. "Aiden Emerson," I say, my eyes never raising to see her expression. But I can hear it in her voice.

"Aiden Emerson . . . that's . . . different." I can't tell what she means. There's a weird edge to her voice, like she wants to say something but doesn't.

My mom stands up from the table and walks to the sink, setting her cup inside. "Sar, he's adorable. He's John and Melinda's kid. You remember them?"

Aunt Sarah nods. "I know who he is, of course."

Of course.

I clear my throat. "We actually broke up, so . . ." *So none of this really matters.* The words hurt to say.

"What?" My mom sounds shocked. "When did that happen?"

I turn around, pressing my stomach against the edge of the island and propping up on my elbows. "A few days ago. But we weren't together. Not really." Even as I say it, I know it's not true. "I mean, we were just for the summer. That's why we broke up."

My mom looks disgusted and a pang of guilt rips through me at the thought that she blames Aiden for any of this.

"It was me. I was the one who decided it was just for the summer." I swallow down the lump in my throat. "He didn't know I was leaving. It was my fault."

The kitchen is quiet as my mother and Aunt Sarah process what I already know: that I haven't been that great of a person this summer. I can feel my chest getting tight and a single hot tear slip out of my eye. I don't wipe it away because I don't want to bring attention to it. Maybe no one will notice, and I can just stop talking about this. Is it possible that I could be that lucky?

"Sweetie . . ." Aunt Sarah's voice is soft and sympathetic. "I'm sorry."

I nod, looking down at my fingertips that are drumming on the striped wood under them.

Mom leans across the counter, mirroring me. "That boy adored you."

I'm not sure why she says it, why she has to cut me with the words when I'm already sliced through in a million spots. All I can do is nod and give a mumbled "I know."

"So do something about this," she says in a firm voice. "If you don't want it to be over, don't let it be."

I look up at a face that looks a lot like mine, her eyes burning with excitement. "He broke it off. He's done." I hate hearing the words come out of my mouth.

"And that's okay with you?" she asks.

Okay with me? It sucks. "It doesn't really matter. I'm leaving."

"For a year. A year isn't that long, Olivia." She's looking at me like I'm missing something so obvious. "If you don't want to, if you're over it anyway, that's fine. But if not, you're being short-sighted. A year will fly by. Look how fast the summer has gone."

She has a point. It's already early August. The summer *has* flown by. It's been three months since Zander and I broke up, and it feels like a literal lifetime ago. I don't leave for two more weeks. Maybe I could even push that out by a week or two—and then the school year isn't even a year. It's nine months. Nine months sounds so much shorter than a year. *Could we actually make it work?*

Just as the excitement of possibility rushes over me, I tamp it down. It's too late. Aiden didn't break up with me because I was leaving. He never even said he had a problem with it. He broke up with me because I betrayed him. Lied to him. Not just once, but twice. Every minute of our time together was a lie, because I didn't tell him I was leaving.

"I'm pretty sure he's over it. I don't think he'll forgive me. I don't know that I'd forgive me."

Mom lets out an annoyed sigh. "You're not a monster. Making a mistake doesn't mean you can't try to fix it. And . . . you've got nothing to lose."

That, she's right about. She must see that I know it too, because her voice sounds optimistic. "All you can do is try. And if he's over it, then you'll meet someone at your new school."

I roll my eyes.

"Or you won't. You'll have an awesome senior year being single, and kissing guys for fun, and . . ."

"Kissing guys for fun is what got me into this." I try to laugh but it sounds sad.

Aunt Sarah's chair squeaks as she stands and takes the spot next to me against the counter. "I think your mom's right." She sounds surprised.

Mom smacks the countertop. "Finally!" She shakes her head, smiling. "I've waited forever to hear that."

Aunt Sarah throws her hands up. "That's not my fault—all you had to do was say something that was actually right," she says.

"I don't know what to do." I pick at a little spot on the countertop where I accidentally gouged it with a knife last year. "Do you think we should sand this?" I say, picking at it.

Aunt Sarah smacks my hand. "I think you need to stop picking at it, and we need to tackle one problem at a time."

"You know what you need to do," Mom says.

"I do?"

"What would you do if this were one of your stories?"

I laugh, thinking about the shelf of books in my room. I haven't even read any this summer, I was so distracted by my own love story. And even as I think it, I wonder if it could be true. If love could happen so fast.

"I'd fight against the totalitarian regime taking over my country?"

Mom rolls her eyes, like I'm just being difficult, which I sort of am. "Maybe a different kind of book."

She's right, I know what I need to do. And just like at the start of summer, I have nothing left to lose. I've come full circle. Just not in the good way.

Chapter Twenty

I liked family dinner better when I wasn't the only entertainment. When I was in middle school, Chelsea and Maddie were in high school, and dinner conversations mostly covered grilling my sisters about their lives. As a middle schooler, I loved hearing Mom and Dad ask them a million questions—how they felt about their upcoming basketball games, which colleges they'd visit. Now that it's just me, with no form of distraction, it's not quite so appealing.

As I fill glasses with ice water and set them on the table, Mom is pulling a pan of chicken out of the oven and asking Dad a full lineup of questions about the next phase of construction on The Annex. I steal a roll from the straw basket my mom has used since I was little, and shove a chunk of it in my mouth before setting the basket on the table and sinking down into my seat.

"Saw that," Mom mutters, and I don't even pretend that I didn't do it. The day I stop eating my mom's food is the day I find her balled up in a corner somewhere, weeping about where she went wrong.

Mom brings the metal baking pan into the dining room, her hands wrapped in rolled-up towels. This chicken is my favorite. Second only to last week's dinner. Ever since my appointment with Dr. Shah, Wednesday night meals have been a medley of my favorites. She's setting the pan down on the table when the door-bell rings.

"John," she yells into the kitchen, where my dad is holding a bowl of green beans.

"On it." He turns for the door and my mom takes her seat across from me. When it was all five of us at the table, Mom and Dad sat on opposite ends, like a king and queen, but now that it's just the three of us, we all sit at one end.

Dad is saying something I can't understand, then there's a slam of the door and he's back in the dining room with his bowl of beans . . . and Olivia.

"Look who I found," he says cheerfully before setting the bowl on the table.

Before I can even process what's happening, my mom is out of her seat and Olivia is approaching her. There's an exchange of names, an offered handshake that's turned down for a hug, and before Olivia has even sat down Mom has retrieved an extra plate and sil-verware. "What a nice surprise." Mom smiles at me, like I'm the one who popped in for dinner. She turns to Olivia, who's sitting next to her. "Aiden didn't tell me you were coming."

I'm about to tell her I didn't know when Olivia beats me to it.

"He didn't know. I had a last-minute change of plans." Olivia looks right at me. "I wanted to be sure to make it to dinner before I left."

"I'm so glad you made it." Mom says before holding a giant spoonful of rice out to Olivia. "Where are you headed?"

Olivia holds her plate out to be filled. She pokes the pile of rice and mushrooms and chicken with her fork. "Arizona." Her voice sounds sad but also resigned. "My aunt got a job, so I'll be there senior year."

"Oh." Mom sounds deflated. *Something we have in common.* "Well, that's too bad." She sticks a forkful of green beans in her mouth.

"Yeah." Olivia jabs at her beans. "I was hoping to snag Aiden before I left, maybe I can steal him after dinner?"

"We don't need him for anything," my mother says, a little too eager.

"You're sure you don't need me to do dishes or take out the trash, or something?" My mom laughs, but Olivia's smile slips for just a second.

My mother dismisses my sarcasm with a wave of her fork.

O L I V I A

When we're done eating, Aiden's mom hugs me, and he walks to the door with me following behind.

I close the door behind us and join Aiden on the little porch that wraps around his house.

He shoves his hands down into his pockets. "What are you doing here, Olivia?"

"Eating chicken?" I say, with a smile that's taking a lot of effort because of the way Aiden is looking at me right now. He doesn't want me here. "Really good chicken."

"Why are you here?" Aiden repeats it, like maybe I didn't hear him the first time.

I push through, smiling. Fake it 'til you make it, that's what they say. And until Aiden forgives me, I'm just going to pretend that he isn't looking at me like he wishes it were anyone else on his porch right now. "I suck. I know I do." I can feel my smile wavering. "But I think maybe I deserve one more chance. Maybe *we* deserve it?"

I don't wait for him to respond. I push forward, my voice nervous and fast. "Meet me at River Depot in an hour?"

"You want me to go to work?" He's trying to be tough but I can tell he's curious.

"Meet me at the docks." I start down the steps and pause at the bottom. "Wear something comfortable." I throw the instruction over my shoulder. "And be prepared to get wet."

I probably don't deserve another chance, so there's a definite possibility that Aiden doesn't show up. But I have nothing to lose, so I'm going to give this a try. I'm going to chase him for as long as he lets me—right up until I get on a plane to Arizona.

AIDEN

When I'm back in the house I decide I'm not going to River Depot. Olivia managed to string me along all summer, and now here she is, weaseling her way into my house with a smile and a hug. For what?

So my mom can get attached to her and I can spend my senior year hearing about "the one who got away"? My mom is in the kitchen, piling dishes into the sink. You can always tell when my dad is doing dishes, because the plates are still coated in food. The only fun part of dishes for my dad is grinding things into oblivion in the garbage disposal. Even though my mom swears up and down that all that crap isn't supposed to be going down our pipes. If it were up to Dad, he would feed corncobs down it like a meat grinder, just to see if he could.

Mom looks up when I come in. "I thought you were going with Olivia."

The only reason I leave the house is to avoid having to talk to my mother about this. She just sat through her first dinner with a girl I brought home (not that I brought her home, or even invited her) and I know the night will hold nothing for me but questions and commentary on all things Olivia. So I'm on my bike, pedaling in the muggy evening air, and before I know it, I'm a block from River Depot. I shouldn't go. Somewhere deep inside me I know that, but also, I can't help but be curious about what Olivia wants. Any hope I have is pushed down remembering that Olivia said, not even an hour ago, that she was still moving. This is just her mending fences before she leaves, and all it's going to do is hurt more.

But even as I think it, I'm pulling in to River Depot, dumping my bike at the rack and skipping the lock. It's seven o'clock, and Beth is checking in the equipment for the night, stacking paddles inside the garage and pulling the door closed behind her as I come down the last set of stairs. She smiles and looks surprised when she sees me.

"Have you seen Olivia?" I don't know why I sound irritated, it's not like it's Beth's fault that I didn't just say no to Olivia and then stick to it.

Beth shakes her head. "Nope. I don't think she was on the schedule today."

"She asked me to meet her." I look at my phone—it's been fifty-five minutes.

Beth puts a hand on my shoulder and pats it as she walks past me toward the stairs.

"Okay. Well I'm sure she'll be here soon." She smiles and I'm pretty sure she doesn't have any idea what's going on. "Have a good night." I wonder if Olivia has told anyone we broke up. Or if she even had to, since no one knew we were together to begin with. The thought of it pokes me in a raw place.

I sit on the little bench next to the docks, where little kids sit while their parents strap them into life jackets. That's what I need right now; something to save me from being pulled under by hope again. I'm looking at my phone, swearing that the second it hits seven o'clock I'm out of here, when I hear my name. My first thought is to look toward the deck, where people are still milling around with their ice cream cones, but I realize it's coming from the river. And the second time I hear it, it's louder. I look toward the river just as a canoe comes into view. Olivia is in the back, her paddle cutting through one side and then the other, until she's in front of the docks, dragging the paddle through the water to bring the boat to a stop. She reaches for the dock but can't quite grab it, and the boat is tipping as she struggles to get closer. Her eyes dart between me and the dock, and I run out and put my hand out to pull her in. She grabs hold and uses me as leverage to bring the canoe alongside me. As soon as the boat clinks along the wooden planks, I release her and put a hand on the boat itself, squatting down to hold it.

"What are you doing?" I say.

"Get in."

"Where did you put the canoe in?" I ask, looking downstream.

"Ellis helped me put it in at the public ramp."

No wonder she looks like she's been through the wringer. The public docks are a trek on your own, especially for someone like Olivia who isn't used to canoeing. I bet she was a sight to see zigzagging down the river from bank to bank. "Get in," she repeats.

"Olivia—"

"Let me take you for a ride." She slaps a hand against the canoe, as if I didn't know what she was referring to. "I owe you."

I look back at the boat garage and then upstream, as if there may be another canoe coming, a better option. Someone to rescue me from making the horrible mistake of getting into this one. But no one's coming, so I do it. We're heading down the river, and there's no turning back.

OLIVIA

As we paddle down the river—and by we, I mean me, because I forgot to grab an extra oar for Aiden—I'm starting to think this was a horrible idea. Because Aiden didn't seem even mildly thrilled to get into this canoe with me, and he looks rigid and awkward in front of me now. Meanwhile, I'm trying to focus on keeping us in a semi-straight line, with only minimal success. *Olivia, what were you thinking?* I've clearly read too many romance novels. We're in a straight section, so I set my paddle across my lap and open the bag I have between my feet. I pull the folded papers out, and now I have to actually talk to the guy in the front of my canoe. The one who hasn't said a word to me. I clear my throat. "Can you read this?"

Aiden doesn't react right away. He stays frozen in place, like maybe I'm talking to someone else on this deserted river. Maybe if the river was filled with tubers and other boats, it wouldn't feel so awkward. I wish we had that noise to lighten the mood. Right now the air is filled with nothing but the heavy feeling that Aiden doesn't want to be here with me. It's engulfing me, like a heavy cloud that follows our boat down the clear blue river. Finally he shifts and turns toward me. His eyes are on the papers I'm holding in my outstretched hand. They don't meet mine. I don't really blame him though. After all, I did ruin our summer.

Aiden

I don't look at her, because it's hard to stay mad when we're out on the water and all I'm thinking about is our first few trips: our escape from the reporters, the first time she saw the sunset from the river, as we forged out into the big lake. I take the papers from her and hold them for a minute before opening them. I'm not sure what I expect. A goodbye letter of some sort, I suppose. Olivia doesn't want to leave with me mad at her, but I don't know if I can give her that. I don't know if I can get over it that quickly and let go of her all over again. The white paper is folded and creased, and I open it to reveal an essay. I read it as Olivia continues to push us down a jagged line through the river: *HOW TO RUIN SUMMER by Olivia Henry.*

When I'm done reading Olivia's essay we're close to the lake and the sky is warm, but it's still another hour until sunset. We cut through the beach, heading into the lake, and I think about the first time we did this; the way Olivia froze up as we neared the end of the river, when I told her we'd be "sucked" out. I didn't know her then, but I do now. She didn't tell me everything over the last few months, but she showed me a lot. And now she's even shown me something I never asked for—her writing. I take the papers in my hands and fold them three more times before tucking them into my pocket. The canoe shifts a little when I do, and I sneak a glance back at Olivia, to see how she's handling this last leg before we hit the lake. The current has picked up now, and there isn't much paddling to do, only steering. Her eyes are ahead, fixed on the horizon, but they meet mine for just a second, and she smiles.

"Thank you," I say, my voice soft, because I feel like I should say more but don't know how—or what.

"You're welcome." She gives me a shy smile and her eyes go back to the water. "I'm going to try not to drown us," she says lightly, and I laugh. "I forgot a few things . . . including the cushions."

"I promise not to drown," I say. But what I really mean is that I would never let anything happen to her. I wonder if she's ever had that, someone who put her above everything, and I realize she hasn't. Zander left her, and her mother is just now acting like she cares at all, and even her Aunt Sarah put her job first; or at least it feels that way to Olivia. I wish I had told her how I felt about her, before she gave up on me the way everyone else has given up on her.

We cross into the lake without drowning, but when we're out in the push of Lake Michigan, it's obvious that Olivia is struggling to keep us from being washed onto the shore. It's much rougher tonight than the first night we ventured this way, but she hasn't given up yet. She's shook though. I can tell by her little gasps every time a wave picks us up, tips us to the right, and then crashes us down to the left. This isn't the kind of day you take a canoe out on Lake Michigan. Every length of the canoe, we're getting closer and closer to land, and by the time we reach the beach that I'm guessing is our final destination, we're running parallel to the shore, about to scrape along the rocky bottom.

Olivia lets out a huge sigh as we begin to wash up onto the sand. I couldn't do anything from the front of the canoe, but now I take a step out and pull the bow up onto the shore.

"Here," I say, holding my hand out to Olivia. She drops her paddle into the boat, slings her bag over one shoulder, and takes my hand, climbing out onto the sand.

"We're here," she says with a smile, but her voice says that she didn't think we'd actually make it.

I laugh. "And no one drowned."

"Thankfully," she says, the stress starting to drain out of her face as her shoulders soften. She doesn't pause at the shoreline, just hoists her backpack onto the other shoulder, and starts toward the grass behind us. "This way," she says.

෨

The sky is shining pink through the treetops as we make our way up the steep dune. Olivia took a hit from her inhaler before we began climbing, and she's taking slow, measured steps. She's leading this time; in control. I follow behind, wondering how we'll get the canoe back up the river in the dark. There's no way I can make it without a light or Ellis to lead. We hike up the last hundred feet of the dune, Olivia charging ahead of me, traversing the trunks of fallen trees and ducking beneath sagging branches. She's not talking to me—and I'm not talking to her—and it's giving me too much time to think. About why she brought me here, at sunset, when clearly I've seen it a million times. This dune held no significance to me, it was simply the perfect platform on which to capture the scene below. A scene I never painted anyway. So why are we working so hard to get back here?

When we reach the top, Olivia steps to the side of the narrow, sandy path, and lets me pass her. "Turn around," she says, just as I walk into the opening.

I do what she says, and stare back at her. Her face is red, but she looks better than the first time we climbed here. She lowers her backpack, strap by strap, and sets it at her feet. As she unzips it, she says, "Close your eyes."

"Olivia—" I argue, but her voice is soft and pleading.

"Please, Aiden?"

I do what she asks, and close my eyes. The air is still hot, even though the sun is making its final descent, but the breeze on the dunes is cool against my heated face, and sends goose bumps across my arms.

Hands fall on my biceps, and turn me around, then they're gone. A hand on my shoulders pushes me forward, one step, two steps, three, until I'm starting to get nervous that Olivia brought me up here just to push me off. Her hands are gone again, and I feel the sand shift next to me. Even though we're not touching, I can tell she's right there, her arm so close to mine that I want to move it just an inch to touch her.

"Okay." She takes a deep breath that seems amplified with my eyes closed. "Open your eyes."

I do what she says, letting the orange of the sky slide past my eyelids. The orange is almost rusty where the sun is slipping below the lake, and as my eyes sweep across the water, I wonder what exactly I'm supposed to be seeing. I look to Olivia next to me, and she pushes me forward another step with her hand on my lower back.

"Down there." She points to the beach below us, and when my eyes drop down, I see why she brought me here. What we made the climb for, why she subjected me to her mediocre boating skills one more time.

Below us—in the sandy gap between the grass that skirts the bottoms of the dune and the blue water that's nipping at the shore—is a message. There are no words, but I still know what it says.

O l i v i a

It took me two days, with a lot of help from Ellis, to get the stones out to the beach. We bought them from a local farmer—they're oddly shaped, dirty, and rough, not pretty enough for landscapers. But after being painted they look beautiful laid out on the beach. On the left is a mass of green rocks shaped like Arizona. And on the right—much bigger—a mitten-shaped arrangement of blue rocks. And in it, a red heart. My heart. There's a line of black rocks that stretches from one state to the other.

I swallow back my nerves. "There's something I need to tell you."

Aiden turns to meet my eyes, and it's not helping my nerves to look into his.

"I'm moving."

His voice is soft. "I know."

"I should have told you, and I probably shouldn't have done any of this with you, knowing I was leaving."

His eyes look disappointed.

"But I did do this, and now I'm in it. Even if I'm not going to be in the same state as you . . . I'm in it. Because nine months without you is going to feel like forever, but not being with you at all . . . ? That just doesn't feel like an option."

Aiden isn't saying anything, he's just looking at me, and I can't tell what he's thinking. More than anything though, he looks confused. He looks away from me, back to the beach, and his hand slips around mine.

"I knew you had an eye for art," he says with a smile.

"This isn't art. It was mostly manual labor."

"They're pretty much the same thing," he says, laughing a little. "Haven't you learned anything this summer, Olivia?"

"You did read my essay, right?" I joke.

"You didn't ruin summer though," he says, looking down at me. "You made it so much better." He cocks his head to the side. "Maybe not the last week or two, but yeah, summer with you was good."

As soon as the words are past his lips, his hand is on my waist. Then his lips are on mine. He pulls me close, so close it feels like he might absorb me. But I think maybe he already has. Because no matter what I do, I don't think I could shake Aiden Emerson, even if I wanted to. Not when the summer ends, maybe not ever.

Chapter *Twenty-One*

OLIVIA

Just as I'm getting into bed, I get an email asking me to come to *Lake Lights* in the morning. I decide, just before I fall asleep, that I won't go, but when I wake up curiosity takes hold. I throw on clothes and make my way into the kitchen, expecting to see my mother with her usual cup of tea. But the kitchen is empty and the house is quiet, and I sip my herbal all alone, wishing I had just a little longer in this house.

Inside the reception area of *Lake Lights,* things look like they did the last time I was here. It was just a few months ago, but it feels like I'm not even the same person. Maybe I'm not. I feel like someone different, someone who has a lot more to look forward to than just a summer internship. There's no one behind the reception desk, so I try a tentative "Hello." I hear a thump, and make my way down the hallway. The first two doors are closed but the last door on the right is open, and I stop just outside. I give a light tap on the door before poking my head in.

"Hel—" I stop when I see the woman standing behind the desk, a box in her hands. "Mom?"

She smiles and sets the box on the desk. "Joanie will be fine around here."

"Wait, what?" I walk into the office and sit down. "What are you doing here?"

"This is my new office." She puts her hands on her hips and smiles, looking around the little room like it's the greatest thing she's ever seen. "I bought *Lake Lights*."

"But—you just—I mean—why? Why would you do that?"

She shrugs. "*Lake Lights* is fifty percent photography. I can do that."

"And it's fifty percent *not* photography."

"That's true. I was hoping you could help with that part." She pulls the cardboard lid off of the box and drops it behind the desk. "Not full time, obviously—you're still in school. But you can help after school, and then next summer, I was thinking you could work here full time."

"You want me to work for you?"

"I want you to be happy. So I bought this place so I could stay, so *you* could stay, and we could both be happy." She bites her lip and looks nervously at the mess of things around here. "You don't actually have to work here. I mean, I can hire staff. I'm *going* to hire staff, anyway. I just thought if you wanted to—"

Old Olivia wouldn't be standing here—she'd have left imme-

diately, slamming the door with angry words about how she couldn't
be bought. How this one thing doesn't change the years of being
left behind and forgotten. She would have hurt herself, just to hurt
Mom. But now I have too much to gain from my mother doing
this. Senior year with Emma. A chance at giving Aiden and me the
best shot possible without a thousand miles and nine months between us.

I don't know why I haven't said anything. Maybe my mouth is
physically incapable of admitting that my mother has done something to help me. I'm broken forever, maybe.

"I know I can't buy you." Mom picks up a pen and sets it back
down. "I'm not trying to do that. I'm just trying to . . . make it
better from here." She looks at me and her voice is firm. "And I'm
listening."

I nod, because I don't know what else to do. This one thing is
giving me so much. It feels worthy of more than a thank-you. It feels
too big to be held in this little room, too big to be held in my heart.

"Thanks." I step around the desk, a foot away from my mother,
and I want to hug her, but also I'm not sure how. I've spent so long
being mad at her, resenting her and thinking of ways to hurt her as
much as she hurt me; but it feels like all summer has been building
to this. I take a step forward and she wraps her arms around me,
taking the matter into her own hands.

"Thank you for letting me," she says, and I can't hold it in any
longer. Tears run down my face and I feel like I'm letting out years'
worth of anger. This doesn't fix it, it can't; but it feels like we're
finally stepping onto a new path—one that takes us somewhere other
than pain and resentment.

I pull away. "Aunt Sarah said it's okay?" It's hard to miss the hurt on my mother's face, but I'm not trying to hurt her now.

"Yeah, it's fine." She gives me a tight smile. "I ran everything by her." I don't get the usual comment about how Aunt Sarah isn't my mother. "I bought the house, so it helps her out too."

"Wow."

"I needed a place." She shrugs. "And this way you can be in your own house."

"That's . . . wow. That's perfect."

"Listen." She pushes her hair behind her shoulders and takes a deep breath. "I know you think I missed out on everything, and maybe I did. Maybe I missed out on all of the best parts—"

"I didn't—"

She holds a hand up to silence me. "But maybe you missed all of the worst parts of me too." She pushes a piece of hair away from her face. "And you're not done needing a mom. You'll need one for a long time. So . . . I want to try. I want to try to be that person. I know I'm not that person yet, Sarah's still that person. But . . . someday."

"Okay."

"Okay." She pulls a stack of folders out of the box and sets them on the desk. "Get out of here. Don't you have a boyfriend to give some good news to, or something?"

I'm fighting the urge to sprint out of this office and all the way to River Depot. "Thanks."

"You're welcome."

Epilogue

AIDEN

8 months later . . .

The sun is bright in my eyes as the ball flies toward me. I dip my hands and catch the pop-up at my waist, squeezing it gently. I missed the way this feels; the once-soft leather, roughened from pelting the ground. The laces raising up under my fingers. I throw the ball back to Zander, and he gives me a solemn nod.

Next to me, Olivia wraps an arm around my waist. We're not going to stay long, but I wanted to be here to cheer everyone on. It's been a long year trying to gain back my friends and teammates. A lot of the conversations I was dreading: explaining why I wouldn't come back despite the fact that my vision is close to normal again, why I needed time away from everyone—away from baseball—to figure out who I was without it.

I've been working with Callahan, the new starting pitcher, since school started. It's nice to be involved, even if it's off the field.

Olivia tugs my hand. "I want gum before we leave," she says, turning for the concession stand. I follow behind her, taking her hand back in mine. At the metal counter she plunges her hand into the clear plastic tub and eyes me with a mischievous smile. "Let's play a game," she says, mixing her hand around. "If I pick a yellow, we go make out in your car . . ." She winks.

"Oh no." I grab the plastic jar from her and set it in front of me. "Fate doesn't get to decide anymore. We are totally making out in my car."

She opens her hand slowly, revealing the yellow candy in her hand.

"Okay, fate's obviously still on our side," I say, pulling a quarter out of my pocket. "Heads?"

She smiles. "Of course."

"Your choice?" I say, thinking about that night at the ruins.

"My choice," Olivia says. She stretches up and presses her lips quickly to mine. "And I choose you."

Acknowledgments

As it turns out, every horrible thing people say about writing a second book is actually very true. So I have to give a huge shout-out to my wonderful agent, Michelle Wolfson, for her professional-grade cheerleading skills. Even when things felt hopeless and deadlines seemed utterly out of reach, you told me I could do it, and actually made me believe it. Amy Stapp, you get me and my stories, and I'm glad fate and chance and luck (and Michelle) brought us together to create these swoony book-shaped things! Thank you for not telling me just how horrible the first unfinished draft of this book was. I definitely knew. And I'm so glad you and Michelle saw past that, and waited to see what I turned that ridiculous mess into. The two of you are my dream team.

A huge thank-you to Daniela and Seth for another wonderful cover design, and to my amazing publisher, Kathleen Doherty, and the whole Tor Teen team, who have supported me and my book babies in an amazing way. I am immensely grateful to be part of the Tor Teen family.

Much love to all of the amazing author friends, writers, and readers who helped push me through: all of the Electric Eighteens and Book 2 Struggle Bussers who were always quick with sympathy and support; SisTOR Amber Lynn Natusch, for helping me to brainstorm on a whim while our fearless leader was on leave; my wonderful CP, Jenn Nguyen, who was always ready to commiserate with me; and Lara Willard, who is always just a message away with brainstorming help. A huge thank-you to my very early beta readers, Courtney and Arden Kurhayez and Simone Nicole, who happily waded through a truly rough draft in just a few days. The bookish community is truly one of a kind, and I'm so thankful to have met so many wonderful and supportive people while going on this strange journey as an author. Shout-out to my amazing street team, and to all of the book bloggers, booksellers, librarians, and readers who supported my debut and made me want to write this second book that much more.

When Summer Ends is the first book I've written since becoming a mom, and so I have to give a huge hug to my sweet little Rory, who gave up some Momma time during hectic drafting deadlines and provided extra snuggles when I was feeling stressed. And I literally couldn't have written this book without all of the extra help from my wonderful husband, Josh, who supports every ridiculous dream I have, and my amazing parents, who pitched in to give me more writing time.

Last but not least, a huge thank-you to everyone who cheered *Love*

Songs & Other Lies into the world and made this second book possible. Having one book published was a dream come true, and having a second out in the world is absolutely surreal. Thank you for reading and letting me do this thing I love.